Praise for *Every Last Cuckoo*

"A story about the profound gifts of time, love, and loss . . . Maloy's message is about affirming the profundity of grief by expressing that energy in positive ways. This story is her generous vision of how things could be."   —*The Olympian*

"The appeal of Maloy's debut—which has the fast-forward quality of a fairy tale—is not in its subtlety but in its conviction."
                                                        —*People*

"Maloy does a marvelous job depicting the kind of tender, steady domestic partnership that is the reward of a lifetime of shared experiences, both good and bad . . . Its tenderly wrought portrayal of elderly life has an unexpectedly powerful effect, revealing fictional possibilities we'd either forgotten about or never considered at all."   —*The Oregonian*

"Maloy nicely portrays the long, imperfect, but still lusty marriage of Sarah and husband Charles, moves gracefully through the shock of loss, and charts the steps back into community. But what feels most original and moving is Maloy's sense of how Sarah sees herself connected to other generations."
                                          —*The Boston Sunday Globe*

"This lovely tale depicts the surprises and changes that come about with aging . . . Maloy has created a truly engrossing novel, with situations at times both joyful and horribly sad and an entirely likable protagonist surrounded by an eclectic cast of friends and family. An excellent book club selection; highly recommended."   —*Library Journal*

"A luminously textured novel that insists that grief need not diminish a life but instead can offer up a bounty of surprises, that choices don't have to narrow as we age but, in fact, can grow more plentiful, and, finally and most important, that love can be as open and expansive as the sky itself. I loved this rich and haunting novel."

—Caroline Leavitt, author of *Girls in Trouble*
and *Coming Back to Me*

"A beautiful, graceful story about a vibrant, beautiful woman."
—*Seattle Post-Intelligencer*

"A wonderful story of human potential and what is possible when strangers become family . . . This heartwarming tale is an excellent read." —*The Roanoke Times*

"[A] moving debut." —*More*

"A tender and wise story of what happens when love lasts. This vivid and original novel seizes and surprises the reader, who is rewarded by an extraordinarily appealing range of the best sort of fully engaging novel elements, from the moving issues of multigenerational family dynamics and aging and solitude to the necessity of confronting our own sometimes violent instincts as creatures living in the natural world. It's a stunning, elegant debut."

—Katharine Weber, author of
Triangle and *The Little Women*

"*Every Last Cuckoo* is an impressive step in a new literary direction."
—MSNBC.com

"Kate Maloy's sweetly inspiring first novel, *Every Last Cuckoo,* is a lovely meditation on what miracles can happen when we simply open our hearts . . . Maloy's novel grabs the reader by the heart—it is rare indeed to find such assured fiction about love that endures over time . . . In this portrait of a long and loving marriage, Maloy gives us a real human family, with all its love and conflict and change, as well as a look at the richness that can come with age." —*The New Orleans Times-Picayune*

"A striking portrait of a marriage that is as imperfect and amiable as its participants." —*Kirkus Reviews*

"This charming novel is an examination of friendship, tragedy, romance, generosity, moral indignation, aging, solitude, and what happens when love lasts and we confront our own inner weathers." —*Rocky Mount Telegram*

"This is a splendid book, written in spare, clean prose, in which the knots of grief and complication are eased to resolution by wisdom and love."
—Peter Pouncey, author of *Rules for Old Men Waiting*

"[A] moving debut novel . . . Maloy's wordplay and startling nature imagery enchant." —*Publishers Weekly*

"Almost every page rewards the reader in some unexpected way: by a glimpse of the Vermont landscape, a moment of intimacy between the characters, a beautifully turned sentence. And every page brings us closer to Sarah, Kate Maloy's remarkable heroine, a woman so passionate, so intelligent and so full of life that most readers will quickly forget that she happens to be in her seventies. This is a wonderful debut."

—Margot Livesey, author of *Banishing Verona*
and *Eva Moves the Furniture*

"What great pleasure Kate Maloy gives us with this lovely, lucid novel of family, landscape, and complications."

—Roxana Robinson, author of *Sweetwater*
and *This Is My Daughter*

Every Last Cuckoo

Also by Kate Maloy

A Stone Bridge North: Reflections in a New Life

EVERY LAST CUCKOO

a novel by

Kate Maloy

Algonquin Books of Chapel Hill
2009

Published by
ALGONQUIN BOOKS OF CHAPEL HILL
Post Office Box 2225
Chapel Hill, North Carolina 27515-2225

a division of
WORKMAN PUBLISHING
225 Varick Street
New York, New York 10014

This is a work of fiction. While, as in all fiction, the literary perceptions and in-sights are based on experience, all names, characters, places, and incidents either are products of the author's imagination or are used fictitiously.

Library of Congress Cataloging-in-Publication Data
Maloy, Kate, 1944–
   Every last cuckoo: a novel / by Kate Maloy. — 1st ed.
      p. cm.
   ISBN-13: 978-1-56512-541-4 (HC)
   1. Older women — Fiction.   2. Fear of death — Fiction.
   3. Vermont — Fiction.   4. Psychological fiction.   I. Title.
   PS3613.A48E84 2007
   813'.6 — dc22   2007016641

ISBN-13: 978-1-56512-675-6 (PB)

10 9 8 7 6 5 4 3

For my mother, ELIZABETH HARDY MALOY, and her mother, BESSIE WATSON HARDY, my first storytellers. For my aunt, ANN FOSTER HARDY, my inspiration for Sarah.

Acknowledgments

WORK ON THIS novel was supported in part by a grant from the Vermont Arts Council in connection with the National Endowment for the Arts.

Every Last Cuckoo

⇒ PART I ⇐

RUNNING ON FEAR ALONE, Sarah Lucas follows her dog Sylvie down a long meadow and onto a disintegrating ski trail in the woods. Sylvie, a black Lab, holds her tail out stiffly from the base of her spine; she is all business. Sarah carries a heavy down parka for Charles, just in case. A sleeve falls loose and tangles between her legs; she nearly goes down. Panic fills her lungs and throat, displacing her breath as she tries to keep up with the dog. Her heart strains, an overtaxed engine. Sarah curses herself for not having said to Charles, "Be careful," as always. She had rushed off with a friend; she had failed to voice the necessary charm. In her last glimpse of her husband, he had his walking stick in hand, his daypack over his shoulder. He was pleased to be setting out — and then he did not come back. Sarah had returned home to find the house empty and Sylvie waiting, frenzied.

Sarah feels both young and old, amazed that she can move so fast but aware that it might kill her. When she reaches the topmost point of the trail, she can see where Charles struck off through recently melted and refrozen snow. It has a thick crust, which he broke with each step. He wasn't wearing his snowshoes.

Sarah wads the parka more securely under her arm and moves carefully off the ski trail. She places her feet in the depressions Charles left, thinking wildly, *Whither thou goest.* Her pace now is unbearably slow. Her pulse thuds in her throat and behind her eyes. She squints to see ahead, but Charles's trail, which descends into a deep ravine, goes out of sight behind a house-size boulder.

Finally, Sarah sees him down. The broken snow reveals that he fell steeply and rolled. His mongrel terrier, Ruckus, is close beside him, a furry appendage. The little dog looks up and whimpers as Sarah approaches, but he stays put. Charles lies sprawled on his back, his head lower than his feet, one leg bent wrong. Sarah reaches his side and falls to her knees. A sudden soft keening escapes her. He is icy to her touch, his lips are blue, he does not stir. Frantically she feels for a pulse. It is there, but faint. She quickly wraps her husband in the parka, tucking it as far beneath his motionless body as she can. He murmurs something, and his eyelids flutter, but he doesn't awaken. She fumbles in the pocket of her coat for her cell phone, her hands shaking violently. She enters a number, hears a crackling emptiness. She wails in frustration, breaks the failed connection, and tries again to punch in 911. When a woman answers, Sarah stammers with cold and fear as she tries to explain where Charles is. She has to give their address, then directions to the entrance of the trail, then an estimated distance to the point at which Charles left the easy route and began breaking through the old snow. She is weeping by the time the operator understands where to send the EMTs on their snowmobiles.

Sarah lies down as close to Charles as she can, trying to warm him with her body and her breath, feeling for his heartbeat. The dogs curl up close as well. Charles does not move.

Chapter 1

THAT FALL AND WINTER Sarah felt events conspiring toward some menacing end. She told herself this was baseless, nothing more than a symptom of the seasonal plunge into cold and lengthening dark, but her anxiety persisted.

Her dread first began to surge during an illness that came over her on a midnight in November. She left her bed at the first roiling and moved to the window seat across the room, not wanting to wake Charles. Cold air flowed down from the stars, up from the river, and through the open casement beside her. She gulped it like an antidote, though it turned the fever sweat to icy pinheads in her pores. She was alarmed by her racing heart, too aware of her skin—how touchy it was with the onset of illness, how furnace-dry beneath the moist sheen.

Sarah held herself perfectly still, trying to quell the swelling nausea by force of will, as she had done since childhood, hating the stink and sound of the body's gross defenses. She preferred drawn-out suffering to the quick but horrible relief.

Hot and cold, she set herself adrift, hoping to sleep again and fool whatever virus or toxin had invaded her. Soon she entered a suspended awareness in which she was conscious yet assailed by images her conscious mind did not produce. Where had she seen that piece of road, that sweet rise and bend that now unspooled behind her eyes? The ocean, or perhaps a lake, lay to the right of it, a fringe of trees and a tucked cottage to the left. Up ahead, around a curve, a causeway crossed the wide water, but from where to where? Sarah tried to remember, but it was like snatching at milkweed fluff in the air. The very attempt sent it out of reach.

This kind of thing happened more with age. Sarah was seventy-five. She had lived many thousands of days, so it was not surprising that scenes from an hour here or a moment there should surface at random. Her memories were beads jumbled loose in a box, unstrung. Everything—people, events, conversations—came and went so fast that only a fraction of the beads were ever stored at all. Few were whole, many cracked; most rolled away beneath pressing, present moments and were gone forever. What was the point?

Still, Sarah felt she should remember that road. Something about it.

Fully awake now, she slipped from the window seat and stumbled urgently across the hallway to the bathroom. On her way she heard Charles utter an inflected snort that meant, *What's happening? Where are you?*

She closed the bathroom door and fell to her knees, thankful that she had scrubbed the toilet just that day. The porcelain was clean enough that she cooled her cheek on it between eviscerating heaves.

Charles knocked softly after a decent interval. He would never just come in, not while she was on the floor, clammy and trembling. "Just a minute," she called, flushing the toilet. She rose and glimpsed her face, gone ashy, in the mirror. She rinsed her mouth, brushed her teeth, rinsed again, and went out of the bathroom into Charles's embrace.

"Why didn't you wake me?" he asked, looking down at her, his white hair standing in tufts, his eyes naked without glasses.

"So you could do what?" Sarah answered, filled with relief, welcoming the pale euphoria that always rose in her when illness faded.

"Well, how about now? Want tea?"

"No, thanks. Just put me back to bed."

Charles, still lanky and straight at eighty, still courtly at moments like this one, held Sarah's arm and steered her to their room and her side of their bed. He lifted her legs and feet onto the mattress, smoothed the covers over her, and felt her forehead. "Hot," he said. "I'll get the thermometer."

"No need," Sarah replied, exhausted. "Fever's going down."

Charles touched her cheek. He might be the doctor in the family, but the palm of Sarah's own hand was accurate within a degree of fever. All those years of mothering.

"What brought this on?" he asked. "You feeling better?"

"Mmm. Just a bug." Talking was an effort, but Sarah added, "Don't you catch it."

"Not this iron man," said Charles, bending to kiss her cheek.

SARAH SLEPT UNTIL NINE the next morning, three hours later than usual. When Vermont's dilute autumn sun finally woke her, she could tell the hour from the position of its diffuse glow through the honeycomb shades. Her body luxuriated in surcease from illness, but her mind dwelt on mortality. This time a fly-by-night virus. Next time — what?

Sarah was rarely ill. Even as a child she had weathered the odd bout of sickness with a calm born of utter trust in her body. She had submitted patiently to everything from colds to menstrual cramps, believing that to be in the best of health she had to be ill sometimes. She had to let her body use its defenses the way an army practices maneuvers during peacetime. Colds kept her immune system fit. Cramps confirmed her clocklike fertility, announced the readiness of her body for babies, familiarized her with the tugging sensation that would so wildly intensify during labor. No matter what the ailment, her health always returned.

Last night, though, Sarah had feared the body-shaking thud of her heart, the weakness in her joints. Her half-awake dreaming had brought unusual images, scenes in which her molecules came unbound and drifted like motes in a beam of light, or her limbs turned to rivers that ran away into sand. She tried to fight panic along with the nausea, but neither had receded until victorious. Vomiting drained away the poisons, but the fear crept back, peripherally.

The telephone rang downstairs. Charles answered. He must have turned off the bedside phone. Sarah heard the rumble and inflections of his voice but couldn't distinguish his words, only that he was friendly, not grumpy. The grumpy Charles emerged more often than he used to, but, then, so did the grumpy Sarah. So, for that matter, did a broader spirit in each of them, a ferocious joy. There was more to being old than she had ever expected.

With that, Sarah dressed and headed downstairs, stepping

through early November sunshine on the landing, pale light made watery by the wavy, century-old glass in the southeast window. As she turned to finish her descent, she felt briefly unsteady and grasped the banister. Sylvie and Ruckus surged up to meet her, a canine tide. She extended her free hand, received their kisses, and fondled their ears. Content, they preceded her down the last stairs and flanked her on her way to the kitchen, tails moving like metronomes, toenails rattling time on hardwood and tile.

Charles was still on the phone, holding the receiver to his ear with his shoulder while pouring coffee. He saw Sarah and held the pot up inquiringly.

No, thought Sarah, her stomach contracting. She grimaced at Charles and went to the pantry for tea.

Charles said into the phone, "She's up. Let me see if she's up to talking." He covered the receiver. "It's Lottie."

"Ask if I can call her back," said Sarah, filling the kettle.

Charles did so, laughed, and hung up. "No, she's never speaking to you again." He surveyed her face and looked her tall self up and down. "You don't look sick," he said. "In fact you look better than you ought to and too young for an old fart like me."

"Eye of the beholder," said Sarah. "What did Lottie want?"

"You, of course."

"She say why?"

"No, but I'd guess the usual," Charles said. "Her parents."

"You mean her mother," said Sarah wryly. "Don't be so judicious. It's only me."

Lottie, their granddaughter, belonged to their firstborn, Charlotte, and was named for her. She'd been given her nickname to avoid confusion, but it suited the girl's light, free-spirited nature. Lately her rising hormones had brought stronger moods, many of them dark. At fifteen Lottie was volatile and given to melodrama. Charlotte, high-strung herself, had no idea what to do with the adolescent changeling in her house, so Sarah was a drawbridge, separating mother and daughter until the traffic on their troubled waters could pass.

The teakettle whistled, and Sarah poured boiling water into a heavy mug, over a pouch of ginger tea. She sat down opposite Charles at the table inside the kitchen's broad bay window. "Thanksgiving's less than two weeks off," she said. "I need to plan, though the thought of all that food's a bit much this morning."

"You going to call Lottie first? She was heading out soon."

Sarah tried, but Lottie had already left on some Saturday jaunt. Charlotte, after a brief and stiffly cheerful conversation, said she would tell Lottie that Sarah had called.

Sarah hung up, disheartened. She gathered cookbooks but then sank into her chair and stared out at the late fall garden, trying, as she had countless times, to remember when she and Charlotte had first lost track of each other. As she often did amid thoughts of her oldest child, she wished her other two, Stephie and David, lived nearby. She felt no tension with them.

Sarah shifted her gaze to Charles, engrossed in a book. "Remember the first time it was just the two of us?" she asked wistfully. "Before the kids?"

He glanced up, preoccupied. "Anything in particular?"

"All that sweaty sex." She smiled and got up to fix some toast.

"Who, us?"

"Us. Don't you ever think about those days? They come back

to me all the time lately. Sometimes I think I remember every minute; other times I think I made it all up. Or I can't tell the difference."

Charles looked up at her, considering. "I prefer the present." With that he closed his book, planted a kiss on the crown of Sarah's head, and started back to his office over the barn. As a young man he had meant to study history, before medicine proved a stronger calling. Now he was writing a Lucas genealogy, conducting his research on the Internet. Since his retirement a dozen years earlier, he had written a social history of their village, Rockhill, and had self-published the diary his mother had kept as a World War I nurse. Charles was disciplined and happy. Sarah often envied his routines—mornings at his desk, errands in town, lunch with friends or meetings with environmentalists, then afternoon chores or rambles with the dogs in good weather. She joined him on those long walks when she could, but her days refused to conform to anything like a schedule. She had her own kind of discipline, which kept their lives and house in order, but she didn't have Charles's long attention span, and she wasn't creative.

Sarah made more tea and began riffling through the cookbooks. She sat planning the holidays until almost noon. The sun circled past her right shoulder. Now and then some high, fast-moving clouds cast brief shadows on her lengthening list of tasks. Before Thanksgiving was over, she would feel Christmas bearing down—the last one of the century and the old millennium.

Chapter 2

CHARLES AND SARAH'S YOUNGEST, David, arrived early from Massachusetts on the day before the holiday. Sylvie and Ruckus reached the door first, barking excitedly. David bent to greet them as Sarah rounded the corner from the hall to the foyer. She meant to embrace her son but stopped suddenly, surprised to see a small child—bright-haired, wearing red—back up a step at the sight of the dogs, her eyes frozen wide, chubby hands in the air. Then she flung herself at Sylvie's neck, accepting wet kisses with glee.

"David!" Sarah cried, delighted. "I didn't expect you for hours. Who's *this*?" She went down on one knee to meet her unexpected guest. "Hello, sweetheart. I'm Sarah. What's your name?" The little girl backed away, as she'd done before the dogs. Her dark blue eyes turned solemn.

David hugged his mother as she rose in some embarrassment. His leather jacket was stiff from the cold, his neat beard coarse and springy against her cheek. Sarah looked up at him and saw the young Charles, tall and handsome. David said, "This is

Hannah, Mom. Hannah's three and a half. And this," he added, drawing a slender young woman indoors, "is Hannah's mother, Theresa McDermott. Better known as Tess."

Sarah smiled and held out her hand. "Forgive me! I was so taken with your daughter."

Tess's hand was warm, her grip firm but not hard on Sarah's joints. "It's good to meet you in person, Mrs. Lucas. I've seen photos of everyone in the family—David has prepped me well." She threw him a teasing glance. She was tall, with the same pale blond hair as her daughter, the same clear eyes and skin. A certain asymmetry in her face saved it from being just another pretty one. Overall, she had an inquisitive, intelligent look.

Hannah tugged shyly at Sarah's sleeve. "What's his name?" she asked, patting Sylvie's broad, glossy head.

"He's a she, honey. Her name is Sylvie. And this curly guy is Ruckus."

"Hi, Sylvie," Hannah crooned. "Hi, Ruckus," she added, extending her hand to the smaller dog, who obligingly licked it and wagged his stumpy tail. "Ruckus is a funny name," she announced, and giggled.

"Well, he's a funny dog," said Sarah. "Go on into the kitchen, all of you. I have a feeling someone there will be very happy to see you." She'd heard Charles come in through the mudroom, returning from errands. Driving into the barn from the village road, a rutted dirt byway through the woods, he wouldn't have seen David's car in front. Sarah suddenly wondered why David had come in that way, through the door on the wide porch. Family usually entered from the barn and mudroom, shedding boots and jackets on the way.

Sarah sent David and his guests ahead of her and took their

coats to the hall closet. She longed for Stephie and Jake to come, too, bringing the whole family together at one time. But northern Minnesota was too far away for a short holiday trip.

Sarah overheard introductions as David and Tess encountered Charles. Hannah entered the spirit of things by telling him, "This black dog is Sylvie. That curly guy is Ruckus."

Charles pretended surprise. "You don't say. And did they come with you in the car, all the way from Cambridge?"

Hannah's laugh rang down the hallway, a wholehearted burst. "No! They live *here!*"

Sarah entered the kitchen in time to see Charles scratch his head, looking confused. "Never saw them before. Now ain't that the darnedest thing?"

An hour or so later, after a light lunch, Hannah explored the backyard with the dogs and came back exhausted and out of sorts. Tess took her upstairs for a nap, while David and Charles toured the property together. Sarah watched them. They adopted identical male postures, legs apart, hands in pockets or pointing at a tree limb that needed pruning, a piece of roof in need of repair, a gate hinge hanging loose. They had confined themselves to practicalities ever since David's adolescent rage against his father had finally faded to politeness. This saddened Charles the way her distance from Charlotte saddened Sarah. They had never dreamed that love would not be enough.

Charles, for reasons of temperament and constraint, would never glean from David the information Sarah wanted. Who was Tess? Where was Hannah's father, and did he share custody? Did Tess see staying power in David? No other woman had inspired more than passing infatuation since David's shattering divorce a dozen years ago. He was forty now. Tess was younger, probably only thirty or so.

Perhaps she was the reason David had come in through the porch door. It could be his way of announcing that they should take her seriously. He had told Sarah only days ago that he and Tess were living together, a revelation that automatically elevated her above David's many other loves. But he'd said nothing about Hannah.

Sarah had been moved by Hannah's instinctive courage, her willingness to forge past her wariness of dogs and new places. She wanted to feel Hannah's weight in her lap, to smell her hair. Her keenness for the child surprised her. She had taken her grandchildren's sequential arrivals in stride—she'd expected their entrance into her life as she expected the seasons to change. But Hannah drew Sarah's eye and ear; she was strong-willed, talkative, and filled with color and light. *A butterfly next to an old bat like me,* thought Sarah, chagrined and wry.

AT DINNER DAVID SAID he had met Tess at a Quaker meeting, the last place Charles or Sarah would have guessed. Tess had been raised among the Friends but hadn't practiced as an adult until Hannah was a year old. She explained that she wanted Hannah to grow up among people who lived simply and worked for peace and social justice. She seemed reluctant to discuss the matter further, though she did add that Quakers believe each person carries a particle of the divine inside. That was the basis for everything they stood for.

Sarah had trouble picturing David as a believer or even a seeker. He'd always seemed too coolly ironic for faith, too tightly bound by flesh and bone and logic—though in recent years he had begun expanding, following artistic impulses that no one had known he had. His chosen medium was clay, his forms were large-scale architectural pieces and sculptures. Still, Sarah thought his nature was more accurately reflected in the finished, cooled shapes than in the fire that cured them.

She asked him what had drawn him to a Quaker meeting, but all he said was, "I went with some friends a couple of times. I liked the silence. It was peaceful."

Tess told Charles and Sarah that she worked as a freelance writer for several museums in the Boston area. She wrote exhibition brochures, captions for works on display, occasional fundraising letters or grant proposals. "It's only part-time. I can work from home, so I'm there for Hannah."

There was nothing unfriendly about Tess, but nothing easy or forthcoming, either. Neither she nor David offered much that was personal. Little by little, though, their story would emerge. In the usual way of families, people would talk to each other, one at a time or in small clusters, and pieces of their conversations would conjoin. David might tell Sarah more in private than at dinner. Tess might talk to Charlotte and Charlotte to Charles. Lottie, in a sociable mood, could charmingly pry and question, worming more from everyone than they meant to divulge. And Lottie would tell Sarah everything.

Tess offered to help clean up after their meal, but Sarah said, "Thanks, anyway. I'm going to mix up some pastry first, so I can make the pies first thing tomorrow." She meant to be up before six. Dinner would be at two. Charlotte would bring side dishes, and Peter and Vivianna Marks, old family friends, would bring wine and hors d'oeuvres.

David and Tess took Hannah upstairs for a bath and a book.

They were using the clawfoot tub in Charles and Sarah's bathroom, directly above the kitchen, and Sarah could hear snatches of conversation through a grate in the ceiling. She was aware, from the variously abashed, accusing, and delighted reports of her grown children, that many private parental talks had made their way into eager ears through that grate. But tonight Sarah, the eavesdropper, heard nothing she wasn't supposed to hear.

THE NEXT MORNING while the pies were baking, Charles and Sarah drove to the village to deliver a turkey for the annual community dinner. The event, held at the town hall, was open to anyone at loose ends for the holiday. People with no family showed up, along with transients, those who were out of work, and others who barely made it on two jobs. A few of the better-off came bearing food; they stayed to help in the kitchen and share the meal. It would all happen again on Christmas.

Charles was handing their twenty-pound offering to Amos Brand, the dinner's organizer — also their friend and attorney — when sirens split the early morning air and shouts followed. Amos, Charles, and Sarah rushed out in time to see state police cars screech to a halt in the small parking lot, while two men hauled a couple of boys roughly from another car. People gathered suddenly from the houses close by, from passing cars, from nowhere, from the air. They stood with their arms crossed. A trooper handcuffed one boy, while another trooper and one of the civilians threw the second boy roughly to the ground after a short scuffle. Murmurs raced through the crowd. The car had been stolen. The boys were on drugs. They weren't from here; an alert had been issued in New Hampshire. The car had New Hampshire plates. That man over there, that big guy holding the boy to the ground, had a police scanner on at home all the time. He was the one who called it in. Good for him. Serves the punks right.

Sarah's eyes darted over the scene, lighting on each face in turn, always returning to the skinny, frightened boy on the ground. The conscientious beefy civilian had pinned his arms and planted a knee in the small of his back. The boy's ear and cheek were pressed against the pavement, hard up against grit and loose rock. He was furious; he was crying. Sarah listened to the crowd's self-satisfied judgments and easy condemnation.

Charles strode angrily over to the man who held the boy to the ground. "For chrissakes, Bill, get off that kid. Your knee's right on his kidneys. He can't breathe with his arms yanked back and all your weight on him." He gestured at one of the troopers. "You take over. Unless you want a dead kid on your hands."

Bill, big as a linebacker, started to hurl a protest, but the trooper motioned to him to be quiet and get up. Then he pulled the boy up and held him by the upper arm. The car thief's face was scratched, streaked with dirt and tears. He was painfully thin, no more than sixteen or seventeen.

"Shame on you both," Charles said to the men, his voice soft with disgust. He looked at his neighbors gathered there and said, "Happy Thanksgiving, everybody." He caught Amos's eye, and Amos lifted a thumb into the air.

Charles and Sarah climbed into their car and left. Sarah fought tears, shaken by grief too great for the occasion. It caught her off guard. Charles reached over and took her hand, and they rode home together.

It was still early, only seven thirty, when they reentered their kitchen. No one else was up, not even Hannah, so tired last night, so late getting to bed.

Sarah put the pies to cool. Wordlessly Charles drew her into his arms and kissed her. He slid his hands from her shoulders down along her spine, gently massaging her back before clasping her hips and pulling her in close. It had been a long time, at least a month. Sarah was a little surprised that desire should choose this occasion, but not this hour. Intimacy often found them in the morning, when their energy was strongest.

She climbed the stairs with Charles, mentally moving her holiday chores around to accommodate this unscheduled break. They entered their room holding hands, then took off their clothes and unmade their bed as if for sleep. Sarah knew this early morning love was about comfort silently sought and silently given. It wasn't she who needed it, having recovered from her reaction to the scene in town.

How many times had she and Charles come together like this, in how many ways? This time was slow, there was no urgency. Whatever happened happened. Their bodies and desires had changed, but almost in tandem. Charles and Sarah took their time now, as if time were still limitless.

Charles was no longer as avid or athletic as he had been when young, but he was no less inventive. Sarah loved his patience. Her orgasms, like his own, took longer to achieve, when they happened at all, but the feelings were the same. What was new, what now entered Sarah each time with Charles himself, was a blend of gratitude and anxiety. *We are blessed,* she thought, *fortunate that we have had this, that we have it still, though each time could be the last.*

Charles reached for the bottle of slick liquid he called Jiffy Lube—essential to their foreplay now. When she was ready, they moved together and fell into the rhythm that made them one. Eventually Sarah called out softly, tightening the grip of her arms and legs. This time Charles didn't follow, nor did he mind. He kissed her and rolled onto his back, his whole length warm against hers, under the covers. This late in life, destinations, and even journeys, mattered less than each moment they spent together. What satisfied each was that the other was there.

Afterward Sarah turned to Charles. "It was because of David, wasn't it? When those two cops manhandled him."

"Yes," Charles answered, lazy and happy, having swum once more in the mouth of the river of their lives.

Chapter 3

CHARLOTTE ARRIVED AT NOON to help in the kitchen. Her husband, Tom, a wiry man with curly black hair and amused blue eyes, helped Charles move extra chairs into the great room and put a wide leaf in the dining table. The two men talked about Tom's pediatric patients while they worked. David went into the backyard to fix the gate hinge. Sarah thought he envied Tom's closeness with Charles. Those two shared medicine and much more — politics, a love of the woods, wry commentary on town meetings — but David found little conversational ground with his father. Even his stories about the math students he taught in Boston, so full of the potential for revisiting his own teenage years, led only to impersonal observations and anecdotes. David probably compared himself unfavorably to Stephie's husband, Jake, who also taught high school math. Jake loved his occupation and excelled at it, earning Charles's respect. David was marking time, hoping before long to make a new living as a ceramic artist.

It must tear him up to think that his two sisters had brought home better sons than he was. If only he knew. If only he had seen Charles protecting that young car thief, that angry, sad boy who'd made him think of David at the same age.

After David finished with the gate, he helped Lottie and her younger brother, Luke, hang an old tire swing they'd found in the barn. They had taken charge of entertaining Hannah, glad for an alternative to boring adults or their own resources. Once the swing was back on its old beech branch, Hannah could be heard throughout the house, begging to be pushed higher. Tess occasionally checked outside but seemed unworried. She moved quietly from one task to another, one group of David's kin to the next, smiling, listening, speaking little. She didn't cling to David; rather it was he who ranged into her proximity, as if for some nourishment his family could not give.

At twelve thirty, the Markses, Peter and Vivianna, came through the mudroom and into the kitchen. They met Tess and Hannah and hugged David, chattering and joking as they unpacked their box of goods for the holiday meal. Peter was stocky and bearish and wore a white beard still threaded with its original red. Vivi was small and angular, with prominent cheekbones, black hair barely streaked with gray, and eyes so dark the pupils were scarcely visible. She was in her midsixties, and Peter was a few years older. They'd been Charles and Sarah's dearest friends for almost forty years. The four of them nearly always shared holidays, with and without family.

"So!" Peter boomed at David, gesturing with exaggerated politeness toward Tess. "This woman looks far too good for you!"

David cuffed him lightly. "You would know, wouldn't you?

Vivi outclasses you by orders of magnitude. You realize that, of course."

"Absolutely. Always marry up," Peter laughed, then clapped a hand over his mouth. He opened the hand and whispered loudly, "Not to be premature or anything."

Tess and Vivi exchanged glances, then smiles. Peter had made them instantly easy together. He made David easy, too, as Charles could not.

Peter was an outspoken, outgoing, occasionally outrageous man descended from a line of Russian Jewish emigrants to western Europe. Many had died in the Holocaust. Peter carried this legacy as lightly as he could. He appreciated humor and savored pleasures, having seen and heard much sorrow. He had been born in New York City to parents who had tried without success to put a good face on life, to shield their son from horror. He loved them, but he never relaxed with them.

In his twenties Peter had settled in Vermont because Vivi would live nowhere else. Through her, he made many friends. He came to love the state's landscape, its people, and its diehard independence. Like Charles, he relished its history, especially the fourteen years in which Vermont had been a tiny, independent nation bordered on three sides by the hard-won new Union with which it exchanged wary looks. Peter had even run for governor once, losing narrowly in the primaries to someone with better connections in the state legislature. Before his retirement, he'd been a newspaper editor. He still wrote stinging op-eds, when he wasn't building rustic furniture in his barn. He sold the smaller pieces at fairs and farmers' markets, the larger ones through galleries.

Vivi was a native Vermonter, a builder's daughter, unflappable and kind. She had met Peter at college in upstate New York before hightailing it back to Vermont. She was a weaver and sold her works through the same markets and galleries as Peter.

Peter and Vivi set out cheese pastries, shrimp, and a horseradish sauce, knowing just where to find what they needed in the Lucases' kitchen. They opened a bottle of wine, and the promise of a quiet interlude after the busy preparations drew everyone into the great room for appetizers.

At two o'clock they all trooped into the dining room, where dinner proceeded as in Thanksgivings past. Afterward they dispersed—David to the great room with Charlotte and Tom, Lottie and Hannah back outside, Luke to Sarah's computer in her office, a narrow room near the kitchen where she took care of bills and other household business. Charles, Peter, and Vivi went outside to walk off their holiday meal in the cold. Thanksgiving day had begun under low, convoluted clouds and spitting snow. Overnight a scant two inches had fallen, the first measurable snowfall of a tardy season. By late afternoon, patches of clear, rinsed blue shone through the gloom, gradually reclaiming the entire sky and spilling sunlight over the landscape, sharpening its subtle browns and grays, its dark greens, and now its first thin cover of white.

Tess and Sarah stayed inside and cleared the table, talking amiably as they rinsed plates and glasses and stowed them into the dishwasher.

"Have you always lived near Boston?" Sarah asked. She understood that Tess was private. She felt a certain tension in the younger woman, as if she were keeping herself apart out of deference to family history and habits, as if she feared she might un-

wittingly step on toes or into crossfire. Still, Sarah was inclined
to like Tess and was curious about her.

"I grew up on the North Shore," Tess said. "My father owned
a fish processing plant outside Gloucester. A lot of my friends
were fishermen's kids. I moved to Boston for college—started
out at BU in art history and later went on to Harvard for my
master's. You'd have thought my father had won the lottery."
She smiled.

Sarah learned a few more things about Tess in their short
conversation by the sink. She was thirty-four, older than she
looked, and she had two sisters and a brother, who among them
had produced five cousins for Hannah, all within a few years
of the same age. Everyone on both sides of the family, including Tess's parents, aunts, uncles, and cousins, lived within forty
miles of one another.

Sarah was about to ask how Tess had managed to spend
this Thanksgiving away from her large clan, when the younger
woman took a hard choking breath. Her whole body jerked into
helpless rigidity, seized as if on a hook. Her jaw stretched open
without a sound. She dropped the glass bowl she'd been rinsing,
and the noise of its shattering broke her frozen spell.

"Hannah!" she wailed, and tore out onto the deck, slamming
the storm door open beyond the range of its hinges, cracking the
wooden frame at the top.

Sarah's thoughts were still colliding when a second cry sliced
the afternoon air, followed by a loud clamor from Ruckus. Then
another cry. It was Lottie screaming, down by the pond.

Sarah raced after Tess. The pond was a hundred yards or
so from the house, invisible beyond a thicket of hemlocks and
yellow birches. It sat near the bottom of the long meadow,

overlooked by a disused cabin on its near edge and bordered by woods on its far one. Tess ran toward Lottie's screams and Ruckus's yelps. Her feet were bare except for sheer stockings. She had kicked off her low pumps for better speed.

Sarah, running behind Tess, glimpsed the shoes red against the snow. Behind her, she heard David shouting. She saw Charles ahead of her and off to her right, loping toward the pond with the Markses right behind. Some aberrant piece of her mind found this amusing, all these old farts running. Then she rounded the thicket and nearly fell. Fear closed her throat like a handful of sand.

The layer of new ice on the pond was marred by a ragged gash, through which Sylvie, barely visible and struggling heavily in the black water, was pulling Hannah's limp and waterlogged form. The streaming dog, straining in every muscle, had Hannah's head above water, the collar of her jacket in her teeth. She had broken the ice all the way from the shore to a large black hole and now was swimming strenuously back through the channel she had carved with her body. It was hard going. Sylvie's head and neck were wrenched sideways with the weight of her burden. Sarah, still running, kept her eyes on the only spot of color in the scene, the small bit of Hannah's red jacket that was visible above the water and ice. It was moving much too slowly.

Lottie stood at the edge of the pond, bent double, keening. Tess had nearly reached the waterside. Charles was already there, with Peter closing behind him, and Vivi trailing.

Then the dog beached Hannah on firm ground. Charles bent over the small form. He put his mouth to the parted blue lips as Tess caught up with him and collapsed to her knees, as Lottie kept wailing from the frozen grass, as everyone else finally arrived amid clouds of breath as dense as smoke. Tess bowed her head while Charles breathed into her child. She stroked Hannah's dripping hair, lifting plastered tendrils away from clammy skin. She mouthed prayers no one could hear and held one hand clenched hard against her breast.

Charles alternated mouth-to-mouth with chest compressions. He did this for so long that his rhythm took hold of the onlookers, who anticipated his every switch from Hannah's lips to her narrow chest. Hypnotized by Charles, by terror, they stood like pillars while Tess's silent supplications gave way to a soft, pleading moan.

At last Hannah coughed, and Charles turned her onto her side. Muddy water spilled from her mouth, past the dam of her tiny, bright white teeth. Charles lay her back again. Her blue eyes flew open, shocked and indignant, reflecting sky. She began to cry, a long, loud, angry howling, as Tess gathered her up and sobbed into her sodden, red wool jacket. Sylvie licked Hannah's dangling hand, then lay panting next to Tess, as close as she could get.

Charles took off his barn coat and stooped to take Hannah gently from her mother's arms. Tess rose stiffly to accommodate him. "We need to get her into the house, Tess." He swaddled Hannah from head to foot in the heavy wool, still warm from his body.

Tess nodded at him, glassy-eyed, as David, in shirtsleeves, took Peter's wordlessly offered down parka and put it over Tess's shoulders. He held her tightly for a second, then turned to Charles. "I'll take Hannah, Dad. I can get her to the house faster." He took the child from his father's arms and looked into his father's face. "Thank you," he said. "Jesus, Dad. Thank you." Then he strode away, nearly running up the hill.

THE EMTS ARRIVED LESS than ten minutes after David got Hannah to the house and called 911. Everyone else was already there—everyone but Lottie and Charlotte, who had stayed behind, huddled near the gash in the water. Charles had swiftly examined Hannah, with Tom standing by, but they couldn't assess her condition without a hospital's resources. They were relieved when the two paramedics stripped the child down, wrapped her in a heated blanket, and checked her vital signs. She tracked one paramedic's forefinger with her eyes and told him her name, where she was, how many fingers he held up, and the names of everyone else in the room.

"No obvious symptoms except the hypothermia," the other paramedic reported. "Core temp's ninety-two, could be worse. They'll run some tests once we get her to the hospital."

"What kind of tests?" David asked. Tess sat next to Hannah, white and silent, taking it all in.

"They'll do a blood gas to check her oxygen level, check for acidosis."

"Acidosis?" David interrupted.

Charles answered. "High acid in the blood. Causes confusion, shortness of breath."

The paramedic chimed in. "She doesn't have those, but they'll test her anyway."

David nodded, and the man went on. "They'll draw blood, maybe urine. They'll do a chest X-ray, in case she aspirated sand or weeds or anything."

Charles said, "But so far, you think she's all right."

"Far as we can tell, but we can't be sure yet. It's probably a good thing the water was cold. Protects the tissues from effects of oxygen deprivation. Might even trigger a diving reflex—slows the heart, sends the blood to the internal organs and the brain."

Charles took a breath and blew it out. He looked haggard. Sarah went to stand beside him, her hand on his arm. "If she does have problems . . ." She couldn't go on.

"The docs will look for lung damage. Brain damage, too." Tess started.

The paramedic looked over at her and said, "The signs look good. She's alert, lucid. Keep your focus on that. Seventy percent of submersion episodes end in death or brain damage. I think your daughter's going to be in the other thirty percent."

Tess rode with Hannah in the ambulance. David, Sarah, and Charles followed, bringing dry clothes and a quilt. Tom offered to come, too, but Charles urged him to wait behind and see how Lottie was doing.

Tess brought intermittent reports to the hospital waiting area. Hannah's tests were normal. She hadn't aspirated any pond debris; she had no fluid in her lungs. It was a good thing she'd had a full belly when she went through the ice; that slowed the onset of hypothermia. It was a good thing Sylvie was right there and had her out of the water in only a few minutes. It was a good thing Charles knew CPR.

Hannah would recover completely. The only thing that worried the attending physician was her silence. She'd clammed up after answering the paramedics' questions.

Tess said, "It's her way of dealing with things. She just needs time."

The doctor wasn't so sure, but he released Hannah after reading the paramedics' account of her clear responses to them. After four hours of tests and observation, Charles went to warm up his Subaru while Tess signed the necessary papers. No one spoke on the ride home; no one seemed willing to intrude on Hannah's quiet.

By nine o'clock the family was seated in the great room. Vivi and Peter had gone home, reassured about Hannah. Luke was in Sarah's office, where he had fallen asleep and missed the crisis altogether. The rest of them were subdued. Sarah's eyes moved from Hannah to Charles and back again. She was comforted by the sight of Hannah on Tess's lap, wrapped in a quilt, but she worried about Charles's gray, exhausted look.

He was sunk in his wing chair, stretching his legs out before him. His face was in shadow, but his eyes caught the lamplight as he watched his son, who sat with his arm around Tess. David looked over at his father and held his gaze.

Lottie would look at no one. She had come inside with her mother almost twenty minutes behind the others, hair tangled, teeth chattering hard enough to crack. Tom had tried to assure her that Hannah would be fine, that the EMTs had seen no signs of permanent harm, but Lottie wasn't convinced. She had wanted to go to the hospital to see for herself, and she was furious when Charlotte insisted they all stay behind and out of the way.

Hours later, seeing Tess carry Hannah back into the house, Lottie had blurted out, "It was my fault, Tess. I turned my back, I threw a stick for Ruckus. I didn't know Hannah would step onto the ice. There were these little tracks in the snow on the pond. I showed them to Hannah. I didn't know she would follow them. I should have known, Tess. I should have watched her better."

Tess put Hannah into David's arms. The child watched solemnly as her mother embraced the older girl. "Lottie, honey, I watched you with Hannah all afternoon. You were so careful. It wasn't your fault."

Sarah could have hugged Tess, for she had overheard Charlotte reprimand her shivering daughter down by the pond. She knew Charlotte would also offer comfort, given time; she knew her judgmental outburst was only the aftermath of terror, but she could not forgive Charlotte for deepening Lottie's misery and shame. Adolescence made Lottie susceptible to the best and worst of her imagination, and the worst was in control tonight. To Lottie, Hannah remained as good as drowned, though she was right there, safe.

Finally, after everyone sat exhausted and still for nearly an hour, Hannah spoke. "Mom, did you know Sylvie can talk?"

Tess shifted Hannah in her lap and looked into her face and said, "Really, Hannah? Did Sylvie say something to you today?"

"Yes." Hannah sat up straight and looked around the room. "Sylvie!" she called. "Where are you?"

Sylvie was right at Tess's feet. She gave a low, canine groan, then stretched and stood and rested her chin on Tess's lap, next to Hannah.

"*There* you are, Sylvie," breathed Hannah, lying back against her mother's chest. "I was telling Mom that you can talk."

"What did Sylvie say, Hannah?" Tess looked down into her daughter's upturned face.

"She said, *Don't be afraid.* That's all. She said that when I was in the water. I was really cold. And I was heavy. But I *wasn't* afraid, because Sylvie was there." She closed her eyes. "I really love Sylvie, Mom."

"I know, Hannah. We all really love Sylvie." Tess stroked the dog's ears, trying not to cry. David pulled her head toward him and kissed her hair.

AT TEN DAVID AND Tess rose to take the sleeping Hannah upstairs to bed. Tess went to Charles and gazed up into his eyes as he stood to embrace her. "I can't find the words," she said to him. "I am grateful beyond words." She rested her head on his chest a moment, then turned to Sarah and put her arms around her. "I hope you'll sleep, Sarah. All's well." She glanced over Sarah's shoulder at Lottie, who looked down at her hands.

Sylvie followed wherever Hannah went, and Hannah, who woke on the way upstairs, groggily insisted that Sylvie sleep with them all in the same big bed. Tess turned and looked ruefully at Sarah. "All right, sweetheart," said Sarah. "Sylvie can stay with you." Inwardly, a different Sarah shuddered at the thought of mud residue on her good linens, but that was the Sarah who had thought all Thanksgivings were the same.

Chapter 4

AT FIVE, SARAH ROSE in the dark. Charles was still sleeping heavily, so she moved quietly about their room, pulling on sweatpants and a heavy sweater against the predawn chill. She winced when she dropped a shoe, but Charles never stirred. He must have taken something.

Sarah went into the hall. As she headed toward the stairs, Tess emerged from another bedroom, wrapped in a faded pink robe, trying to close the door soundlessly behind her. She started when she saw Sarah, then smiled and caught up with her.

"You too?" she whispered. "I thought I was the only one awake."

"Didn't you sleep at all?" Sarah whispered back.

"Like a rock at first. But David kept thrashing, and Hannah would have slept inside my skin if she could. Then there was Sylvie," she added. "Four bodies in one bed."

Sarah made a face. "Now there's a picture. Would you like something to help you sleep now?" she offered.

Tess shook her head. "No, thanks. Hannah will wake up early. I need to be here."

"Then let's go brew some coffee," Sarah yawned. "I'll stoke up the fire."

They moved silently down the stairs, where Ruckus greeted them by wagging his whole body and whimpering with relief.

"Poor baby," sighed Sarah. "You miss Sylvie, don't you, boy." The two dogs normally slept together in a corner of Sarah's office on an old green cushion from a long-ago glider.

Sarah raked the coals in the furnace and threw on several chunks of wood that soon caught fire. She poured water into the top of the coffeemaker but found no filters. She went into the pantry for a fresh package, and there she saw the pies she'd made less than twenty-four hours earlier, one apple and two pumpkin, all untouched.

Tess came up behind her and said, "Ooooh, look at those. You know, the holidays aren't official without leftover pie for breakfast. May I?"

"Of course. I'll join you."

"Which would you like?"

"A slice of each," Sarah declared. "How about you?"

"Same." Tess took plates and mugs down from a cupboard. "Where are the forks again?"

An hour or so later, Lottie came sleepily out of Sarah's office, dragging her feet in an old pair of her grandmother's sheepskin slippers. She wore borrowed flannel pajamas and a cabled woolen throw around her shoulders. Her mass of ash-brown hair was tangled as a brush pile. Tom and Charlotte had wanted her to go home with them, but she had said she was too tired. Sarah thought it more likely that Lottie, like Sylvie, couldn't bear to be far from Hannah.

Lottie slumped down into a chair next to Sarah, across from

Tess. The sun was not quite up, but it lit the sky over Apple Mountain in the distance. Through the bay window by the kitchen table they could see over the backyard and across the high end of the meadow that led down to the thicket and the pond. The light shone like pearl. Soon it would turn to the gradual morning blue that Sarah loved. It was a peaceful scene, but the memory of yesterday's headlong rush down the slope was all too fresh.

Sarah squeezed Lottie's hand under the table. "Want some pie, kiddo?"

Lottie shook her head mutely.

"Oh, come on," Tess urged, gesturing with her fork toward a second serving on her own plate. "This pumpkin is the *best*." She took another bite and mimed ecstasy, her eyes heavenward, her left hand on her heart. She reached for a can of Reddi-wip, bought specially for Luke and Hannah, and pointed it at Lottie, grinning.

"How *can* you?" Lottie burst out. "How can you eat pie? How can you act . . . goofy?"

Tess stopped clowning but was still amused. "You want to know? I'll tell you, Lottie. I'm eating pie and I'm goofing around because I'm incredibly happy. I'm celebrating. I'm finishing Thanksgiving dinner with praise in my heart. Total joy."

"Yeah," said Lottie. "After I almost killed your daughter." Her brown eyes filled, and she stared fixedly out the window so that the tears would not spill over.

"That's not what happened at all," Tess said firmly. "You took the very best care of Hannah that anyone could. You jumped every time it looked like she might get hurt—on the swing, running around the yard, trying to climb the deck railing. I saw all that."

"It wasn't enough," cried Lottie, finally looking straight at Tess and letting the tears come.

"Right," Tess agreed, matter-of-fact. "It wasn't. That's a tough lesson."

"I don't understand," said Lottie.

"You shouldn't have to," Tess told her. "You shouldn't have to know yet that you can't protect the people you love. You do what you can, but perfect safety just isn't possible."

Lottie opened her mouth to say more, but Tess shook her head. "Look at the sky turning blue out there, and eat your grandmother's pie, and get it all the way through your head that Hannah is perfectly okay. And so are you."

Lottie gave in and eyed the pie disappearing from Tess's plate.

Just then they heard Hannah scampering down the hall with Sylvie at her heels. She stopped at the kitchen doorway in footed purple pajamas, holding a tattered stuffed rabbit by one ear and smiling brightly at the three women sitting at the table.

"I *wondered* where you were!" she said, putting her small, balled hands on her hips. The bunny swung at her side. She went to Tess and kissed her, then dispensed her affections to Sarah before scrambling up into Lottie's lap. Lottie looked apprehensive, as if Hannah might dissolve into mist, but she made a circle of her arms and loosely enfolded the solid, warm child.

Hannah looked across at Tess and declared, "Mom, I need breakfast."

Tess laughed. "We're all having pie. Want some?"

"Pie for *breakfast*?" Hannah crowed. "Is there pumpkin?"

IT'S ALREADY TWILIGHT. Sarah croons softly to Charles as she listens once more for someone to pick up a ringing phone. Lottie answers and spins into fear at her grandmother's nearly incoherent voice. *"Mom!"* she shouts, then yells into the mouthpiece at Sarah. "Nana, I can't understand you! Slow down!" Dimly, Sarah can hear Lottie's alarm, but she has no time for it.

"Mom?" Charlotte asks, after seizing the phone from Lottie. "Mom, are you all right?"

Sarah takes a ragged breath, which feels like the first since she started toward the woods with Sylvie. Finally, she is able to speak. Charlotte stays calm while Sarah tells her what has happened and where she is. Sarah is immeasurably grateful for her daughter's coolness in this dizzying moment. "Mom," Charlotte says again, steadying Sarah. "We're leaving right this second. Lottie will know where the trail is. We'll be there in twenty minutes. I just made tea; I'll bring a thermos. Keep Dad warm. He'll be fine."

She hangs up, and Sarah turns back to Charles. "Don't go, don't go," she begs him.

The EMTs arrive at last, having followed Sarah's route on their snowmobiles. One tows a rescue sled — a sleek, enclosed bubble on runners, with room inside for a patient, an attendant, and emergency supplies. Moments later, Charlotte and Lottie come racing down the trail, half falling, half sliding. Charlotte has a large flashlight in her hand, turned on against the gathering dusk. It's

been half an hour since Sarah reached her husband's uncon-
scious body, and he has not so much as moaned since the first
small sound. Three rescue workers check his vital signs, which are
weak but steady. They take off his wet outer clothing and wrap
him in a lightweight, heated blanket before moving him to the
rescue sled.

"His body temp is just over eighty-six, which isn't too bad,"
says one of the paramedics. "We can only warm him part way out
here. Too much external heat sends the cooled blood back to the
organs too fast. Shocks the system."

They explain more as they work, telling Charlotte what they
see. Charles's heart rate is steady, but the least wrong move could
drastically disrupt it. They move very, very gently with him. They
think he has broken his knee. They're not too worried about a
cut on the back of his head, though. The snow has kept it from
bleeding much.

Finally the team installs Charles in the rescue sled. Charlotte
goes and pours hot tea into the thermos cap for Sarah. "You'll
need this, to make it back home, Mom." She sees a paramedic —
a tough, abrupt young woman — gesture to her. "Time to go,"
she says briskly. "Try not to worry. He seems pretty tough for his
age."

Charlotte barely has time to say, "Go ahead," before the
woman climbs into the sled with Charles and yells to the driver,
who speeds off; then her remaining colleague climbs aboard the
other machine and follows. Charlotte watches the taillights rapidly disappear. She turns to Sarah, who is sipping tea, cradled in
Lottie's arms but still shivering.

"Mom, we have to get you home. Now. It's almost dark."

"Yeah, Nana," Lottie adds shakily. "Come on."

Sarah looks blankly at the two women. She knows perfectly well who they are, but their voices are slurry, their features do not hold still. It isn't until Charlotte and Lottie each take an arm that Sarah heaves herself painfully upright, pushing on a fallen log for leverage. She wants to say something but cannot. Her jaw will not open, she cannot form words.

Neither can she walk. She trembles. Her knees buckle every few steps. Charlotte and Lottie make a chair for her, interlocking their hands and wrists in a foursquare pattern. Sarah manages to hold the flashlight steady in her lap. Gradually, they make their way home, stopping now and then to rest. Sylvie joins them, having first run ahead with the snowmobiles, which soon outraced her. Ruckus stays with the women all along, his head low. When they finally reach the house, Charlotte tries to put Sarah to bed. "Lottie can stay with you, Mom. I'll go to the hospital and call as soon as I know anything."

Sarah nearly agrees. She is desperately tired. Her limbs are smoke, they will never hold her up again. But as Charlotte turns to leave, Sarah suddenly bolts up in bed, burning. "No," she cries. "Wait." She will not be placated, she will not lie down. The more Charlotte reasons with her, the more unreasonable she becomes. Finally she turns to Lottie. "You help me, right now. I'm going with you." Lottie ignores her mother's disapproval. She puts her hands under Sarah's arms and lifts, as if her grandmother were a small child.

Chapter 5

PETER AND VIVI LIVED six miles closer to town than
Sarah and Charles, in an 1830s farmhouse fronting
on a dirt road. The house was older but strung together like Charles and Sarah's, its two-story main unit linked to
the barn by a long ell. This design kept farmers and their hired
help out of the elements. It was too easy, in a January whiteout,
to get lost just stepping outside.

Peter and Vivi had adapted the design to their own uses. The
barn was now Peter's woodworking shop, and the adjacent part
of the ell, once used for storage and as quarters for farmhands,
was Vivi's textile studio. The rest of the ell had been hollowed
out to make a single, high-ceilinged room that was beautiful and
always messy. It held an enormous kitchen and dining area with
two big couches, bookshelves, and a woodstove. A wall of windows faced southwest, overlooking broad meadows and wooded
hills beyond. Peter and Vivi scarcely used the main house at all,
except for their bedroom and bath.

Everyone, including Sylvie and Ruckus, arrived at the Markses' in two cars. Charles was out of sorts, ill-tempered ever since he'd risen around noon. No pie for his late breakfast; he would not be sweetened.

When the extended Lucas family entered, Vivi had a Brunswick stew simmering and cheese biscuits ready to bake. Hannah asked Peter, "Where's your dog?"

Peter bent down over a padded rocker and scooped up a hefty black-and-white cat. "Here he is," he announced to Hannah.

She pursed her lips severely and shook her head at him. "That's a cat!" she exclaimed.

Peter gave her a look of horror. "Sshhh!" he said. "Don't tell Boojus that! He *thinks* he's a dog!"

Hannah ducked her head and giggled, her hand over her mouth. "Why?"

"Just watch," said Peter, putting Boojus down. "See how he sits?" Boojus sat. "Any self-respecting cat sits with its legs all close together and its tail wrapped around like a ribbon on a package. Boojus here sits all loose and sloppy, just like a dog. See how his lazy old tail's just lying there, straight out? He'd wag it if he could figure out how. He also fetches. And follows us around, and begs at the table."

"Can I see him fetch?" Hannah begged.

"Well, sure." Peter tore a piece of waxed paper off the end of a roll, crumpled it noisily into a ball, and threw it across the wide oak floorboards. Boojus pricked his ears up at the first crinkling sound, watched Peter's hand in tense anticipation, then scrambled across the smooth floor in pursuit of the ball, skidding past it as he tried to stop. He doubled back, batted the wad of paper around a few times, then picked it up in his mouth and trotted to Peter. He dropped it at Peter's feet and looked up at him expectantly.

Hannah said, "Let me!"

Tess laughed, "I never saw such a thing!"

Charles, Charlotte, and Luke stared coldly at Boojus, unamused by his performance.

"Oops," said Vivi, interrupting the play and tossing Boojus outdoors. "Forgot about the Lucas family allergies."

Hannah buried her face in Sylvie's fur and burst into tears. "I wanted to make him fetch!" she cried.

Vivi looked distressed. "Oh, dear, I never meant . . ."

Lottie soothed Hannah and shyly offered to take her outside in pursuit of the cat. "I promise, we'll stay close," she said to Tess, not noticing Charlotte's anxious look. Tess agreed readily. Luke followed Lottie and Hannah. In the small commotion of their leaving, Charles corralled Peter and David and led them into Peter's shop. Sarah saw them go and knew it would do Charles good to decompress in the company of men. She was glad to see him invite David and not Tom, who sat next to Charlotte on the big couch. Soon she heard distant, deep-chested laughter drift back into the kitchen. Charles's bad mood was loosening its grip.

Hannah's increased, meanwhile, and soon after dinner David and Tess decided to take her home.

"Never mind," Vivi said, when they apologized for leaving early. "She just needs you two to herself for a while."

Tess carried Hannah to David's car. The dogs followed, and David drove off with Hannah crying loudly, wanting both to stay and to be far away from all those people.

After they had gone, the others sat back down at the table with coffee and the last of the pie Sarah had brought over. Peter asked where David and Tess had met, adding, "Is Hannah's father in the picture?"

"Don't know," Sarah answered. "They haven't mentioned him."

Lottie hesitated, then said. "Hannah's father is dead. He was murdered."

Charlotte jumped as if stung. "How do you know that?"

Lottie looked uncomfortable. "I don't know if I should've said. She told me today, at our house. We were alone in the kitchen. I was still feeling really guilty about Hannah, and she told me she knew what that was like. She said she blamed herself for a long time after her husband got killed, even though she was only trying to keep him safe." She looked at them all in turn and added, "His name was Ian. She was really in love with him."

Sarah stared at Lottie and Charlotte as if into a time-lapse mirror. Her own face at fifteen, and at forty-six. She caught her breath, caught herself suddenly tapping rapidly at her breastbone with her fingertips. Her hand knocked at her heart; her heart knocked back.

Charles moved his chair closer and casually slung an arm around her shoulder.

Tom asked Lottie, "What happened? How was Tess trying to protect him?"

"She made him take the car," Lottie said. "He had to go out late at night, and there had been a bunch of muggings in their neighborhood. He wanted to walk but she made him take the car. Then he got carjacked. He probably resisted, and that's when he got killed. Shot. They never caught who did it. Or found the car."

Vermonters were used to different hazards altogether—ice, cold, dangerous roads, even deer ticks. Human violence rarely threatened, except in close quarters made tense by winter, poverty, or alcohol.

Sarah ventured. "When did this happen?" She'd finally identified what puzzled her about Tess. It was as if she didn't fully inhabit the space in which she moved. This seemed less strange now, given the startling news.

Lottie answered. "I think Hannah was still a baby. It's been a couple of years."

"Does Tess have family?" Vivi asked.

Sarah spoke about the close-knit clan Tess had described. "I wonder whether that's when she went back to the Quakers. I wonder what her husband was like. Ian."

Charles answered. "He owned a small computer company. Troubleshooting, systems management, bunch of services. But his passion was music. He played piano—jazz, blues, classical." Seeing Sarah's surprise, he said, "Tess told me this afternoon, before we left the house. She didn't tell me how Ian died, only that she couldn't have survived another loss."

THAT NIGHT, BEFORE CHARLES came to bed, Sarah sat on the window seat recalling her assumption that David and Tess's story would gradually emerge over the long holiday weekend. Instead, only this grim tale of murder was out. She shuddered and remembered as well the simultaneous birth and death of Andrew, her first son. It had happened a month after Charlotte started kindergarten, while she was still thrown by her daily separation from Sarah. Stephie was an adventuresome four-year-old, a handful for Sarah, who was tired before she even rose in the morning. Her pregnancy was hard. Nausea dogged her throughout, along with spotting, cramping, and shortness of breath. Charlotte grew more demanding, even as Sarah lost patience and energy. She was no help to her daughter. Instead, she had sown the first bitter seeds into the ground of Charlotte's being.

The landscape between mother and daughter had changed as the seeds put forth their shoots, and it seemed from then on as if every small misstep on either side nourished a crop of frustration and misunderstanding. Sarah realized that her memories exaggerated the early disaffection, but she knew as well that small rifts do grow large over time, fed by any incident that furthers the pain of the first one. Through the years there had been many such incidents. Charlotte took everything to heart, and Sarah's efforts to comfort her and heal the rift met with failure every time. Eventually a pattern formed and seemed indelible. By now, neither Charlotte nor Sarah could break out of the role each had taken with the other.

Yet Sarah could bring to mind whole scenes from her past with Charlotte, capturing them in greater detail than she had in years. She remembered seeing in her newborn daughter's face those of older generations, which passed fleetingly over the tiny new features like the shadows of high summer clouds. Later, she and the toddler Charlotte had delighted passionately in each other, mother and firstborn, utterly in love. Their connection seemed telepathic, especially at night, when Charlotte would awaken just as Sarah was dropping off to sleep, as if the child could not bear for her mother to go beyond conscious reach.

Sarah never thought about the end of her troubled third pregnancy without mourning as well the loss of her closeness with

Charlotte. Memory would simultaneously place before her the image of her daughter's scowling face at age five and the sorrowful sight of her motionless infant son. The nurses had tried to whisk the baby away, to keep Sarah from seeing his lifeless body, but she howled at them to let her hold him. They consulted Charles, a doctor they knew well, and he instructed them to comply, even as he absorbed the loss himself, haggard and grieving.

Finally the nurses cleaned Andrew up, wrapped him in a blue blanket, and laid him in Sarah's arms. They invited Charles into the delivery room, but he declined. He had seen his dead son as the nurses were swaddling him, and he thought Sarah needed to be alone with the small body. For hours after Andrew had died on his way into life, she felt powerfully that he had come from unreachable realms with knowledge she needed urgently to learn. Yet there he lay, swaddled in her arms, looking entirely at peace and not at all like a failed emissary. His face was closed; she could read nothing in his blank, perfect features except her own loss. She had given birth to death, and she felt its claim on her. She held Andrew until he was cold and his chill entered her body and heart.

Charlotte turned with ever greater need toward her father after the loss of Andrew. Charles at first tried to revive Sarah's attention to their bewildered daughter, but soon he simply gave in and turned toward Charlotte with an eagerness of his own. He had never before been the primary parent.

Stephie entirely ignored Sarah's coldness, bringing her small body close as if to warm her mother. She asked many questions about baby Andrew and where he had gone, and then she went about her childish life as happily as before.

Sarah grieved a long time for her lost son, barely getting out of bed for weeks and forcing herself up after that. Unmoved by her daughters, she was finally reborn as a mother when David arrived, squalling and robust, just over a year later. She had not planned that pregnancy and did not believe in it. She and Charles had made love so seldom, and with such tepid ardor, that the pregnancy seemed without substance. Evanescent. But when David lay in her arms, she finally woke up and was herself again, if more inclined to bouts of dread—she, who had grown up free and fearless, even in hard times.

THE REST OF THANKSGIVING weekend was quiet. An old friend of David's dropped by on Saturday. Peter and Vivi came and went. Charlotte and Tom showed up, too, running from Lottie and Luke. "Honest to God," Tom said. "They ignore each other when they're home alone. I know that because neither one is dead when we get back. They save their constant bickering and snarling for our loving ears." Charlotte elbowed him when he added, "Kids are overrated. Nobody tells you that while you still have a choice."

The next morning, Sunday, Hannah sat in Sarah's lap during a late family breakfast, displaying a sudden affection that pierced Sarah with sweetness and regret. David and Tess were leaving that afternoon, and she hated seeing them go.

An hour later Charles and David went out to stack the last of the green, split wood that would dry over the next year. The house was heated by a room-size, dual-unit furnace that could burn either wood or oil. Sarah and Charles used wood almost exclusively when heating oil costs were high, as they were now. This year's fuel supply, ten cords of hardwood, was dry and ready inside the barn. David and Charles were stacking next year's wood outside. Charles loved the sight of a perfect woodpile, squared at the ends and flat on top, covered with sheets of tin, its quartered hardwood sections forming a handsome mosaic along the face.

Standing inside the porch door, Sarah was pleased to see Charles and David laughing and talking volubly. This change in their connection seemed miraculous, yet it made sense. She would never forget the look David had given to his father as he took Hannah from him, wrapped in his coat. Sarah had not seen her son's face so naked since he was younger than Luke — not even when his ex-wife sliced him up and laid the strips to dry like jerky. That had toughened David, but now, near the end of this visit, he seemed easy in his skin. He'd looked at Charles with an open adoration he had not bestowed in thirty years. He had broken the ice and found warm currents underneath.

Chapter 6

THE FIRST BIG SNOW came down in the middle of December, taking out trees and power, often simultaneously, as when a tall old maple or fir, rotten at the center, fell over onto electrical lines with a slow creaking and a final crash. Anyone who lived in rural Vermont lived also with the sound of trees falling in the forest. Wind, wet snow, age, or disease downed them, especially in dense stands where overcrowded hardwoods grew to fifty feet without roots deep enough to support their nearly branchless heights. Many of these trees fell with a breath of wind; others were cut deliberately. They all made the same heavy sound as they came down.

A century earlier, 80 percent of Vermont had been clear-cut for pasture and farming. Now the proportions were reversed, reflecting changes in regional economies and demographics. The trees had simply grown wherever the cleared land was no longer needed, and the result was miles of dense young woods. In time, nature took care of the crowding by taking out the weaker trees. Charles, however, had been unwilling to wait.

In the forty-three years that he and Sarah had occupied their acreage, Charles had thinned several acres of their woods, providing the household with firewood in the process. He'd had an old pickup truck with a winch that he used to engineer the fall of each tall tree that he culled from its fellows. He told Sarah you could plan which way a tree would fall if the trunk was thick enough. You made your cut, and as you deepened it you inserted wedges that would force the fall in the direction you wanted. But these spindly trees allowed no such control. So Charles wrapped the trunks with chains he attached to the winch cable. He secured the chains above the site of each cut. Then, when he made the cut and turned the winch on, the cable pulled the tree over within a few feet of the spot he had chosen. Sometimes he had to angle the cable around another stump or a boulder to control the tree through its dreamlike, slowly accelerating fall. Sarah watched, in the earliest years, and thought of Charles as the choreographer of a large, lumbering ballet. She had liked that word, *lumbering.*

Eventually she grew so accustomed to the sound of trees falling and chain saws whining that she scarcely noticed. The racket became her children's lullabies on summer nights, when Charles could work in the woods until well past nine. He would come home from his office by six, sit down for dinner, and then rattle the junky truck down the meadow to whatever section of woods he was thinning. He would limb the trunks of the felled trees, remove smaller branches from thicker ones, and haul the bare lengths out with the winch to be bucked into sections and split. He piled the brush in gullies or under large outcroppings of rock, leaving it behind as winter cover for small creatures before it rotted slowly back into the forest floor. Today the trees he had left uncrowded in the light had thick, strong trunks. Their broader branches started lower to the ground and spread more widely. Their canopies were lush, their shapes graceful.

Sarah knew how much pride Charles took in husbanding the forest well. It was not what he'd been raised to do. He had been born into a wealthy Boston family that had sent generations of sons to Harvard and then into commerce, law, or politics. He had even been named for the city's famous river. But he had spent his childhood summers in New Hampshire and Maine at rented cottages with his mother and sister. His father would come on weekends. On Friday evenings Charles would watch him wash the urban grime away in whatever sparkling lake they were visiting that year. On Sunday nights his father would head back to the city, his eyes reclaimed by anxiety or a distant cogitating look. Charles had often told Sarah how it had saddened him to watch this, but how it pleased him to see the changes in himself when he was outside more than in, when he could learn the names of birds, trees, animals, and insects.

Charles slowly pulled back from his striving peers and family as he came to feel increasingly at home in nature and taught himself more about it. He read, observed, and explored. Finally, in his high school years, when his mother rented the same large cottage three summers in a row, Charles found a mentor, a farmer and town clerk near the Connecticut River, a man only a decade older than himself. Bony, slow-moving, wry Albert Graves had taught Charles how to shear sheep, card and spin the wool, milk cows and goats, make cheese, tap a sugar maple, build a barn, drive a tractor, harvest corn and hay, cut down trees, and split wood. In his apprenticeship to Albert, Charles not only learned a lexicon of skills but came to learn and love his own body, its sliding wiry muscles, its sweat, its smells, its strength, and its surprising intuition about tools and their uses. He did not make the leap to a career in medicine until he fought and was wounded in a devastating war—until he saw firsthand how bodies could be split like firewood or torn like a bobcat's prey and sometimes, miraculously, made whole again. He had told this to Sarah the first time they slept together, when she first saw the shrapnel scars on his back.

Those high school summers displaced Charles's thoughts of Harvard farther north to Dartmouth, where he could stay close to woods and mountains and could now and then visit Albert on his farm across the river. Soon Charles was unfit for the partnership his father had planned for him in his law firm. He meant, instead, to teach history and run his own small farm. Above all, he wanted to escape the moral imperative of his parents, which, as he had explained it to Sarah, was to make a lot of money and do a little politically expedient good. After history gave way to medicine and Charles opened his practice in this small, poor state, he reversed that equation. He felt he did a lot of good every day but never got rich doing it. From the beginning, patients without money or insurance paid him in whatever currency they could. Charles would take anything—tires with decent tread, a cord of wood, a cement mixer. Even if it was not of value to him, he would find someone who could use it. All he really wanted, in a material way, was to provide for his family and permit himself the twenty-two acres that recalled his youth.

SARAH HAD BEEN RAISED in the Northeast Kingdom, the poorest part of Vermont. Her father, William Everett, was a teacher. Her mother, Louisa McGill Everett, was a housewife with a huge garden, the overabundance of which she sold every summer from a vegetable stand at the end of their long driveway. Even as a small child, Sarah had helped with that enterprise — weeding, harvesting produce, and putting it into baskets or bunches. She kept her mother company in the shade of the roadside stand and could still remember the buzz of insects, the close heat of the small shelter, the dust in the air as people came and went in their boxy black automobiles or horsedrawn buckboards.

Sarah was an only child, so the family had few enough mouths to feed and was well-off by local standards, which were spare at best. Early in Sarah's life, though, her family's welfare suffered along with their neighbors'. By the time she was seven, the poverty that already surrounded her grew desperate under the weight of the Great Depression. Soon her parents' big, peeling farmhouse filled up with relatives who had been wiped out by hard times.

Uncle Burton Everett, William's brother, was the first to show up, having hitchhiked from Boston lugging a satchel and wearing a heavy tool belt, ready to work. With William as his helper, he started right in, tearing down the empty barn and salvaging enough wood to add two rooms to the back of the house and build a two-seater outhouse. Sarah watched the men and handed them tools, once Burton had taught her the difference between a wrench and pliers, a claw hammer and a ball peen, a hacksaw and a crosscut. Uncle Burton was big, loud, and sweaty, entirely unlike Sarah's quiet, reflective father — except for the storytelling. Uncle Burton's tales were wild and silly, her father's more sly, but the family resemblance was there. That had reassured the young Sarah, whose world was changing.

Burton's labors brought the toilet seat count to four (two indoors, two out) and the bedroom count to eight if one included the converted dining room and what had once been a sewing room, hardly bigger than a closet. Each would prove necessary, for the Everett household gradually swelled to a commune of sorts, with ten adults and eight children eking out an existence on fifty rocky acres. William kept teaching, though the three towns that employed him could seldom pay. Burton and three uncles on Sarah's mother's side — Harry, Hollis, and Warren McGill, who came with their wives and children — got so good at tearing down disused buildings and erecting habitable ones that they soon had a small barter business going. They worked for gasoline, flour, milk, butter, used clothing, tools, seeds, and medical care.

Sarah's mother and aunts enlarged the garden, raised chickens for eggs and stewing, canned and preserved produce and wild fruit, and altered hand-me-downs to fit the various members of the extended family. They ripped out moth-eaten sweaters and used the wool to knit new ones. It sometimes took the yarn from three or four small or holey sweaters to make another that would fit one of the larger men or boys. The effect was odd and patch-worked, except when Sarah's Aunt Jane Lacey, Louisa's widowed sister, was the knitter. Aunt Jane knitted moons or stars in contrasting colors, or stripes and zigzags, or a white birch against a two-tone field of blue and dark green. This last sweater went to Sarah's father, who wore it until the elbows gave out. Sarah still had the stretched and threadbare garment mothballed in a trunk somewhere.

The last of the live-in relatives and friends moved on when Sarah was halfway through high school. She had almost no memory, by then, of ever having been an only child; cousins and a few unrelated children, boarded out by their struggling families, had always surrounded her. She had known the whole lot of them were poor, but in her mind that was not a bad thing when there were so many other children to play with, and they all had three meals a day.

While Charles had spent his wild times alone, Sarah had spent her liberty in a pack, like a young coyote. She and her cousins, and one or two refugee boarders in their midst, had discovered every last hiding place, swimming place, wading place, climbing place, berry-picking place, and flat-rock sunning place on the fifty acres. From her companions Sarah learned to be fearless in woods, beside headlong rivers, and in shallows where fish bumped her legs and snakes now and then swam by, writing black esses on the surface of the water.

Only later did Sarah learn more about the adults' fears and quarrels in those years, the confinements and necessary dependencies that grieved them all and strained their relationships. When Louisa mentioned the strife to Sarah and Charles, just before they were married, her account lit up memories that Sarah had never understood—an aunt locking herself away in one of the outhouses, shouting out her demand to be left alone; uncles quarreling, possibly drunk; another uncle weeping with a strangled sound that nearly drowned the crooning comfort offered by his wife.

Hearing of those depression years, Charles had been moved by Sarah's sense of security in such hard times. Though his own family had not suffered want—not with their ironclad trusts and securities and their properties that could simply sit until their value rose again—many of Charles's classmates had been

forced to leave the private schools he attended. Some of his parents' friends had lost everything. "Nobody ever told me we were
going to be okay," he said to Sarah. "And I saw so many people
ruined overnight. It just made me determined not to stake my
life on money."

In Sarah's last year of high school, she learned she could attend college in Vermont on a full scholarship, an opportunity
that opened up for girls when the boys left to fight in World
War II. The day after graduation, she moved to New York with
a girlhood friend, Adelaide Jones. It was 1945. Though the war
was ending and the men would soon return in weary droves,
Addie and Sarah raced to join the last shallow wave of New
Women, the adventuresome young females who had inspired
them by becoming journalists, teachers, and factory workers.
Sarah and Addie were eager for careers, a heady plan for two
young women from the remote Northeast Kingdom. No other
women in their acquaintance had ever finished college—most
had not started—and there they suddenly were, earning more
in a year than their parents had sometimes been able to earn in
two or three.

Sarah joined a magazine called *The Life and Times of Women*,
which throughout the war ran stories about her own generation
and their older sisters, young women in search of new expression
and new roles in a world gone inside out. Sarah excelled as an
editor and hoped that she would eventually move to the top. She
wanted to choose which stories to run, which writers to nurture,
which models of success and intoxicating independence to provide for thousands of readers determined to resist conventional
womanhood.

Then, in the late spring of 1946, Wendell Burnham showed

up with his empty left sleeve, his clips from *Stars & Stripes* and *Life*, and his brand-new graduate degree in journalism from Columbia. The publisher of *LTW* hired Wendell not because he was uniquely qualified but because the returning soldiers had earned special consideration. They had families to care for, lives to pick up again. Some of the editorial, secretarial, and production staff bowed to this, but others just up and quit.

Wendell rapidly reversed *LTW*'s editorial direction. With a growing staff of men he had known in the war or at Columbia, he ran more and more articles pitched at women but serving their husbands and the magazine's advertisers. The rhetoric covered a single idea from countless angles. Now that the men were home, the nation needed its women back at their traditional stations—the kitchen, the bedroom, the nursery, the garden.

Sarah was dismayed that peace should suddenly bring shackles for women who had thrived on adventure and change. Though she did not question the courage of those who had taken part in the war, she wanted more than the dubious freedom of devotion to others.

By the time Sarah met Charles, she had gone through two other jobs with two other magazines, one on amateur photography and one on gardening. The latter made her think she should study horticulture and one day open a nursery or landscaping service back home in Vermont. Having neither land of her own nor savings to buy any, she registered for botany classes at NYU and took yet another job, this time in the medical school's student affairs office, so she could qualify for free tuition.

That was where she met Charles. She noticed him because he was tall enough that she would not feel ungainly beside him. But then, she always noticed tall men, if only in an idle way. As

Charles came and went through the office where she was employed, she heard the other secretaries laugh at his dry jokes; she saw that he was not flirtatious but simply quietly friendly; she drew close enough to notice how light his eyes were in contrast to his dark hair—the same coloring that attracted Charlotte to Tom decades later.

Charles eventually noticed Sarah noticing him. He was used to female attention, which he usually shrugged off as untimely, but, as he often told Sarah when they relived their intimate history, something in her pale freckles, green eyes, and thick light hair and lashes made him think of summer in the open fields of Albert's farm. As he sought out excuses to speak with her, he learned she spoke with an accent that likewise recalled Albert. She was direct and unpretentious and carried her tall self fully upright, not slouched or apologetic. She had elegant long fingers and skin so fine it seemed to have no pores. Charles found her beautiful, and he loved spending time with her. Even so, he thought he could not afford a commitment until he was established as a doctor. What seized him was what Sarah told him about the childhood that had formed her. The more time they spent together, the more he could see that she had always had what he had always looked for.

Charles was one of several medical students who had seen combat, but he was the only one who seemed to have shed the war along with his uniform. Many veterans clearly carried the conflict within them, just below their skin. Some were arrogant, others seemed wounded, jaded, or half-belligerent, as if they could not break habits of vigilance or control the lightning reflexes of self-defense.

Many women besides Sarah were attracted to Charles. She

was not the only one to sleep with him, just the last to do so. As they grew closer, he was frank with her about having had lovers before and after the war—not many, three or four altogether, but enough to qualify him in her eyes as sexually experienced. This was a good thing; she didn't want them both to be clumsy fools the first time they made love. She had made out with boys in high school but had scarcely seen an eligible young man throughout the war. That had ended three years ago, and Sarah was impatient. Curiosity and desire had ramped up almost beyond her endurance.

Charles later told her that he would have taken it slowly. He had begun to think of Sarah as his future, and he wanted to court her, tantalize her, and gradually teach her the ways of his body while learning the ways of hers. She was having none of it.

They were finishing dinner at Sarah and Addie's apartment. Sarah had roasted a chicken with vegetables. She had set the table with candles and real linens to dress up the unmatched plates and flatware. With Addie in Vermont for her mother's birthday, Sarah meant to take full advantage of the privacy that was so hard to come by, both for her and for Charles, who lived in a flat full of students. She drank two glasses of wine but ate sparingly, not wanting to feel heavy or drowsy. Besides, her stomach kept fluttering, and her lower abdomen tensed up—pleasurably, nervously—every time she thought of what she hoped would happen that evening.

Charles lavishly praised Sarah's cooking and raved about the peach pie she had made for dessert. He overdid it a bit, and Sarah wondered if he knew what she had planned for later. When at last he rose to clear his plate and utensils away, she followed him

to the cramped kitchen. She set her plate on the counter as he
stood at the sink, rinsing, and she put her arms around his waist
from behind.

"Never mind the dishes," she murmured. Her hands were flat
against his stomach, one above the other, and she began moving them apart, one stroking upward, the other down until it
reached his belt. She hesitated only a second, then went farther down, then up again and down again, slowly. She pressed
herself against his back as she caressed him and felt him grow
hard under her touch. He turned toward her and reversed their
positions until Sarah leaned against the counter and he leaned
into her, rhythmically pressing and pulling away, his legs apart,
his breathing low and soft, nearly a moan. He put his hands on
Sarah's hips, steadying them as he moved against her. She held
onto his backside and thrust her lower body forward, matching
his slow rhythm. They kissed deeply, then lightly, teasing each
other with their tongues, tasting, nipping gently.

Sarah said, "Not here," and ducked away from Charles and
took his hand.

"Are you sure about this?" he asked, following her to the bedroom she shared with Addie.

Her answer was to shut the door behind her and light candles
that she'd placed around the room.

Charles went to her and took her face in his hands, looking
into her eyes. She looked back steadily as she pulled his shirt
from his trousers and slid her hands underneath and up along
his back. His body was strong, his skin smooth over the hard-
ness of muscle and bone. Feeling him was not enough, she had
to see him, every inch, and she needed his eyes on her as well.
Every one of her senses clamored for satisfaction.

They undressed each other until they were naked from the waist up. Sarah had thought she would be shy, but it was as if, wherever Charles looked at her, his gaze touched her skin; she heated up, she wanted him to look at her forever. Her nipples hardened before he touched them, and when he did touch them, she shuddered from head to foot, as if light coursed all the way through her. She wondered whether she could make him hard, perhaps even make him climax, without touching him at all, just by looking at his penis. She laughed at the idea, and Charles grinned at her. "What?" he asked, holding her breasts, rubbing her nipples gently with his thumbs.

Sarah was bolder than she had ever thought she could be, but this last thought was more than she could utter out loud. So far she had not even seen this much-imagined penis; she had only fondled it through clothing. Ignoring his puzzlement, she kissed Charles and unzipped his fly and reached in, briefly fearing she would fumble hopelessly, but, no, there it was, alive in her hand, its heat and springing energy astonishing. She had never imagined. She broke away from Charles's kiss and bent her head to see. She had no thought of restraint or seemliness as she unbuckled his belt and let his trousers fall and then swiftly pulled on his undershorts until they were at his ankles. She rose quickly, overcome by the nearness of her mouth to his erection.

Charles shuffled clumsily backward until he sat on the bed. He kicked his cumbersome clothes away and bent to remove his socks. He lay back, smiling at her. "Now you," he said softly.

"You do it," she answered, drawing close so that he could remove the last of her clothing. Charles took her skirt off and lay his cheek on her belly. She had bought extravagant, satin lingerie, none of it like anything she'd ever worn before. He unfastened her stockings from her garters and carefully rolled them to her ankles and lifted each foot in turn to take them off. She steadied herself with her hands in his thick hair.

Next he dealt with the garters themselves. All the while Sarah stood before him like a schoolgirl or, rather, not like a schoolgirl at all, since now his mouth was on her stomach as he slowly drew her lacy tap pants down, over her backside, letting them drift to the floor. She stepped lightly out of them. He ran his hands over her hips, pulling her closer, kissing her belly harder, until he moved his hands lower and found the center of her longing. She gasped, and he drew her down beside him, and she felt for the first time the intimate length of him next to her, skin on skin. He entered her slowly, measuring his urgency until her virginity gave way with a sharp twinge. She cried out softly, then was overtaken by sensations that were entirely new but felt as if she had always known them.

They married halfway through his residency, in 1950. Less than two years later, with Charlotte on the way, they moved to a small house in Montpelier, near Charles's new one-man practice. Sarah's thoughts of running a botanical nursery lapsed as she decorated a different nursery for her first child. After she and Charles moved to the house outside Rockhill, she contented herself with her own gardens. She joined the generation of housewives that Wendell Burnham's *LTW* had helped to create, but Vermont's Yankee culture and her own upbringing saved her from the worst of her time and station.

Chapter 7

THE DAY AFTER CHRISTMAS, flakes as light as torn tissue eddied in the middle air. Sarah sat at the kitchen table in the early afternoon and watched as they changed from dark against the sky to white at eye level. The snow was coming down fast and thick, an inch an hour, with more than a foot predicted by evening. The hemlock boughs bent under the weight, their branches scarcely visible. They assumed fantastic shapes—gnomes with white robes and soft pointed hats falling sideways or bearlike creatures with heads bowed, shoulders hunched, limbs loose.

Charles and their grandson William had been out cross-country skiing all morning. William, who had arrived just before the last storm, was the younger of Stephie's two sons, a sophomore at Carnegie Mellon University in Pittsburgh. He usually opted for Christmas in Vermont, not wanting to risk the longer trip home to Minnesota in winter. No one else had come for the holiday. Stephie and Jake did not travel between November and

May, and David and Tess were spending Christmas with her large family.

The two men had returned a half hour ago, carrying cold into the house with them, stomping their boots, joking and steaming in their down vests and wet wool sweaters.

"Nana!" William hollered from the mudroom. "Thanks for the snow!"

Sarah grinned. Once, in the car, when Stephie was two, she had objected to the bright, late-day sun in her eyes. "Turn it down, Mama!" she had demanded, having recently seen her first dimmer switch on an electric light.

The story grew and changed until it became a well-worn piece of family folklore that Sarah had powers to control the moon, sun, tides, and weather. But nature was Charles's domain, not Sarah's. She never went into the woods alone. Wild weather got under her skin. She no longer swam in rivers. Even simple aging confounded her, the relentless flight of her remaining days.

Charles, on the other hand, seemed fearless, undaunted even by his own mortality. He had seen so much death in his practice, in the war, on Albert Graves's farm, and even in the very woods where he felt so fully at home. Once, he had come home from an unusually warm and sunny early-winter trek, stinking outrageously and guffawing almost to tears as he told her about rounding a head-high outcropping of rock and tripping over a tall, entirely unexpected structure. "God, Sarah, it was the weirdest thing," he had told her. "I fell and found myself in a cage — a ribcage! Of a moose!" He caught his breath and added what Sarah's nose had already told her. "Lord, it was ripe. Critters had eaten the organs, thank God, but hair and flesh were still sticking to the bones, and most of the bones were still there — gnawed, but not clean. Those ribs held me like a hand. You don't quite realize how *huge* a moose is. I fit in there like a baby. A moose papoose!"

Mysteries riddled this story. Why had the rib cage been upright? It rested against the steep rock, and so the moose would not have been able to turn onto its side in that direction. But why not the other? Why had it died with its ribs skyward, its legs in the air? And why were its bones so porous?

Finally Charles discovered the answers. The moose had had late-stage osteoporosis. This, his research informed him, was common among the bulls, which shed their enormously heavy antlers after each mating season and grew them anew the next year. The process leached calcium from the rest of the body and endangered the entire skeleton. Charles thought that this particular moose had fallen because of his weakened bones. He had struggled to right himself and in the struggle had broken his diseased neck or spine. He had died flat on his back, leaving his upright ribcage as a trap and a puzzle. Charles had found his way out of both.

That story, too, was legend by now. Charlotte and Stephie had told it to their children, who might pass it on forever. But they left out the stink, the carrion eaters, the osteoporosis, the reason the moose had died with its legs in the air. Really only the punch line remained from Charles's telling, though fictional details were added. For instance, when Papa looked out at the woods through the bars of bones on his cage, a bear came wandering by and roared at him, making Papa glad he was jailed. And so on. Getting the children to laugh was the whole point. Still, it pleased Sarah to think that she and Charles might one day enter the minds of children they would never know, who might nevertheless believe in them as the Nana Who Ruled the Sun, and Papa the Moose Papoose.

WILLIAM LEFT TWO DAYS later, having repeatedly skied the trail he and Charles had beaten down with their snowshoes. He skied alone. He skied with Charles, with Tom, and even once with Charlotte. He had tried to persuade Sarah to ski with him. "Come on, Nana," he teased. "I know you ordered up this snow just for me. We'll go slow."

Sarah had relented, but on her own terms. "Oh, fine. I'll go try out your trail with you, but I won't ski. My bones are too old. Let's just hike." She enjoyed the woods, as long as she had company.

So they had set out together on the well-packed trail, Sarah and her tall grandson. The air sparkled with powdery crystals. Here and there were shallow furrows where snow had fallen from branches and rolled lightly down small slopes. Sarah saw the tracks of a mouse going in and out from under a half-rotten deadfall, perfect cover for a tiny creature, guarded as it was by a tangle of brush. William spotted a porcupine at the very top of a white spruce. He had brought binoculars, and he zeroed in on the fat ungainly thing asleep in its swaying perch. He handed the glasses to Sarah, who wished Charles were there to see it.

So a few days after William had gone, Sarah said to Charles, "Let's go for a hike. Maybe we'll see that porcupine."

"Good idea. Bring your snowshoes, so we can go off the trail to a spot I know. Maybe I can show you something else."

They had just finished lunch. Sarah grabbed a ski pole to use for balance and called the dogs. They often went with Charles on his walks and were good about staying close, so he never leashed them. This time, though, Charles signaled the dogs to stay. He explained only that they might interfere with his plans.

Charles and Sarah set out under a pale winter sun and light clouds. He carried a water bottle, thermos, and snacks in a light backpack that also held first aid supplies. Years ago, Sarah had worried when Charles went into the woods alone. She couldn't recall when she had finally learned to trust him completely, but he was a good woodsman and a careful hiker. He knew his way around.

They followed William's ski trail for a little over a mile. They didn't speak as they walked along, carrying their snowshoes. The silence between them was as familiar as their faces, their bodies, and the synchronized rhythm of their days. Sarah kept up with Charles easily, but he would have gone faster on his own.

Sarah's ski pole took some of the strain off her lower body, especially on the ascents. Otherwise she didn't tire much, though the weight of her snowshoes, tied together and slung over her shoulder, made her feel clumsy. The cold, diffuse light of this January afternoon spilled all around them, down through the trees, clear as water, alive. Sarah noticed everything. Deer tracks on the trail, its beaten path an unwitting favor to animals that would otherwise struggle in deep snow. Old wounds on red maples that had scabbed over in the years since moose incisors had scraped the bark away. Copper and blond leaves still clinging to the lower branches of beech trees. The humming energy in the air, the sound of her breath, and the moist warm fog it made in front of her mouth.

But Charles noticed more. He knew where to look, for his memory had banked a wealth of tiny signs left by animals going about their business. He pointed out bear hairs still clinging to a tree that a female had rubbed and clawed last spring, marking the territory in which she was keeping her cub safe. He showed Sarah where he had most recently seen Stallone, a big bull moose who wintered high up in their woods. He took her off the trail a few feet so that she could see where an ermine had recently scurried home carrying prey in its mouth. Tiny spots of blood made a dotted line beside the small weasel's tracks, and the tail of the mouse or vole that the ermine had held in its teeth made a dragline connecting the dots. Later, they saw hoof and belly marks where a deer had done just as they were about to do themselves, which was to leave the packed trail for the unbroken snow.

They laced on their snowshoes. "Where are we going?" Sarah asked.

"Bobcat country," he told her. "After that first storm, I came up here and saw lots of sign. It's right above a deer run, so this smart old cat comes here a lot."

Sarah shivered a little. "Well, at least the bears are asleep."

But she was fascinated, half an hour later, after they had climbed steadily, to find herself next to Charles at a high, cliffy spot that dropped off sharply to the game run he had mentioned. Far beyond the run she could see four ranges of the Green Mountains through the naked trees, the nearest slope lit gold by the winter sun, the others variously blue-green, gray-green, or dark cobalt.

Sarah thought such perspectives were good for the soul. She felt in her neck and behind her knees a vertigo that had nothing to do with geographic elevation. This spot had an odd intensity, as if she and Charles, like the deer on the run below, were being watched. Sarah would never dare come here alone.

"Look," Charles said, pointing to a tiny black spot moving erratically on the nearest range. It was scarcely visible through the leafless cover of hardwood trees. It crossed a small open space and then darted into a stand of conifers and was gone. It looked like a scurrying insect.

"What was it?"

"Fisher," Charles said. "They like high country."

"Horrible thing," Sarah muttered, believing one of the large, muscular weasels had carried off her favorite cat six years ago. They hadn't had a cat since. They'd scarcely had cats at all, and none that could come in beyond the mudroom, given the allergic gene from the Lucas side.

A moment later, when the fisher appeared again in the clearing, she got out the binoculars. "I've never really looked at a fisher," she said, scanning the range and then focusing when she found the animal in her sights. "What do you know," she cried. "He looks rather sweet — all that thick fur, those little round ears."

"Sweet like needle teeth and a lousy temper," Charles answered. "That's a furry little killing machine."

Sarah lowered her binoculars. "And here I was trying to be open-minded."

"Let's go a little higher," Charles said. "You okay?"

Sarah nodded, though tomorrow her muscles would ache.

They climbed another dozen yards and then went straight ahead a quarter mile. The sheer drop was to their left. Sarah was looking to her right, at the massive girth of a grandfather beech, when Charles suddenly caught his breath. She turned, and he pointed, far down below the cliff, to an animal stock-still in its tracks. He put his fingers to his lips. Sarah dared not move. She stared down at the bobcat as it hovered beside the carcass of a deer, switching its stunted tail. It had lifted its head, perhaps having heard Charles's quiet gasp. But the cat did not look all the way up to discover them. They stared breathlessly at the powerful body, the lovely, dense, ticked fur, the silvers, grays, and spots of black that disguised the cat well in dappled summer woods or in falling snow, when everything turned gray, black, and white. Warily it returned to its feast of red meat, the brightest color in the landscape. They watched until suddenly the cat bolted away so fast it might never have been there at all but for tracks that went into a thicket of brush.

Charles took Sarah's hand and drew her back from the edge of the cliff. They backtracked a bit and sat down on a flat rock, which Charles cleared of snow with his forearm.

"Have you ever seen that before?" Sarah murmured.

Charles shook his head. "Cat a couple times, running, but no prey. You hardly ever see a bobcat; they're too reclusive."

"Did it kill that deer? It looks too small to bring down a deer."

"Not if it leaps down and gets a good fast shot at the neck," he said matter-of-factly.

"Too bad we interrupted his feast," Sarah said, disguising her squeamishness for nature's dripping teeth and claws.

"He'll be back," Charles said, reaching into his backpack. "He might even circle around while we're eating, if we keep our voices down."

Charles took a thermos of hot tea from the backpack. He served Sarah, and they sat companionably, their legs straight out, propped by the backs of their snowshoes. After a while, he rose and stole expectantly to the edge of the cliff. "Nope," he said softly. "Still not there." He sat down again. "I was surprised to find bobcat sign at this elevation. It's pretty high for them. Means there aren't any lynx nearby, because they'd claim the high ground."

They both fell silent as they finished their tea. Sarah was content until she saw that Charles looked more preoccupied than peaceful.

"Anything wrong? You're pretty quiet."

He shrugged, and Sarah threw him a look.

"Oh, yeah," he said, smiling over at her. "*A shrug is not an answer.* How many times did you have to say that to David when he was a teenager?"

"Is that who's on your mind?"

"Since you ask—and since you already know—yes. I've been thinking about him a lot since Thanksgiving."

"Me, too," Sarah told him.

Charles looked over at her from his perch on their rock and held her eyes. He looked away and seemed to gather himself. "It's David as a father that floors me!" he said suddenly, his eyes reddening at the edges. "I've just never seen him the way he is with Hannah. I'll never forget his face when he took that child from me, all wrapped in my coat. God, Sarah, he looked like *me.* I knew every thought in his head, I could read his eyes right down into his gut." Charles turned to her. "I haven't felt so close to him since he was ten. I haven't *known* him since he was ten. Thirty years. What have I missed?"

Sarah put her arms around Charles and felt his whole body tighten up. She pulled back and looked at her husband. His eyes were still young, even amid the pleats of skin that held them fast. They gazed back at her, those old young eyes.

Then Charles kissed her on the mouth, first lightly, as had become his habit, then with growing intensity. It was the first searing, searching kiss they'd shared in years, a kiss much older than the slow sex life they now enjoyed. Sarah responded exactly as she had when she was young; she felt her lower abdomen contract, felt, even lower, a blossoming heat and soft twinge that once had signaled the copious flow of sexual moisture. Later she would remember that kiss, and her body's instant warmth, and she would consider it the most important gift of that holiday season.

THE QUIETUDE OF NEW Year's Day 2000 was interrupted only by phone calls from children and grandchildren. Stephie, as always, was the last to call, waiting until those on eastern time would already have phoned.

Of the three children Sarah and Charles had raised in north central Vermont, Stephie, a year younger than Charlotte and five years older than David, was the truest Yankee. By nature independent, frugal, and resourceful, she was possessed of tart wit, a soft heart, and a love of woods and wildlife. As a child she had spent whole days in the countryside, always with a large dog or two at her side, always returning scratched, sunburned, itchy, and enthralled, with twigs in her hair and anything from bird wings to orphaned fox kits in her hands. Once, she had struggled home with a rack of moose antlers. Sarah, though anxious, had made herself trust that Stephie knew her boundaries and observed the safety lessons Charles had taught her.

And so Stephie never did catch fear from Sarah. Her school science projects won awards at the state science fair, and her senior project, on methods of tracking bird migration, had garnered honorable mention at the national level. When she went on to Middlebury, she met Jake Campo in a first-year biology class and was immediately as sure about him as everything else in her young life. Right after graduation, twenty-four years ago, she and Jake had spent their honeymoon trekking in northern Minnesota. There, the passion between them had spilled over to embrace the lakes and woods, so much like home but far from childhood. They had traded their Ph.D. plans for two openings at a small Minnesota high school, where Jake still taught math, Stephie biology. They had raised two sons, now men, in their years away. Sarah missed Stephie as much as ever.

Now Stephie was telling her about the group of juniors she had recently taken on a winter field trip. Her enthusiasm for the outdoors turned a surprising number of her students into avid birders or animal trackers. Sarah thought of Lottie and her pink-haired, tattooed, pierced, and studded friends, unable to imagine them traipsing through wetlands to observe otter sign or moose wallows.

Sarah, in turn, told Stephie about the bobcat and the half-eaten deer she and Charles had seen. "How can you be so at home with all the predators and prey?" she asked. "You and your father—it never bothers him either; he just accepts it."

Stephie, amused, said, "What's the alternative, Mom? Everything lives on the death of something else. Including us."

Sarah had known this all her life, and recent articles recounting the remarkably bloody course of the twentieth century had forcefully reminded her of it. But something in Stephie's casual remark drew her up short. She looked out at the long meadow and watched a blue jay fly overhead, carrying some small creature in its beak. It soared into the evergreens beyond until it vanished like the bobcat that had moved so rapidly out of sight. Like the fisher, into the trees.

IT TAKES CHARLOTTE, Lottie, and Sarah forty minutes to reach the hospital, a new facility with a high-tech trauma center, east of Montpelier near Barre. When they arrive, Sarah says brusquely, "Let me out, then you go park." Charlotte pulls over. Sarah gets out of the car without help, and Lottie leaps out after her. Sarah walks up to the reception area, asks where she can find Charles Lucas, and stalks off in the direction of her informant's pointed finger, Lottie behind her. She is suddenly angry, and glad for that. It keeps her fears at bay.

Charles is in intensive care, but they expect to move him in the morning. The nurse in the unit explains, "It's just because of his age. We don't know too much about older people and hypothermia. And we don't know how long he was down, out there."

"He's strong," Sarah snaps, annoyed that her voice is shaking. "He's been active his whole life. He's a doctor, too. Dr. Lucas. You take good care of him."

A tall young physician overhears; he walks over to them. "I know Dr. Lucas," he says, taking Sarah's hand. "I'm Jason Quesnel. I think you know my parents."

Sarah does. Her eyes well up at Jason's kindness, but she blinks the tears away. "How is he? Can I see him?"

"He has a badly sprained knee—not broken—and a cut on the back of his head. We stitched that up. The worst of it was the hypothermia, but he's warmed up now. He should be just fine."

Charlotte runs up breathlessly. Lottie stands by, scanning each face. Later she will tell Sarah, "I wanted to scream. This *pressure* kept rising up into my throat. Then I remembered how I screamed when Hannah almost drowned, and I swore to myself I'd be quiet."

Jason Quesnel puts his hand on Sarah's arm. "You can see him, just for a minute. No one else, please. He should be stronger tomorrow, but he needs rest."

He shows Sarah to Charles's room while Charlotte and Lottie take seats in the waiting area. "I'll be back soon. You go on in. Just remember, he's better than he looks. He's been through an ordeal, but he's in good shape for his age."

Sarah wishes everyone would shut up about Charles's age. People live to a hundred all the time. She pushes the door open and tiptoes in and stands at the end of Charles's bed. A little color has returned to his cheeks, but she can see the gray beneath. Oh, God, he looks old. How can he? He never sits still long enough for time to catch him.

She pulls up a chair and sits beside the bed, taking Charles's left hand in both of hers. She wants to crawl between the sheets with him. She tries to believe she will once again feel his long body beside her in bed. For now, she puts her forehead down on his pillow, briefly resting it there, wordlessly praying. Then she reaches up and touches his cheek. "Charles," she whispers. His eyes fly open, disoriented, and Sarah clutches his hand. "Oh, Charles, it's Sarah! I'm right here."

Charles grunts and tries to focus on her face. He makes an incoherent, interrogative sound, keeping his eyes on her.

"You fell in the woods, my love. You're in the hospital, but you'll be home soon."

His eyes close heavily, and he disappears behind them. His breathing is labored but steady. Sarah strokes his arm over and over, and her hand shakes every time she raises it from his skin. She inhales deeply, smelling clean sheets, soap, a heavy confusion of medicines and disinfectants, and, just barely, Charles's own scent, earthy and warm. Hot tears slide from her eyes. She stares and stares at her husband, seeing in his face all the men he has been in nearly fifty years. All those young and old, wise and foolish men, those good men.

"Sleep," she whispers to him at last, knowing her time is up. She starts to rise but his eyes open once more and lock onto her face. "Charles? What is it?"

He tries to clear his throat, making small coughing sounds. A broad smile flashes and fades. Or is it a rictus of pain? Is he gasping or laughing? He lifts his hand and gestures for her to lean closer. He clutches her wrist. His mouth works. Sarah bends toward him. His voice is strained, rough, barely audible. How can he sound so weak and yet hold her so tightly?

Finally Charles says, amid the sounds that might be laughter or might be outbursts of pain, "Sarah, oh, you wouldn't believe what I . . ." He half smiles at her, or winces, and holds his free hand out, palm up, as if giving her something. His hand drops, he falls into sleep again and lets go of her wrist. She sits there, Charles's heart beating beneath her palm, until Jason Quesnel returns. It is barely seven o'clock. Sarah feels as if days have passed since she found Charles down.

Tom and Luke are in the waiting room, huddled with Lottie and Charlotte. Vivi and Peter stand up, and Sarah walks mutely into Vivi's arms, laying her head on her friend's shoulder. Vivi holds her for a long time, cradling the back of her neck. Peter tries with his short arms to wrap both women fully and contain their fear and fragile relief. His eyes are red.

Jason Quesnel expects no change in Charles overnight, so Sarah's family and friends take her home. They make soup and stay with her until she is quietly rejuvenated and confident of Charles's recovery. Charlotte wants to spend the night. Vivi does also, but Sarah says, "No. Really. I'm fine on my own. You heard what Jason said. Charles will be out of intensive care in the morning. Probably be home in a day or two, restless as an old bear."

Chapter 8

IN ALMOST ALL OF January there was no new snow. The ground was still covered, but heavy winds blew the trees bare early in the month. Day after day, the skies were intensely blue, deceptively inviting. Temperatures dropped far below zero and stayed there for three weeks. The longed-for thaw just would not come. Sarah thought she had never known a span of winter so implacable, so bitter in its grip.

One morning when she went out to the barn for kindling, she found a frozen, scrawny cat near the woodpile, no doubt a feral tom. The poor thing looked old, a feline Methuselah. Its coat was lusterless and patchy, striped dully in black and gray. She had no idea what to do with this pitiful carcass. Perhaps Charles would toss it down into the woods, where carrion eaters would find it after the thaw.

Sarah thought she understood something new about cold, the reason adults in their prime insisted that winters had been colder and snow deeper when they were children. It was because, in their full strength, they felt the harsh winters least acutely. The very young and the very old measured by a different thermometer.

Even the strong could be stupid, though. Sarah read in the paper about Josie Koval, the pregnant daughter of an acquaintance, who had gone to visit friends in Wolcott. Driving home after midnight, she had been stranded by a broken driveshaft. Counting unwisely on her ten-year-old Ford and its heater, she had dressed inadequately against the cold. She wore thin, ankle-high boots and a short woolen coat. She had gloves but no hat, just the loose hood on her jacket. Beneath the jacket she wore knit cotton pants, stretched to their limit over her almost eight-month belly, with a man's loose sweater and turtleneck on top.

Josie's car broke down on a five-mile uninhabited stretch of Route 12, a two-lane secondary highway. Woods and rock outcroppings lined the road. Guardrails now and then formed squat barriers against steep drops into ravines or creekbeds. She told the reporter from Montpelier that at first she decided to keep the engine running and wait for another car to come along. She tried that for half an hour, keeping one window half open to ventilate any carbon monoxide, trying to point the heat straight at her feet and hands. The heater fought a losing battle against the frigid air streaming in. No one came, and there wasn't much gas left in the Ford's tank. Josie could be stranded all night and frozen by morning. She had to get out and walk, not knowing how far she could make it. She could be miles from help.

Utter blackness engulfed her when she turned off the ignition. She was stone blind unless she looked up at the thin cloud cover and sparse stars. They illuminated nothing on the ground. Josie found a weak flashlight under the backseat of her traitorous car, but she used it only intermittently, fearing its batteries would die altogether. So she walked along, flashing the dim light before her, then switching it off until she reached the limit of what it had shown. She set out this way, in spurts of faint light whose black-rimmed scenes she held in memory until she could bear the dark no more. Not one car passed her on her pitch-black journey.

Josie walked for at least a thousand steps — almost a mile, the newspaper said — stumbling and ungainly, carrying her unborn child before her, oblivious in its warm bath. But even the amniotic sac was in danger of cooling down, because Josie's coat did not span her belly. When at last she smelled wood smoke and saw a single light a few yards off the road, she shuffled into a half run on feet she could no longer feel. She fell weeping into a blessedly overheated trailer as soon as the door opened. She lost two toes to frostbite, but she could well have died.

"Stupid," Sarah muttered, putting the newspaper down. She knew what that drowning blackness was like, having once been stranded herself on a remote back road. That was in summer, and she had not feared for her life, but she had been seriously unnerved. Since then she always kept a flashlight and fresh batteries in the car. In winter she stocked the way-back with blankets, extra hats, mittens, scarves, and chemical toe warmers.

Sarah called Josie's mother to commiserate. Rose said Josie's labor had started prematurely, but her doctor had been able to stop the contractions. Josie was still in the hospital, abashed, mourning her toes but rejoicing in the safety of her child. Sarah could picture her — smiles, tears, and new wisdom mingling in her face and voice. Vermont kids could be as unwise as any, but at least they tended to own up to it.

• • •

SARAH AND CHARLES, IN this subzero weather, were irritable, gripped by cabin fever. Each snapped like a twig at the other's least misstep. Sarah indulged in small fits of rage at a broken pickle jar, a dropped bundle of kindling. She stabbed viciously at the fire in the great room, scattering sparks, enjoying her own fury. Charles prowled the house from window to window. He peered out and hated the cold that kept him in. When Sarah spoke to him, he scarcely bothered to answer. Furious, she would heft the woodstove poker speculatively—then roll her eyes and clatter it back into its rack with the other iron tools.

Sarah remembered a much longer time, decades ago, during which she had harbored genuine bitterness, not this passing aggravation. That was the dead spot in their marriage, a bitter season when neither was real to the other; each, in the other's eyes, was the ghost of some half-forgotten being.

David was a baby when it began, Charlotte seven, Stephie almost six. Even as Sarah mothered them all, allowing no lapse in her attention, she felt severed altogether from their father. That lasted two years and part of a third. It had seemed endless, and yet an ending. In a later decade, she and Charles might have divorced. Looking back, though, their icy standoff had proved a tiny fraction of their long shared time, and it had headily spiced the relief that followed. Still, Sarah had despaired.

She was fat then, and chronically exhausted. She bore on and within her body the evidence of her four heavy pregnancies and their labors—splayed-out rays of stretch marks, mottled thighs, breasts gone low and loose after nursing. She was ashamed in front of Charles, who kept his distance, kept his silence, and—Sarah was sure—did not desire her. She undressed in the bathroom and slept with her back to him. A few times, half-defiant, fully on fire, careful to make no sound, she had satisfied herself while he slept. Her body, which had been so filled with Charles and then with his children, three living, one dead, now swelled with loneliness and prickly anger. She grew steadily uglier with Charles, believing she was already ugly in his eyes. In this way she preempted him. Certain that he would reject any softness or longing, she showed him a hard shine in her eyes, iron in her backbone, a deliberate stillness about her hips. She carried herself carefully around Charles and let him see in these mute demonstrations that she could do perfectly well without him.

Charles never mentioned Sarah's ruined shape or complained about her ill temper. He never overtly confirmed Sarah's assumptions. But Sarah remembered how openly he had praised her body while it was young and taut, and she knew just when he had fallen silent on the subject, which was during her second pregnancy. He had still wanted her enough, even so, to make her pregnant twice more, but with David's birth he seemed to feel his work was done. He had given her the child who would heal her grief, and so he need not touch her again. So Sarah believed. Charles no longer came up behind her in the kitchen to nuzzle her hair. He had stopped gathering her into the hollow of his body in bed, stopped sliding his erection against her backside before turning her around for the caresses she had taught him.

The truth was much more than this, as Sarah later thought she should have known. But it took her a long time to heal and forgive, to see that Charles was not repulsed by her outward changes, but by her unkind self-perceptions and the bile with which they laced her spirit. Yes, he had found her unattractive, but not for the reasons she supposed.

Sarah never knew what prompted Charles to turn again in her direction. She never knew whether a patient of his had confided an anguish and self-loathing similar to Sarah's, or whether he was too sexually hungry to wait. Maybe he'd had an affair. Or maybe another woman had scared Charles just by letting him know she was interested.

Whatever his reasons, Charles began to court Sarah again when David was going on three. He began with small, wry gestures that at first only bewildered her. He bought books, but only for their titles. He left them lying about but never mentioned them. The first one Sarah noticed was called *The Paradise Lost-and-Found,* a novel about wayward people and the emotionally charged objects they left behind at a shabby piano lounge in a Midwestern hotel. That was the only one she actually read before she caught on. It was badly written, and she wondered at Charles for buying such a thing. She didn't remember what the other books were about or whether she had tried to read any of them, but she remembered their titles in the order they had appeared on the kitchen counter, her dresser, the table beside her chair: *The Silent Treatment, Charlie Blue, Family Man, Ice-Melt.* Many others. Eventually she began with some reluctance to enjoy the silent word game. She kept her eyes peeled for new titles and finally laughed out loud the day she found both *Pound Foolish* and *Skin Deep* on the upstairs hall table, next to a full-length mirror. Charles knew she was softening. He began venturing jokes and tentatively kissing her good morning, good night—chaste dry pecks on the cheek or lips.

Sarah wanted to welcome his patient overtures but also took some pleasure in viewing them askance, in hurting Charles back for what she saw as his betrayals. She refused to let him see her amusement, but Charles persisted. Sarah began to see that he, too, had been hurting. The things she did to preempt his power over her had sometimes broken him. She had half deliberately shoved Charles outside the family circle, hoarding their children and only grudgingly serving up the bread he brought home. His patients, his vegetable garden, his summer nights felling trees—these were the only nurture she allowed him until finally he seized on others. His approach was entirely characteristic of him, marked by analysis, action, humor, and indirection. As he patiently worked his methods, Sarah began to see the harm she herself had done.

Healing finally took firm hold of Sarah on a chilly spring day when she caught sudden sight of Charles heading down to the woods to buck timber. There he was, any man in a buffalo shirt, small against the backdrop of the softly rounded mountains and known to her, at this distance, only by the way he held his chain saw on his shoulder. Sarah was seized with love for him. Seeing in Charles all humanity, moving about on the earth under the weight of grief and joy and the endless heavens, she deliberately chose him all over again.

Later she seduced him, also with deliberation. That initiative had to be hers; Charles could risk only so much. So Sarah waited until he was sound asleep one night and then began caressing his body, timing her movements and adjusting the pressure of her hands so that he would stir only after he was already hard. Charles would know exactly what she was doing—giving him her own greatest pleasure. She loved being slowly awakened to urgent desire unmediated by conscious thought. It aroused her more intensely than anything else Charles ever did. And now it aroused him in just the same way. He groaned in his sleep, then he half woke and rolled toward Sarah, who was naked. He touched her with a blind man's hands, drinking her in with them, learning her all over again before entering her and crying out, saying her name.

Charles, in his forties, and Sarah, at the end of her thirties, spent the next year in a sexual haze whose tendrils still could bind them, even today, now that they were old. Their memories never aged. They still reached for each other.

Chapter 9

A T LAST A LATE January thaw broke the hold of
bitterest winter. The temperature climbed almost
sixty degrees on that first morning, from twenty-
five below overnight to freezing by noon. Thirty felt tropical,
and Charles went out hatless into the sun, grinning at Sarah
as if the two of them had not spent those past weeks as edgy as
two knives in a drawer. The dogs followed as Charles set off on
a short walk into the woods. They leapt and ran in the sun and
grinned like Charles, like Sarah as she answered his eagerness
with her own.

Sarah had an outing planned, too. She needed things in town,
and on the way she would stop to see a neighbor who raised
merino sheep. He sold hand-dyed, hand-spun wool, and Sarah
wanted to take some to Josie Koval, still confined to bed. Sarah
knew from Rose that Josie was a knitter, and she remembered
eyeing a lovely tweedy yarn, spruce green flecked with cream
and brown. If any was left, it would be just the thing. Sarah had

wanted it for herself, but she could no longer knit without pain streaking through the base of her right thumb.

In town Sarah bought a box of clementines, which prompted thoughts of gingerbread to serve with them. She decided to invite someone to dinner. She thought Molly Chalmers, with Adelaide Jones and Leila Briggs. Sarah was in the mood for female company after her long confinement with Charles. Old females, she thought, smiling. Addie and Leila were her own age. Molly was thought to be nearing ninety, a benevolent crone schooled in forestry, herbs, and gardens, a lifelong environmentalist, stooped and white-haired, with pink scalp showing at the crown of her large head. Her halo of white fluff inevitably brought to mind dandelion seeds, delicately spoked before the breezes carried them off. Molly had been big once, before the decades had shrunk her. Her broad knuckly hands were scarred and gnarled with use, but elsewhere her skin was heavy old silk, fine-lined and softly folded, bearing no spots or stains. She must have prized her rose white skin, the way she always covered it with long gauzy garments and broad hats in hot weather. It was her only outward beauty. She had never married or seemed to regret it. She wandered as she pleased, and Sarah could recall Molly's figure trudging roadsides and meadows for as long as she and Charles had lived here. She made ink drawings of local trees and flora and used them on labels for the infusions and decoctions she sold from her home. The income from that couldn't possibly be enough to live on. No one knew for sure how Molly supported herself—probably with an old, well-managed trust.

Adelaide had been Sarah's best friend through high school. Long after their giddy flight from college to careers, long after Sarah had returned to Vermont with Charles, Addie had stayed in the city, climbing the marketing ladder at a prestigious publishing house. What no one in Vermont knew was that Adelaide stayed for the sake of Leila, her lover, a book designer in the same publishing firm. Later Addie would wonder aloud to Sarah which of her sins would have shocked Vermonters more, lesbianism or miscegenation—assuming it was still miscegenation when no progeny could result. Leila was black, and in those days some Vermonters went their whole lives without ever meeting a black person, let alone contemplating the scandal of a lifelong, interracial, homosexual liaison.

Sarah settled on her guest list, adding Vivi and Peter so that Charles would not be the only man amid sharp-tongued old women. She set the date for Saturday, a few nights away, then made her calls and got a yes from everyone.

SATURDAY AFTERNOON, SARAH WAS taking gingerbread from the oven when she heard a loud *whump!* and nearly dropped the pan. She went to the window and looked out. A heavy icicle had hit the railing on the small kitchen deck, punctuating the deep note of impact with the crack of splintering wood. Impatiently she pulled on a down vest and slid her sock feet into loose boots. She grabbed a snow shovel and traversed the perimeter of the house and barn, knocking icicles down over every entrance. Just what they'd need, a friend speared through the scalp while bearing food indoors.

That done, Sarah calmed herself. Charles had gone to the village for lemons with which to sauce the gingerbread. Sarah's other contribution to the evening's potluck was an Italian pie made with layers of polenta, cheese, and roasted vegetables. Sarah had no idea what the others would bring or whether the flavors would blend or clash. She didn't care. She had grown up with potluck.

At seven on the dot, as Sarah sat in the great room with a glass of wine, she heard Leila holler, "Sadie! Where are you?" Smiling, Sarah pushed herself up from her chair. No one else would dare call her Sadie. She got to the door in time to see Leila stomping snow off her boots and waiting for Addie, who was bumping the car door closed with her hip. Addie bore a casserole like a chalice, holding it out from her stocky, bosomy body in both hands. A strong gust whipped her straight, gun gray hair and the tails of her coat. It sprang up from nowhere, unwrapped her muffler, and escorted her roughly inside.

Charles came downstairs, smelling of soap, just as Leila was putting her boots on the rubber mat in the foyer and rooting in a tote bag for some fuzzy slippers. Addie handed him the casserole and said, "This should go into the oven to reheat." Charles brought his sneakered heels together and bowed, lifting the foil that covered the contents. "Curry," he said, inhaling the spices. "Smells good." He took the dish into the kitchen and set it on the stove. "Drinks?" he asked over his shoulder as they followed him.

Addie handed him a jar of chutney she'd taken from her coat pocket and said, "Scotch, rocks." Leila seconded the order. But Charles already knew what they wanted and reached for the bottle kept just for them.

Sarah had left her glass of wine in the great room. She headed back that way, ushering Adelaide and Leila before her and leaving Charles to greet the Markses, who were just pulling in. Molly would be late, as always, but she would bring something fragrant with the herbs she grew year-round in her greenhouse.

When Peter and Vivi came in with Charles, they brought guacamole and corn chips. "I meant to make something more exotic," Vivi said, hugging Adelaide and Leila, "but Jonathan called from Siberia and we talked too long." Her angled face was lit with fond joy. Her only child, born when she was forty, was half a world away, and she worried about him, though she would deny it. At twenty-six Jonathan was levelheaded and focused.

"What's new with him?" Addie asked. She had her own soft spot for the boy who used to play his guitar with Addie on piano and Leila on flute. He would make them laugh until they hurt, introducing sly jazz riffs and musical jokes into their classical repertoire, straight-faced and innocent.

"He's a hero!" Peter declared, nodding to Vivi to tell the story, which she did with glee, acting out the drama between tree-trunk Jonathan and a scrawny fellow postdoc who went outdoors one night, fell down drunk, and could not, or would not, get up. Jonathan, working late, found him snoring when he went out to let the subzero night dissolve his sleepy stupor. The sodden drunk fought his rescuer, threw up into the snow, and went back to sleep. Jonathan shouldered him like a sack of sticks, lugged him home, and flung him snoring onto his bed. The next morning his friend, a slightly older man from Virginia, looked at Jonathan red-eyed and resentful and said in his soft Tidewater accent, "I would rather be dead than live through this hangover. If you saved me, as I believe you did, I do not thank you."

"Then you can go shit in your hat," replied Molly, appearing without a knock or a noise and striking a theatrical pose. She had a drink in her hand and a long paisley shawl over her shoulders. She didn't smile, but her old eyes glittered.

Sarah hooted and embraced the old woman—*really* old

woman, older even than Charles. She giggled as she tried to find the bony body hidden in the depths of the shawl, which tangled them both and splashed Molly's drink. Scotch. Not her usual, but it had been sitting out on the counter.

Over the dinner of Italian pie, Greek salad, West Indian curry, and French bread with rosemary and garlic—following, of course, the Mexican appetizer—they drank an Israeli wine and reminisced about Jonathan and his young years. He had been a funny, easy kid all his life, blessed with native optimism and an intelligent sweetness that likewise blessed his parents.

"You were so incredibly lucky," Sarah told Vivi for at least the hundredth time. "Stephie was our only easy teenager."

"But at least you don't have kids today," said Molly. "Thank God for that. It gets worse all the time, what with drugs and sex and AIDS and . . ."

"Who would *be* a teenager today?" sighed Leila. "How's Lottie handling it?"

"We only know what we see," Charles answered her. "Which all seems okay. We do sometimes wonder what the whole story is."

"Anything in particular?" Addie prompted.

"You name it," said Sarah. "Lottie's friends are mostly fringe kids, arty, geeky. Bright but bored by school. There's a lot of rebellion and acting out. Lottie's like them but not like them."

"Her grades are good, right? And I've never seen her surly." That was Peter, whose thick brows drew down to the bridge of his nose.

"Ha!" Sarah answered. "Believe me, Lottie gets surly! And her grades are pure ego. She likes showing that she can rebel and still outshine the preppy kids."

"What about drugs?" asked Molly, returning to her theme.

"And sex?" Sarah thought she caught a wistful note in Molly's voice. Had she been a wild child seventy years ago? A different world, the 1920s, but there was that *roarin'* part.

"Who knows?" Sarah moaned. "I'm her grandmother, for crying out loud. I do know that the school estimates a quarter of the kids are using marijuana, or alcohol, or harder drugs. And Lottie says it's more like *three* quarters."

"So what's your guess?" Vivi asked.

Glancing a little uneasily at Charles, Sarah replied, "My guess is Lottie smokes marijuana. I'm pretty sure she doesn't drink, because she's allowed wine at family gatherings and always turns it down. But *God* you should see her friends! Pierced in the most painful places. Every color of hair, tons of makeup, leather and chains and studded *dog* collars of all things. Even some of the boys wear black nail polish."

Charles leaned back. "Don't worry about Lottie," he told Sarah, stretching his legs under the table. "Long as everything else is okay, it won't hurt her to smoke a little pot now and then. Assuming she doesn't get caught."

Silence fell as surprised glances traveled around the table. Sarah was about to remind Charles of the very different tune he had sung about their own children when Addie cracked up. "Charles, I'm so glad to hear you say that! Leila and I couldn't *live* without pot. Can't *tell* you how it helps arthritis. And migraine. Not to mention flu and cabin fever and anxiety and acid reflux." Leila nudged Addie conspiratorially, watching the reactions of the others.

Molly humphed. "Think you'd discovered the stuff. Bet I smoked it before the first beatnik did." She reached into the pocket of her long skirt, searching. "Anybody want some?"

Charles grinned and said, "Why not?" and darted a look at Sarah.

Once again she was about to pounce on him, but suddenly the lights went out. In the darkness they could hear the wind rolling like a boulder over the roof and whistling in around the door.

"Well, when did that come up?" grunted Charles, pushing his chair back and feeling his way to the cupboard that housed the kerosene lanterns and matches. He came back ghostly, carrying a soft light in each hand. The glow threw his face into relief, blackening its furrows, bathing its surfaces. The shadows leapt upward, making him devilish. He mugged at his friends and Sarah as he set the lanterns down. "Okay, Molly old soul, light that thing."

One by one, they inhaled the sweet herbal smoke, some tentatively, others with familiar ease. Sarah realized later that she and Vivi had been the only obvious novices. She couldn't imagine when Charles would have smoked marijuana before that night. She would never have guessed, after David's drug-laced adolescence, that he would try it himself or tolerate it in connection with Lottie. Watching him draw in the smoke and hold it, she saw him suddenly young and charged with energy. How adventuresome and funny he'd been; how mischievously he had known and teased her body. Maybe he was looking for that young self.

The seven old friends stayed at the table until very late, laughing and telling familiar stories, their faces softened and made young again by lantern light, memory, fondness, and intoxicating smoke. Sarah felt floaty, sentimentally aware that these friends had enriched her marriage to Charles in uncountable ways. All those years of comfort, hilarity, listening, and escape. Friends gently and indispensably let off the pressure that could build inside the deepest intimacy, days and years in the same house with the same person.

Long after midnight, they all parted reluctantly.

Over breakfast the next morning, Sarah prodded Charles about his changed attitude toward marijuana. He shrugged. "I read the medical journals. Those health benefits Addie and Leila mentioned—they're real. Alcohol and tobacco are much more dangerous, and those poisons are legal."

Sarah hooted at him. "Don't give me that, you old fraud. You *liked* that pot. And it wasn't the first time."

Charles gave her a look of innocent surprise but said nothing.

Sarah popped him lightly on the arm and said, "You're up to something. Secret drug use, new lenience about Lottie." Suddenly she knew exactly what Charles was up to. "It was David!"

Charles tried without success to keep a straight face.

"So that's what was going on! You three guys, in Peter's shop the day after Thanksgiving. No *wonder* you didn't invite Tom; he'd have reported you!" She burst out laughing, knowing at last why Charles's grumpy mood had dissolved like fog in a wind that day. "When else?"

"Stacking wood. David's offered before, you know. I just never accepted until this visit."

"Uh-*huh*." Sarah nodded, considering. "It took Hannah's accident, didn't it? Your son got you high, and now the two of you can finally talk. I saw you out there, by the woodpile."

Charles gave her a wide smile. "I only wish it had happened years ago."

Chapter 10

THE WIND CAME UP again the next week and took out power lines from Montpelier north and east through three towns. Crews worked around the clock, but no one could say how long the blackout would last. On Sunday the town clerk called Charles and Sarah. Could they house a young couple and small boy? Without electricity, their trailer had no heat. Charles and Sarah could. The clerk would call the Hanks family and let them know.

At three that afternoon, under a calm, overcast sky, Bob Hanks arrived with his wife, Sandy, and their four-year-old son, Tyler. The three of them followed Charles shyly into the great room. "Mr. Lucas, Mrs. Lucas," said Bob, as Sarah rose from her chair by the woodstove, "it's nice of you to help us out. I hope we won't be a bother."

"We're happy for the company," Sarah assured him. He was a broad young man with a blond beard and acne scars showing above it. He smiled at Sarah and introduced his wife, a small woman with light brown hair, green eyes, a prominent slender nose, and a round, compact young body. The little boy, Tyler, studied Sarah with the blank, frank gaze of the very young. He whispered "Hello" when prompted.

"Well," said Charles, "let's have your coats. Hall closet's this way. I'll show you."

Bob followed Charles, while Sandy looked uneasily around the room with her solemn son now riding on her hip.

"Sit, please," urged Sarah, gesturing toward a soft armchair on rockers. "That little guy of yours looks heavy."

Sandy smiled and murmured, "Thanks." She kept Tyler on her lap and eased into rocking him. "I hope he doesn't get too rambunctious for you. It's hard to keep a four-year-old quiet." Her eyes surveyed the room nervously, as if looking for breakables.

"If it makes you feel better, we'll put a few things up on shelves. But we've had two generations of kids in this house. Believe me, we don't keep priceless *vah-zes* on tabletops." Sarah drew the word out with an affected drawl, making Sandy laugh a little. Tyler wriggled down from her lap but didn't venture away from his mother's knees.

"We have two dogs; I hope that's not a problem," Sarah said. "They're very gentle."

Sandy said, so low that Sarah could scarcely hear her, "Tyler will be fine. He hasn't been around dogs much, but I don't think he's afraid of them. Are you, honey?"

Tyler dutifully shook his head no. His eyes looked a little unsure.

Sarah made a few more stabs at light conversation, but Sandy spoke so softly it was a struggle to get anything going. She was relieved when the men came back in. Bob was not so reticent, apparently. He was saying to Charles as they entered, "Yeah, I love the winter, 'specially ice fishing. Me and some buddies have a shanty on Lake Elmore, go up on weekends long as the ice is thick enough."

"How do you know when the ice is thick enough?" Sarah asked, glad of Bob's blustery voice. "I seem to remember there's some kind of formula. I see pickup trucks out on the ice, even after a week of thaw. Scares me to death."

Bob's smile lit up his face. He had good eyes, with fine crinkles at the corner. "All's I know is you drill a hole and measure. You need seven inches of black ice under the white stuff on top. That's strong enough for people and shanties. Don't know for sure about trucks and snowmobiles, but we just add a few inches for good measure. Never gone through yet." He stood near Sandy and ruffled Tyler's hair. "Can't wait for my boy to get old enough to go with me. Huntin' too. Got a six-point buck this year. Sandy makes the best venison stew you ever tasted."

"We could bring some over," Sandy offered shyly.

Charles said, "Great idea! Love venison." Charles had never shot so much as a squirrel, even in the long-ago days with Albert Graves. Sarah's mouth twitched a little at this heartiness.

Sandy looked over at her husband, who grinned and said, "Don't know how long we'll have to put you folks out. Maybe we'd best provide supper tonight, while we know we can. I can dash on home, be back in half an hour. Stew can thaw right on the stove."

"Wonderful," Sarah said, putting more enthusiasm in her voice than she felt in her heart. "I'll make salad and biscuits."

FOR THE NEXT TWO nights, the Hankses slept by the woodstove in the great room. Charles spent his days in town or in his office above the barn. Sarah ran errands, took care of what household chores the chill allowed, or read in their temporary bedroom—the one nearest the furnace room below, which the radiant heat warmed just enough. Sarah also spent time with Sandy and Tyler while Bob was at work. He was an electrician, rarely idle. Just now he was working with the power company crews on the downed lines. He told Charles they were living in their trailer until they could save enough to build or buy a house.

Sandy was more relaxed on Monday and Tuesday. She drove Bob to work in the mornings so she could have their car, and she spent much of the day out and about with Tyler or playing with him in the slowly melting snow. The two of them built an impressive pair of snow bears, a mama and cub. Sandy textured the fur with a stick that she cut like a brush at the end, and Tyler found smooth round stones for noses, digging in the front driveway where the snow was plowed to only an inch or two. When Sarah exclaimed over the artistry involved in the sculpture, Sandy smiled, embarrassed. "Tyler and I like to make things. We draw, we make bread in funny shapes."

Sandy was from Ohio and had no family in Vermont except for Bob and Tyler. She had no schooling beyond twelfth grade, but she read avidly and made art out of almost everything she touched, whether snow, paper and pencil, or food. Bob had been right about her venison stew. The dish was heavenly, spiced with herbs, lots of garlic, red wine. There were turnips and kale in the mix, along with potatoes, carrots, celery, mushrooms, and apples. "I never make it the same way twice," Sandy had told them, ducking their praise. "I just kind of dump the produce bin into the pot."

Tyler never did open up during their stay. Outdoors with Sandy, he chattered volubly and ran about with the dogs. Indoors he stayed quiet. He sometimes lay on the floor with Ruckus, scratching the rough curls around the little dog's ears or rubbing his shaggy belly. He looked at books or drew pictures in colored pencil. Twice he watched a video called *The Snowman,* which had once belonged to Lottie. But he seldom spoke. When he did, he was articulate and occasionally even funny, but he definitely saved most of his conversation for his mother. Sarah sensed he was a little uneasy with men. He stayed buried in a project when Charles or Bob was around. He sang to himself often, strings of meandering, tuneless notes that he seemed not even to know he was producing. When the power came back on Tuesday afternoon, he took his farewell from Sarah with an obedient handshake and a soft, scripted, "Thank you, Mrs. Lucas. It was nice to meet you." Then he patted Ruckus and Sylvie, shouldered his small duffel bag, and followed his mother to the car without looking back.

ON THE FIFTH OF February, Vivi called to say Molly had been in an accident with her car. She wasn't badly hurt, just bruised, with a wrenched shoulder muscle. Still, she was hampered in her daily activities, and Vivi wanted Sarah to go with her to visit, take in wood, and drop off some food. Sarah agreed.

"How did it happen?" Sarah wanted to know. "When?"

"Last night, just after dusk. You remember, the temperature dropped all of a sudden. She hit a patch of black ice and slid into a tree. Luckily she hit slantwise, not straight on."

"It amazes me she still drives at all. It amazes me that *I* do, come to think of it."

"I know. I keep expecting her to give it up, but her eyesight's good, and she has all her wits. Why not keep going as long as possible?"

Vivi picked Sarah up at two. They said good-bye to Charles as he was calling the dogs and heading out for a hike. They drove to the co-op and bought organic fruit and greens, a crusty baguette, and a bouquet of dried flowers in bright pinks and purples. At Molly's they let themselves in by a door near the kitchen, leaving their coats and boots in the mudroom. Garden tools hung from pegs, and a mesh bag full of work gloves, bandanas, and baseball caps bulged fatly from a hook. A bicycle rested on flat tires against the inner wall, adjoining the kitchen door. Stacked-up boxes of overflow, neatly labeled, towered in a corner near a long dowel on which jackets, slickers, and barn coats hung over a mat for boots, shoes, and clogs. The mudroom walls were its best feature. Molly had papered every inch with empty seed packets. In the middle of one exterior wall was a door, also papered and therefore nearly invisible. This opened into Molly's greenhouse.

Inside, the kitchen was spare, all the surfaces clean and bare except for the wide sills of sunny windows, crowded with houseplants. The largest bank of windows was taken up with a view of Molly's barn, a big block of weathered red against the snow and blue sky. The curving gully beyond it ran fast with a white-water stream in early spring and then dried to a pebbled bed with barely a trickle most summers. Beyond the streambed was a small apple orchard. Molly's place was heaven when her perennial gardens were in bloom, aswarm with butterflies and hummingbirds. Her vegetable garden, between the house and barn, was laid out in raised beds each summer, all orderly and weed free. Molly had managed all of it herself until just a few years ago. Now she paid a teenager to help.

Vivi and Sarah deposited their wares in Molly's fridge and cupboards. They found a vase for the dried bouquet and took it with them through the living room to Molly's sitting room, hollering her name before them. She lay on an overstuffed chaise longue with books and magazines strewn around her and a pot of tea on a wooden tray at her elbow. She was expecting them. The teapot was wrapped in a thick hand towel, and three cups—thin, translucent china with a shamrock pattern—sat next to it, along with a matching milk pitcher and sugar bowl and a plate of molasses cookies.

"You must be feeling better if you've been baking," Vivi said, leaning over to buss the old woman on the cheek. Sarah presented her with the flowers, and Molly thanked them both.

"Can't stand sitting still," she said. "Busy's a habit old as I am, and that's damn old."

"So what happened?" Sarah urged. "Vivi told me you got banged up a bit."

Molly stretched the neck of her baggy sweater and uncovered a massive, technicolor bruise that extended from the inside of her collarbone to the outside of her left shoulder. Gratified by her visitors' gasps, she told them, "It was on that wicked little low-down curve on the Rockhill-Worcester Road, the paved part of it. Can't remember how I hit exactly. Must have been wrenching the steering wheel round, trying to keep from going into a ravine, when I slammed into that tree. Anyway, this is the worst of it. It's stiff, but if I keep moving it loosens up."

"You were lucky," Vivi said. "My God, Molly, you could have dropped, what, fifteen or twenty feet?" She shuddered.

Molly laughed. "Bless that little maple."

AFTER SEEING HER FRIENDS and family out, Sarah roams her house, uneasy about going to bed without her husband. She wanders from window to window, peering out, listening for night sounds. The moon is bright. Four deer pick their way across the snow, and their long shadows walk with them. The does, pregnant at this time of year, will drop their fawns in some wooded spot early in the spring.

Spring seems very far away.

Sylvie and Ruckus stay close to Sarah as she moves like a prowler through her own house. Finally she lets them follow her upstairs to sleep on the floor of her room. She takes one of Charles's sleeping pills, waits for the drowsiness, and climbs onto the window seat, avoiding the bed. There, in moonlight, she finally gives in to numb unconsciousness.

Sarah dreams. The keening wind enters through cracks around her windows. A baby shrieks somewhere in her house. Sarah, freezing in her nightgown, races from room to room and cannot find the child. *Whose* child? Her bare feet pound up and down the hall and stairs, and the screaming goes on and on. Then Sarah jerks upright from her druggy sleep, staring into darkness. The high howling follows her into consciousness. It comes from Sylvie, who is no dream. Sarah fumbles for the light, thinking she is in her bed. She can't find the switch. She gives up and begins howling in the dark herself, knowing now what the dog knew the instant it happened. Sarah and Sylvie voice together their hair-raising grief, ancient and ceaseless, and Ruckus takes up their crying. The room must surely burst apart in this noise of unbearable loss.

Amid the wailing, the phone shrills—three times, five times. The machine picks up but records only the breaking of the connection. Sarah hears none of this, nor does she need to.

PART II

Chapter 11

EVERYONE CAME, FAMILY and friends from Vermont and all over the country. Then they left. Sarah pictured the house swelling up with a deep intake of air, drawing tiny, weeping people in with its breath and then blowing them out mournfully to zigzag in the stinging cold. The inhalation held her aloft; the exhalation gave her some brief peace in its wake.

There was no funeral, just a memorial gathering at the town hall, as Charles had wished. He didn't want a church, and home was too small; but the town hall, with its tall windows, creaky wooden floors, folding chairs, and echoes of town meetings, had just the plainness that appealed to him. And it was large enough to seat two hundred.

Sarah learned all of Charles's last wishes from Amos Brand, whom they'd last seen on Christmas Eve while dropping off a ham for the community feast. A few days after Charles died, Amos came to the house with the will, though Sarah had offered to meet him at his office. When he arrived and she saw how distraught he was, she understood—he didn't want his grief on display among his colleagues and staff. He tried to subdue it even with Sarah, but his shoulders shook when she embraced him. She served him coffee while he recovered himself, and they stayed in the kitchen to soften the formalities.

Amos sat at the table, across from Sarah. She said, "Charles never opened his eyes again after I left the hospital. His heart just stopped. They don't know why." It wasn't the first time she had said this out loud. She said it often, as if repetition could resolve the mystery, but it never did.

The will was a predictable document, duly stated in legalese and properly signed and witnessed. Charles had written all other instructions on light gray paper in his own angular longhand. For a doctor, he'd had a legible, even elegant script, which had always drawn comment. More than once, he'd said, "I wish people would just think about this. Doesn't it seem odd to *expect* doctors to have poor hand coordination? Isn't that a little scary?"

Amos read both documents aloud to Sarah. "This is my job," he said. "I think Charles is watching."

The will stipulated some modest bequests to environmental causes and a medical foundation. Otherwise the estate went to Sarah, who, in turn, would leave it to their children and grandchildren, as the two of them had discussed. Charles's personal letter went into greater detail. He chose the music for the opening and closing of his memorial service—Shostakovich first, Schubert at the end. He wanted to be cremated beforehand, so his ashes could attend in a discreet urn. Later, he would like his family to scatter these last remains in the long meadow in warm weather. He wanted no flowers except an arrangement in honor of Sarah, which was not to look funereal. No mums, no glads. Anything else, in yellow, blue, purple, and white. There would be no formal speeches or prayers, please. Instead Amos would read another letter, written by Charles for his friends and neighbors, recounting his favorite stories about them and his appreciation for their affection.

These instructions were so like Charles, and his voice so audible in them, that Sarah and Amos laughed and cried throughout. They didn't break down until the very last, when Amos could barely get through Charles's coda.

My dear friend Amos, if you are reading this letter to my beloved Sarah, then your own similar documents remain sealed and you are still alive. In that case, I alone will know which of us has been right in all our arguments. Or, rather, *if* I know it, if I am someplace where consciousness and memory survive, the very knowing will prove me wrong. At least I won't have to face you yet. I will have time to develop a taste for crow.

If, on the other hand, I have gone to the eternal oblivion I anticipate, I will be proved right, but without the pleasure of gloating.

In case you think I'm a loser either way, let me say right now that I hope with all my flawed heart that I have been wrong, wrong, wrong in every syllable of my logic and conviction. Because, if I am wrong, I will be reunited with Sarah. I will lose nothing and no one. I will win, eternally.

Please care tenderly for Sarah. She will be in pain, but she is strong and a gifted alchemist. She will turn her grief into new forms of grace and courage. Just you wait.

Thank you for everything, Amos, friend. Sarah, thank you for marrying me, for being my darling and my life's greatest joy.

After the memorial, family and some friends went to Sarah's for a catered lunch—another detail Charles arranged. He didn't want another potluck. "My life was not haphazard," he wrote. "It had a certain order, which I made with Sarah and loved for a great many years. Allow me to plan my final lunch with my friends." And he did, setting out the menu and naming the wine. Charles had thought of everything.

Still, he could not orchestrate grief. Its crescendo and resolution differed for everyone, an emotional cacophony with as many different tempos and chords as loved ones. Sarah went numb after her animal dirge in the night with Sylvie and Ruckus. Lottie wept openly and often, and Luke acted out angrily or with sullen petulance. Tom went about red-eyed. Charlotte kept her tears to herself once the news sank in. She focused on seeing that her father's wishes were met to the letter.

Stephie, Jake, and their sons stayed for nearly a week. Stephie grieved more openly than Charlotte, but she found equilibrium in the stories that drifted like music or air throughout the house. All the while, she kept her eyes on Sarah. Tess was similarly attentive, and the two of them, in their shared concern, bonded quickly.

Stephie and Jake told Sarah they would teach one more year after this one, and then move back to Vermont. Their children were grown; many of their friends were moving away; they were homesick. "Besides, we missed out on too much time with Dad," Stephie said.

During the hours after the memorial, Stephie and Jake held each other together for the sake of the guests, and Sarah. They became the hosts, refilling glasses, accepting condolences, plundering people's memories for tales, inciting laughter with recollections of their own, encouraging the guilty pleasure of humor.

Then there was David. He was inconsolable, his grief a motley parade of silence, weeping, and regret. Sarah at last saw the fire in him, which she had not known was there. She'd held him close to her the day after Charles died, when he arrived harrowed and shocked with Tess and Hannah beside him. She'd told him then about Charles's passionate identification with David as a father. And on the day of the memorial she had said to him, "Don't try to be like your father when you're not, or not completely. You have a different kind of imagination. He was a craftsman, but I think you are an artist." She understood this only as she said it.

Chapter 12

S IX WEEKS AFTER CHARLES'S death, Sarah sat at the kitchen table and watched the spring snow come down, thick, fast, hypnotic. The dogs slept at her feet, Ruckus snoring lightly, Sylvie now and then taking a long breath and letting it out in a series of little, high-pitched woofs. Sarah half heard the other soft sounds of the house around her—the hum of the refrigerator, the electric whir of the clock over the counter, the ticking of the teakettle as it cooled. Now and then there came a slide of snow from the roof. Otherwise, all was muffled inside the house, inside the blizzard. Sarah imagined herself a tiny figure, sitting and sipping tea inside a glass globe. Someone had shaken her life up hard, and now everything was still except for the whiteness falling all around.

Sarah knew that life would go on for others even as it remained suspended for her. She had seen it happen before, the slow, cool shrinking back of friends when a person was thought to mourn too long, to fail at getting on with things. She could pretend when she had to, but nothing remained to be gotten on with. She got out of bed each morning with heavy reluctance, hating the look of her side rumpled and Charles's undisturbed. She took to lying flat in bed, pulling the covers up smooth over her outstretched form, then folding the top sheet over the edge before slipping out from underneath. Thus the bed was as good as made and the absence of Charles was less blatant before she even stood up. With that accomplished, she had sixteen hours to fill before unmaking her side of the bed once more.

The house felt strange, food went bad, the oil furnace ran instead of the wood-burning one. Sarah avoided dealing with wood. It brought too vivid images of Charles raking the coals and tossing logs into the red mouth of the firebox. His clothing flashed similar scenes. A coat hanging limp from a peg in the mudroom would fill up with Charles as Sarah watched, and then Charles in that coat would take his stick and shoulder his pack and walk as no one else on earth walked, out the door and off to the trails in the woods.

This emptiness was as unnatural as a hole in water. Sarah returned again and again to Charles's prediction that she would transform her grief into something of value. She was letting him down. She remembered, too, the last words he had said to her, which lodged in her mind like a memory that would neither let go nor reveal itself. *Sarah, oh, you wouldn't believe what I . . .* What he had carelessly done to land at the bottom of a ravine? What he had seen in the woods that had fatally distracted him? What he could see before him, beyond the skin of life? Charles, a steadfast nonbeliever—had he seen more than he expected to? Had he died because he was too curious to resist a closer look?

Above all, Sarah remembered Charles's kiss in the woods and felt again her answering passion and caught her breath at the sweetness of that fleeting moment and its passing beyond repetition.

These memories plagued Sarah. People persisted in trying to take care of her, but to Sarah they merely intruded on her obsession. They called, they stopped by. Politely, but with determination, she got rid of them. All but her children or Vivi.

So when the phone rang on this morning, Sarah meant to ignore it until she heard Vivi's voice on the machine. She made herself answer and sound better than she felt. Vivi would notice her false cheer but would not challenge it.

"I need to ask a favor," Vivi said after their hellos.

"What's that?" Sarah felt wary, but something moved in her. The thought of being the one to help and not the one in need.

"How would you feel about renting out your cabin for a while?"

Sarah had thought Vivi would give her an errand to run or phone calls to make for some cause or other. She sat up straighter, marshaling objections. "Rent the cabin? To whom? Vivi, it's filthy, it needs work. Nobody has stayed there for years. There are probably animals living in the furniture."

Scenes flashed like a slide show in her mind, summer images full of scattered light. She and Charles had sometimes moved into the cabin when the children were at camp or visiting grandparents. It had felt like a holiday right on their own property. Sometimes they slept naked on the screened deck, overlooking the pond. They made love in the afternoon, then swam with schools of small, tickling fish. Even now, the cabin and the pond bespoke Charles. How could she let anyone disturb the spirit of him, so vivid in that vacant, lonely spot?

"Peter's cousin," Vivi was saying. "Mordechai Luz. He's taking a sabbatical from the University of Tel Aviv. He's writing a book and needs a quiet place to stay, starting in a month or so. He wants to get out of Israel for a while. The elections are just over and everybody's euphoric about Barak. Mordechai worked on the campaign. Now he's tired and wants a break."

"I don't know," Sarah said. "It's such a mess."

"Hire Lottie and her friends to clean it up. Rent one of those furniture shampooers. It can't be that bad."

"Why doesn't . . . Mordechai, was it? Why doesn't he stay with you and Peter?" Sarah knew the question was ungracious.

Vivi paid no attention. "We asked him to. He says he'd never get any work done if Peter was around all the time. They haven't seen each other in about three years, and they'd never stop yammering and bickering and one-upping each other." After a short pause Vivi added, "That really is true, Sarah. Mordechai does need the quiet. But my darling, patronizing Peter also thinks you need a man on the place."

"Oh, for Pete's sake," snapped Sarah. "*Peter's* sake. Kick him for me."

"Done. Just let me say that Mordechai isn't like that. He won't try to be your watchdog."

"Well. What *is* he like?"

"You met him once about ten years ago, you and Charles, but it was only for an evening. He was up from a quick trip to New York to give a paper. He's . . . not ordinary. Sweet. Easy. But . . . I don't know . . . an Israeli. Or at least no longer an American. A hybrid."

"So he was born in this country?"

"Yes. In New York. He's seven or eight years younger than Peter, sixty-one, I think. He was born Mordechai Nussbaum, but he changed his last name to Luz when he moved to Israel in the late sixties. There's some story about the names. Nussbaum means 'nut tree,' and I gather 'luz' is a kind of nut tree that grows in Israel. Mordechai and his wife did the kibbutz thing for a while. Her name was Rachel Skolnik. I don't remember whether she changed it or not."

"Where is she?" Sarah asked, trying to recall this cousin of Peter's.

"Oh, she died ages ago. Along with their baby. Mordechai never remarried."

Sarah was sure she had never met anyone named Mordechai. A man who had experienced a grief perhaps worse than her own. A young wife, a baby. But by now an old sorrow. Sarah drew a breath and sighed and said, "All right. I suppose so. I'll have to go down there to see what needs doing."

Chapter 13

EARLY IN APRIL THE warm breath of spring released ice and snow in torrents from their frozen imprisonment. Rivers and streams ran fast and muddy, breaching their banks in low places but otherwise furiously contained. Like the rivers, Sarah's grief ran fast and readily spilled over in low, private moments. She could picture herself sinking into sorrow as she'd done over her stillborn son. It was so easy; she could simply lie back and let herself go dark. Death moved ceaselessly at the edge of her awareness, just out of reach, stalking her. She would startle when its immovable reality met her squarely in her thoughts. Surely she would be next. She was ashamed to feel so afraid. She half hoped she would lose her wits before her life. If dementia claimed her, she would never see her own death coming. There would be nothing to fear. Already she was not herself. How much was left to lose?

AS THE SPRING RAINS came down, the dirt roads braided themselves with glistening, axle-deep ruts full of sucking mud.

Sarah began walking in the early mornings to stir herself out of her torpor. She stayed along the edges of the mucky roads but still came back with her boots caked over their tops. With her blood beginning to flow again, whether she wanted it to or not, she sought escape from the stale misery that was everywhere indoors. With no other intention than to flee, she soon made a habit of walking. As the cold that had encased her grief gave way, so did its anodyne effect. Now Sarah's pain rose up fast and raw, undiluted, unrelieved.

Hating her bleak self-pity and likewise her fear of giving herself fully to sorrow, Sarah clung to the hope that the worst would pass when the days warmed further and she and her family could scatter Charles's ashes in the long meadow. But first she would look for the return of the bobolinks, Charles's favorite birds. This was another reason to walk each day, to visit the meadow when she got back home. When she saw the first bobolinks, she would begin checking the weather forecast for an extended period of fine weather—unlikely but not impossible in Vermont's fickle spring—when her family could come from however near or far. Sarah was on edge, waiting.

At six o'clock one morning, after lying awake for hours, Sarah finally threw the covers back and hurriedly dressed and called the dogs. She went outside with them, feeling jittery and walking too fast to keep her own pace.

The day grew lighter and the rivers rushed along. Sarah stood on a steep section of road beside a swollen brown stream gone mad with spring. It leapt and splashed and foamed; it tumbled with wild energy. Sarah imagined herself within the cataract, her rag-doll body flung against boulders and tree roots.

She grew cold and moved on, shivering. The sun had not yet cleared the tops of the trees, so she headed for the meadow, seeking the morning light in open space. She walked toward the barn. The dogs raced ahead like horses smelling oats. The rest of the day, they would mope along with Sarah, but in the brief moment when they reached home after these tame new outings, they ran with joy. Sarah was sure they expected Charles to be there, waiting. They understood nothing, not even their own grief. Daily they hoped and daily were disappointed, but Sarah envied them their fleeting happiness.

With the sun finally up and her nighttime anguish easing its grip, Sarah heard the bobolink before she saw him. His song was a rising and falling ribbon of bright notes that stopped her in her tracks. She whirled to the south and scanned the sky and there he was, a black and white bird with a yellow cap, flying across the meadow from the thicket of birch and hemlock toward the other side of the pond. His pathway through the air undulated like the joyous music he made in flight. Sarah watched him go, then circle around and fly back to the meadow. He landed in the top of a bare maple at the edge of the pond. His plain brown mate hopped onto a branch nearby, appearing from within the depths of the tree. They would be only one pair of several. It had pleased Charles to think that this small grassland would support bobolinks long after he had died. Their habitat was shrinking everywhere, giving way to malls and developments and forcing the bobolinks ever eastward.

THREE DAYS LATER A heavy spring blizzard came down. Sarah, searching for a hat in the back of the hall closet, saw Charles's old Nikon hanging there in its cracked leather case. On impulse, she decided to take it with her. It was already loaded, with twelve exposures left. She slung the strap over her shoulder like a bandolier and headed out with the dogs.

The camera gave her new eyes. Most mornings, she had walked in thrall to her thoughts and sorrows. Now, surrounded again by a world muffled in white, Sarah stopped several times just to look. She photographed the dogs, the woods, and a stream rushing past with new ice forming from its banks. She snapped a clutch of pines through the falling whiteness and then caught a small flock of sparrows spaced on power lines like random musical notes. When she reached a narrow bridge not far from her house, she leaned against the railing and looked down at the North Branch covered with old ice and fresh snow. She could see black water rushing beneath holes in the ice. It swallowed the fast-falling snowflakes as soon as they touched its surface.

On the way home, she took a shot of her neighbor's flock of merino sheep huddled together in the lee of his barn, their dense winter wool dirty and matted, sorrowful against the purity of the new snowfall that blanketed their backs. Then she held the camera with one gloveless hand and extended the other before her, palm up, and waited. She wanted to capture the image of a single fat flake before it melted against her skin.

DAVID, TESS, AND HANNAH came two weeks later in a different world, sunny, greening, and warm. This time, they pulled up into the barn and entered at the mudroom door. Sylvie and Ruckus were waiting, and Hannah delightedly threw herself upon them both. She had been unnaturally quiet after Charles's memorial. She hadn't understood until then that Charles was

David's father. Once she grasped that, and put it together with the fact that her own father had died, she worried. Sarah had heard her ask Tess, "Do fathers always die?"

David had brought with him some sketches for his first official commission, a bathroom mural he'd designed for a fellow teacher at his school. He showed these to Sarah after supper that night, while Tess bathed Hannah. They could hear the child giggling through the grate above.

David stood next to Sarah at the table, pointing at his drawings and explaining details and processes to her. She watched his long hands and forearms below the shoved-up sleeves of his sweatshirt. He had her fair skin but was built just as Charles had been; he had the same well-defined musculature, the same sharp angle in the joint at the base of his back-curving thumb, the same corded veins wriggling over the backs of his hands.

Sarah turned to the pages he had placed before her, which showed both the main panel of his mural and a series of tiles that would border it. Each tile was a fish or part of a fish, and each design element would be embossed and then glazed to contrast palely with the background. Together, the tiles would show a school of fish, undulating, playing. They were simple and stylized, but lively, as was the main panel, in which a necklace of green islands ringed a wooded coast amid steep waves. There flashed in Sarah's mind the winding road she had tried to remember that night back in November, when she was ill. There was water to the right of the road. Surely there had been islands on the water?

"Can glazes really do this?" she asked David. "Make a slab of clay look like a painting?"

David explained that the rich effect suggested in his sketches required layers and layers of color, each applied and fired separately. The endless firings were unbearably suspenseful. "Every time a piece goes back into the kiln it's at risk. Nothing's precise. The clay can crack. The glazes can crack. You never know."

Sarah put her hand on David's, and he sat down next to her. "I feel kind of cracked myself," she admitted.

STEPHIE AND JAKE ARRIVED next, followed right away by their sons, Paul and William. On the Saturday Sarah had chosen for the scattering of Charles's ashes, the whole family, along with Vivi, Peter, Molly, Adelaide, and Leila, carried food and chairs to the meadow. Sarah held the urn against her breast. Luke and Lottie ran ahead with Hannah, and the dogs leapt beside them. Racing clouds, brisk air, and a light wind worked like wine in everyone, and there were no long faces.

Sarah and Tess spread blankets and put out food for the picnic. Charlotte and Stephie moved about from one group to another, videotaping the scene and the people. And then it was time to uncap the urn and disperse the last remains of Charles Lucas, beloved husband, father, grandfather, and friend of those present.

Sarah had thought hard about this moment, dreading it whenever she felt obliged to mark it with memorable words. She had made a stab at a speech but had given up. The two of them alone had known the full measure of their time together. She could not capture that in words, and she feared that trying would shrink the power of her memories.

She decided instead to speak about the human legacy before her, as much to remind herself that it was there as to celebrate it. "Charles was right when he said he designed his life and loved its order," she told her family and friends. "His life was his art, and all of you, alone and in connection with each other and with us, are his masterpieces. And mine and yours. Ours. No one has ever done a better thing."

Sarah cleared her throat. Her eyes were dry, her hands steady. She was learning to master herself, she thought, gratified.

"All right," she declared. "It's time." She picked up the urn, a plain, brushed-steel vessel, and held it against her for a moment with her eyes closed. Then she lifted off the smooth round lid and reached down inside. *Charles.* His ashes were rough as pumice and light as powder, warm from the sun on the urn. She filled her hand and pulled it forth and held it straight out, shoulder high, and walked a few feet through the stubble from last year's mowing. The breeze caught the lightest dust and lifted it all in a cloud, like a ghost. A few heavier fragments fell straight down. "Good-bye," Sarah whispered and handed the urn to Charlotte, her firstborn.

One by one, each person paced the meadow, spreading Charles far and wide, seeing him sift down into the stiff, brown grass and float lightly on the breeze and out over the pond.

"Look! The fish think he's food," Hannah exclaimed at the edge of the water. Indeed, small circular ripples pocked the mirrored surface but left the floating bits of ash behind. "They don't like how he tastes," she said, and buried her face against Tess's belly. That's when Sarah knew Tess was pregnant. She knew before Tess did.

Chapter 14

HANNAH WAS CERTAINLY CALM about the idea of Charles turned to ash," Sarah said the next morning. "Or fish food," she added, surprised by the giggle that escaped her. She looked at Tess across the kitchen table.

"We explained that Charles was more than his body. We said he outgrew his body—that he's just energy now, like a light, all done with things that could slow him down. We also told her that she would still need her own body for a very long time, and David and I would need ours."

"That's perfect. I would never have thought of that."

Tess looked down briefly. "Sarah, you know about Hannah's father, of course. Ian."

Sarah nodded. "I do."

"Well, I got a lot of help and a lot of . . . practice . . . with Hannah, during that time. And later. But she was so young, just a baby. And now, the older she gets, the more questions she has." Tess drew a slow breath, which shook a little as she let it out. "I don't think the questions will ever stop for Hannah. Not in her whole life."

"What questions?"

"The usual, of course. 'Where did I come from, where did my daddy go, where did Charles go?' But with Hannah, I don't know, the questions are . . . demanding. Like she's forgotten something and it's driving her crazy."

"She forgot about Sylvie talking."

Tess blinked. "Yes. She let go of that completely. But other things seem to come back to her, and she can't quite get hold of them. Or she'll remember things she's never even known. Like Ian, for example. She smelled some soap at a friend's house recently, and she said, 'That smells like my daddy.' She couldn't have remembered that. And I never kept that soap around after he died; I couldn't bear it."

Sarah hesitated, revisiting her certainty that Tess was pregnant. "Haven't you ever known things you had no way of knowing?"

"Yes—just not the right things. I didn't know Ian was going to die. I couldn't save him."

"Maybe we're not supposed to know things that could change someone else's fate."

Tess looked at her sadly. "You'd have changed Charles's, too."

Sarah nodded. "Maybe we're all born remembering another world, which we have to forget in order to live in this one."

Tess regarded her curiously. "Or maybe intuition keeps us connected to that other world. I wonder if we remember it at the end of life."

Sarah, oh, you wouldn't believe what I . . .

Tess went on. "All I know is Hannah is obsessed with where she came from. She wants to know if she was made of light, like

Charles, before she grew inside Mom's tummy, before she had a body." Tess shrugged. "I tell her yes, she was. It's a good Quaker thing to say. But I'm not sure I believe it myself."

"David was a lot like Hannah at that age. Or maybe a little older. I would find him sitting perfectly still, on his bed or outside on the steps. And then he would try to ask me something and couldn't get the question out the way he wanted to. I remember he asked me about time once. How did we know it was there if we couldn't see it? How could we tell how much of it there was? Something like that. Only he got very, very angry because he couldn't make me understand what he was really after."

Tess brushed her hair back. "I'm not surprised."

Sarah bent her head to her coffee, then asked, "How did you handle it, Tess? Losing Ian."

Tess hesitated, then said, "Poorly. I crawled into a dark, angry place. It felt very tight and small, much too small for all the hatred I felt. Hatred for the person who killed Ian. Hatred for myself, blame, too. My family took over for me. Someone was always with me. They loved Hannah and kept life as normal for her as they could. I'm grateful to them and grateful that Hannah was so young, just a year old."

"Do you still feel the hate?" Sarah asked, turning around to face Tess.

"No," she said, "I don't."

"How could you not?"

"I don't know."

They both went silent. Sarah got up and poured more coffee. Tess took hers black; Sarah poured half-and-half into hers and watched the pale liquid move like smoke.

"Charles was lucky, and so am I, and yet I can't bear it that he's gone. I see him out of the corner of my eye, I talk to him, I reach out to touch him in the middle of the night." Her voice was matter-of-fact, but she couldn't meet the younger woman's eyes.

"You spent most of your life with Charles. It's a lot to mourn." She rose and dumped her coffee into the sink. "If you'd like, I could stay a few extra days and help you go through Charles's things. If you're ready."

THEY BEGAN THE NEXT morning with Charles's office. They had the day to themselves, since David had driven back to Cambridge to teach his classes, and Hannah had gone off with Vivi. Tess followed Sarah up the dim, narrow staircase inside the barn door. At the top they stepped squinting into dazzling light. Three pairs of mullioned, double-hung windows faced east-by-northeast, all their panes ablaze. The room was awash in sun.

Tess stopped and stared around her, clearly surprised by the spacious room that opened up after the cramped, unpromising stairway. Charles had built it about ten years earlier. Its ceilings were high, its walls a pale blue-gray trimmed with natural wood. Hardwood floors were bare except for two large, worn kilim rugs in shades of red, tan, and blue. This was Charles's aerie, well stocked with coffee and staples, equipped with a tiny kitchen and bath, and furnished with a shabby hide-a-bed couch, a matching wing chair, and a cast-off coffee table. Beneath the windows, which were flanked by tall bookshelves, was a long desktop made from an irregular slab of polished maple. It sat on a pair of low cupboards with shelves and shallow drawers.

Sarah lowered all the miniblinds and adjusted the louvers to soften the blinding light. She stood back, her body striped by sunlight and shadow, and conferred with Tess about how to proceed. Tess offered to transfer Charles's electronic files to CDs so that Sarah could donate the computer to some worthy cause. Sarah would sort through the paper files, and the two of them would empty the bookshelves.

By early afternoon Sarah had gone through six out of eight file drawers. The seventh was crammed with manila envelopes full of photographs. Some, creased and faded, dated from Charles's childhood. Most, thank goodness, were labeled on their backs. Otherwise Sarah would never have known which aunts and uncles, in which years and parts of the country, were posed against their boxy cars or on their front steps or on beaches in baggy, modest bathing costumes.

Sarah lost herself in the whole collection, going motionless inside a stream of time that seemed to slow around her like resin gelling to amber. She first went still when an image she hadn't seen in decades fell from an envelope. It was a formal portrait of Charles and his mother, Eliza, dated 1920. The soft sepia had faded, but the faces and forms were in no way obscured. Charles, less than three years old, much younger than any of his own grandchildren, looked out with serious, pale eyes from under his Buster Brown bangs. He wore short pants and a tiny waistcoat with a broad, round collar. Shiny little boots, ankle high. He stood on fat toddler legs on a wooden stool, with his mother's hand on his shoulder. How beautiful his mother had been! Sarah had scarcely known her; she'd died only a year after Charles and Sarah were married.

In the photograph Eliza wore a loose, straight dress, belted at the hip and closed at the throat with a cameo. She wore a long strand of pearls as well, and pearl earrings. Her brown hair had not yet been bobbed—that would shock the family later—but was pulled back into a heavy twist that left waves draping softly over her ears and above her high forehead.

And now, in a time that young mother could never have imagined, the elderly wife of her small boy was sifting through hundreds of photos that covered more than a century. There were even images of Charles's paternal grandmother, who had died before Charles was born. There were heartbreaking scenes of Charles's brilliant, lively sister, Diana, who had died of breast cancer in her forties, leaving no children. There were dozens of Charles in his boyhood, on Lake Winnipesaukee in New Hampshire, on the Belgrade Lakes in Maine. Then there was Charles on Albert Graves's farm, a young, strong, grinning Charles on a ladder, or loading milk cans, or holding up a wheel of cheese he had made himself. Charles in uniform, looking stern to hide the raw green fear he later confessed to Sarah. Charles the medical student, asleep in his chair, surrounded by books. Some of the later pictures had never made it into the albums—failed shots, near duplicates. Not many of the candid shots included Charles, who was usually behind the lens. Nevertheless, there were a few in which he was holding his babies, putting toys under the Christmas tree, hammering or sawing or stacking wood. So many snapshots, over such a long, long time. Charles and Sarah at a cabin in the Green Mountains, with friends, a year before their wedding. Their first apartment, in New York. Sarah and Addie. Leila, introduced as Addie's roommate, nothing more. So young, all of them.

Time slid through Sarah's hands, one slipstream image after another. She remembered her small David's questions about time. You *could* see time. There it was in front of her, more of it than she could comprehend. So many dead people who had carelessly allowed their effigies to survive them. How many arrested images, all over the world, in envelopes, shoeboxes, albums, frames, and now digital files?

All those generations. Charles was dead and Sarah would follow, either soon or less soon. Tess had a baby coming. All of Sarah's children were parents now, and before long some of her grandchildren could be, too. Sarah pictured Christmases with four generations gathered at the tree. It made her dizzy, this sense of being dead still within the flow of time, which, having slowed around her, now picked up speed again. Endless others had come before her, thousands of ancestors whose sad or passionate, arranged or happenstance unions had all led inexorably—as it turned out—to her, to Sarah Alice Everett Lucas sitting there sorting photographs. Countless others would come after her, if the world did not end first. Sarah's own blood in unseen future bodies.

It was odd to think that she, Sarah, represented a multitude in both directions. How could both past and future narrow down to her, to Sarah her very self? As, of course, they narrowed down to every person, sooner or later, one way or another.

A question from Tess broke Sarah's reverie, and she was relieved to escape the vastness. They took a late lunch inside the house, talking little but eating companionably. At four, when they declared themselves finished, Charles's computer was ready for its next owner and all of the bookshelves, desk drawers, and file cabinets were empty. Seven boxes held paper files, letters, and other memorabilia that Sarah would keep for the rest of the family to deal with. Twenty-six boxes of books sat ready for any school or library that wanted them. Five boxes contained books that Sarah would either store here or transfer to shelves in the house—books she knew Charles would have kept or one of their children might want. She had resisted the sad temptation to leaf through those. She stayed businesslike after her time travels, her trance.

This was not possible the next day, when Sarah and Tess dealt with Charles's personal belongings throughout the house. They removed his items from the bathrooms and pulled his clothes from closets, drawers, and pegs. Sweaters and jackets carried his scent, and Sarah now and then buried her face in the folds of well-worn corduroy or wool. "I wish I could bottle this and wear it as perfume," she said to Tess, weeping as she stood next to the window seat, which was strewn with garments and shoes and empty hangers. "I will lose the smell of him the way I've lost his voice and face and body." Looking away, through the window and down across the meadow, she wailed, "I just can't imagine where he's gone."

LATER SARAH FLED TO town on unnecessary errands. She wandered past familiar brick buildings, among pale people welcoming spring. Around the bowl of the town, the mountains rose up, round and wooded, hazed now with the barest hint of a soft red veil, the buds of new maple flowers. Sarah strolled idly, poked around in a bookstore and a clothing shop and stopped to pick up the photographs she'd taken with Charles's camera. She put off looking at them, afraid to see what else was on the roll of film—the last shots Charles would ever take with his camera, the last images his eye would ever compose.

Just before dinner, lying in a steaming, scented bath, Sarah

dried her hands and reached for the packet of prints. She steeled
herself and slid the photos out of their envelope. The first ones
were Charles's, and all but three, which showed their quiet
Christmas, were from Thanksgiving, taken before Hannah's
accident. David and Tess stood in the fenced backyard, next
to Hannah, who sat in the tire swing, her light hair tangled
from flying high. Lottie and Luke flanked Hannah on the deck,
each of them holding one of her hands and bending toward her.
Hannah wore her red jacket, and the shoes they later threw away.
Peter and Vivi, in another picture, set out their hors d'oeuvres.
Finally, everyone sat at the table, which was laden with food and
color, the chestnut brown of the turkey, the greens of broccoli
and salad, the russets and yellows of sweet potatoes and squash,
the ruby of cranberries, and the flame tones of fall flowers. As
usual Charles himself was nowhere in view.

She turned next to the *after* images, the ones she'd snapped on
that recent snowy morning. She was startled to see them starkly
black and white — just snow and the dark shapes of trees and
rocks and utility lines — after the colors of Hannah's jacket and
the holiday dinner. Fitting, she thought.

Most of the photos were just what Sarah expected, pretty
shots of winter, well composed but anticipated. She slid the pictures one by one to the bottom of the stack, until she came upon
one she didn't remember taking. At first she wasn't sure what
she was looking at, but then she recognized the North Branch
as it had looked when she leaned over the railing on the bridge.
There were the dark waters, surrounded by melting ice, with
snowflakes falling down into them. She'd stopped the waters in
their rushing just as they'd broken into milky foam over rocks
beneath the surface. She could make out the image now — now

that she remembered. Yet it could just as well be a portrait of
the night sky. The blackness of the water was so complete that it
could be the dome of the heavens; the stopped, falling snowflakes,
stars. The borders of thick ice, rounded and irregular, could be
layers of dense cloud against the night sky. The pale, blurred
streaks, created by the stream breaking over the rocks, could be
thin cirrus clouds. *Terra Firmament,* Sarah thought, surprised at
the instantaneous appearance of the words in her mind.

Sarah turned to the next shot. This was the picture of her own
hand stretched before her, a single snowflake hovering just above
her palm, not yet melted by the heat of her skin. Sarah studied
the image of her fingers curled upward and saw that they could
be grasping the snowflake or letting it go; it could be falling or
rising. She thought of Charles, the last time she had seen him,
either grinning or grimacing.

Chapter 15

TESS COOKED FOR everyone on Wednesday night, when David came back up from Cambridge. It proved easier than Sarah had thought to let her take over the kitchen. The two of them ate tuna sandwiches for lunch with Hannah, then Sarah obediently sliced vegetables and located utensils for Tess. Otherwise, she sat drinking tea at the kitchen table, sometimes talking with Tess, sometimes reading to Hannah from a book of myths and folktales. The rest of the time, Hannah amused herself, covering half the table with paper, coloring books, crayons, and pencils. She grew bored with coloring ready-made pictures, preferring to create her own, and she drew skillfully for a child not yet four, adding unusual detail to her work, especially when she drew people. The figure of a little girl bore rows of small parallel lines at the wrists and waistline that clearly stood for the ribbing on a sweater. Faces had eyebrows and sometimes dimples, as well as the usual cluster of eyes, nose, and smiley mouth. Hannah even drew ears, which she shaped like question marks and filled with a couple of squiggles. The effect was remarkably earlike.

Next she drew a tree. She started a little below the line that represented the ground; then she drew upward and branched her line just as a tree would branch. Each time she added a new branch, or thickened one she'd already begun, she started her line back down near the ground. With each repetition of this action, the trunk broadened and developed a rough texture; the branches took on weight; the impression of roots became stronger. When Hannah was satisfied with the shape of her tree, she added leaves. These she drew individually, oversizing them and letting their outlines intersect so that they overlapped each other and the branches and trunk. Then she handed the tree to Sarah and said, "I made this for you."

"Thank you, Hannah, how beautiful. Tess, look," said Sarah, holding it up. "I've never seen anyone make a tree *grow* like that, right on a piece of paper."

"David taught me," Hannah said. "He showed me how to make tree trunks and branches. But I figured out how to do leaves by myself."

"The leaves are wonderful," Sarah told her. Remembering David's sketches for the mural, she added, to Tess, "David's become quite a good artist, hasn't he. He never used to draw as a child."

"Really?" Tess sounded surprised. "I guess he did start late, come to think of it. He told me he used to be afraid to draw freehand, for fun, but he made himself practice. In college, I think he said, or maybe after. I'm not sure."

All the hours, adding up to years, that Sarah had spent as a mother, and now she barely knew her children.

"What does he draw?" she asked Tess.

Tess, busy whisking milk into a bubbling *roux,* answered absently. "Oh, lots of things. Mostly people. He likes the body's engineering." She picked up a bowl of freshly grated cheese and sprinkled it into the sauce, still gently whisking. "Maybe he gets that from Charles. He told David he became a doctor because he liked the way the body *worked.*"

Sarah nodded. Charles had loved human mechanisms, the beautiful interlocking of bones and muscles, the touching interdependence of organs, the looping around of blood vessels, the rhythms of it all. David, it seemed, was able to translate a similar love into art. But where did his talent come from? Not from Sarah, and not, as she now realized, from Charles. It must have originated with David himself.

DAVID DROVE IN AT five, an hour before the others were due for dinner. He had put in his day of teaching and had graded the papers that had piled up. He was caught up, for now.

A roasted-pepper lasagna was assembled and ready to bake, as were stuffed portobello mushrooms. The dough for a focaccia was rising, fragrant with rosemary beneath a striped tea towel. Only the salad still had to be made before everyone sat down to dinner, and Sarah was in charge of the salad. Tess was upstairs taking a bath.

When Hannah heard David's car, she ran through the mudroom and into the barn and flung herself at him as soon as he got out from behind the wheel. Sarah got to the mudroom's far end in time to see David lift her into the air and kiss her cheek with a noisy smack and set her back on the barn's dirt floor. He tickled her lightly, with brief little boxerlike jabs, and she spun away from him, then spun back in, grabbing his left hand and giggling.

"I made some trees, just like you showed me," Hannah announced, pulling him toward the kitchen. She had run to the barn wearing a short-sleeved T-shirt and denim overalls, oblivious to the chill in the April air. "Come on, I'll give you one. I made some pictures for *everybody*! I even drew Boojus, he's for Vivi. Vivi showed me how to weave and she bought me a book, it's about a cat named Henry who has to cross-country ski to get away from a *coyote!*"

David entered the house, shaking his head and chuckling. "Slow down, slow down, Hannah." He hugged Sarah and ducked through the door, with Hannah skipping at his side. Sarah had never seen the child so excited.

Tess reappeared a few moments later, her long hair pulled back and tied at the nape of her neck with a watercolor silk scarf. She wore slim black pants and a blue silk shirt. Elegant and understated without makeup or jewelry, she carried the faint scent of lavender. As she greeted David with a light kiss, her wrists crossed behind his neck, something in her reserve seemed to Sarah more intimate than any passionate embrace. Her quietude was knowing as a whisper, and Sarah looked away as Sylvie and Ruckus came in from her office, awakened, no doubt, by David's deep voice amid the altos and sopranos they'd grown used to.

"How did the work go?" David asked.

"Fine," Tess told him. "I think we're finished, aren't we, Sarah? But there are a *lot* of boxes to stash or haul. We'll need some muscle."

"Sure. Tomorrow. When's dinner and who's coming?"

At six thirty-five, half an hour late, Charlotte and Tom drove in with Lottie and Luke. It wasn't like them to be late; Charlotte never allowed that to happen, so she must be the one who had held things up—a disheartening sign. She had objected strongly to Tess's helping with Charles's personal possessions.

"Mom, she's not part of this family! She barely knew Dad."

"Oh, Charlotte, honey, I know that, but I can't refuse her. People feel so helpless after someone dies. Tess just wants some practical task to do."

"And what about me? What about Tom and the kids? Weren't you even going to *ask*?" Her voice had been tight, whether with resentment or with grief half swallowed, Sarah couldn't tell.

She'd sighed and said, "I'm sorry. Really, I am. Why don't you come and help us? Can you?"

But Charlotte couldn't, or wouldn't. And tonight, having finally dealt with all of Charles's possessions, Sarah was suddenly contrite. She hadn't anticipated how powerfully his personal belongings would invoke his presence, how intensely they would echo his entire personality, all his expressions, his passions, his scent and voice, his way of moving. She had kept her daughter at a distance and denied her a final, physical connection with her father. A last farewell.

Sarah realized that if Stephie or David had been available to help with the sorting, she'd have invited them without prompting. But she was more comfortable with Tess, whom she barely knew, than she was with Charlotte, so she had accepted Tess's offer the minute it was made, without a second thought.

Shame inexplicably brought to her mind the long-ago cold spell in her marriage. With new and jarring clarity, Sarah saw that Charlotte had had her father to herself from the age of five until she was more than nine years old. Her estrangement from

Sarah, which had begun with the loss of baby Andrew, had only intensified when Sarah and Charles had grown apart during David's infancy. Charlotte had been old enough by then to sense the tension between her parents and to choose sides, drawing ever closer to her father. What a shock, then, to watch numbly as her parents slowly reconciled. What a loss to her, and what jealousy she must have felt! Why had this thought never entered Sarah's head, either at the time or in all the years since?

Shaken, Sarah felt more responsible than ever for her daughter's unhappiness, not only on this night but in their whole history together. Meanwhile, Charlotte was chilly with Tess, as if Tess were overstepping yet again by hosting a family dinner on only her third visit to this house. Sarah watched with dismay, hoping Charlotte would not keep taking out on Tess the anger that properly belonged at Sarah's own feet.

David took drink orders as soon as the coats were hung. Everyone stood about awkwardly, aware of change and strangeness. Sarah held herself apart from them and watched their slow jockeying as if her home were a stage and none of these people were known to her. She was the audience now, not the director. Always, before, she'd have placed those who were at odds far enough from one another for the taut cords between them to fray, thread by thread, until the tensions slowly gave way. Now she was startled by distance, suddenly unconcerned even about Charlotte's mood. There was nothing Sarah could do about Charlotte tonight. She could only let the evening unfold as it would.

Luke escaped with Hannah after she gave him his drawing of a dog with a ball—a black dog, Sylvie-like. He offered to show her how to make an origami dog, and she followed him happily into Sarah's office in search of colored paper. Lottie sat close to

David and Tess on the big couch but followed the younger children with her eyes. She treated Tess like a big sister, Hannah like a little one, and didn't quite seem to know where she belonged herself. She had turned sixteen only a few weeks after Charles's death, and the occasion had been marked forlornly.

David now crossed the room to a side table. He opened a drawer and brought out a box wrapped in paper the color of paprika. He stood before his niece, tall and lanky in denim shirt and khakis, trying unsuccessfully to hide the box behind his back. "Lottie, I'm sorry this is late, and I'm sorry we couldn't be here to celebrate—but, hey, happy sixteenth, kiddo. This is from both of us, Tess and me." He held it out, and Lottie's eyes lit up, darting from David to Tess and back. She ducked her head, which hid her face inside a sudden fall of curls. She neatly untied the indigo satin bow, set it beside her, and slid her fingers under the tape at the folds in the paper. Inside the unwrapped box, in layers of tissue, was something soft. Lottie held her breath and slowly lifted a shimmering garment from its crumpled bed. It was a loose, flowing jacket of heavy, rain gray silk, handpainted front and back with Japanese street scenes. Spare, stylized skyscrapers rose beside each lapel and looked down upon a sea of black umbrellas and shiny wet cars and buses. Rain dashed down in slanting streaks, recalling Hokusai or Hiroshige. The only spots of bright color were the Japanese characters on neon signs. Otherwise everything was blue-gray, silver, black, or indigo.

Lottie gasped, and held the extravagant piece of work up to her and stood on tiptoe at the small mirror above the side table. "Oh my God," she breathed. "This is *gorgeous*! Uncle David, Tess, thank you, thank you. I *love* it!"

"Put it on, sweetie," Tess urged. "Here, let me." She held up Lottie's hair in one hand and helped her slide her arms into the jacket's sleeves. "Let's have a look," she said, stepping back.

Lottie turned to face Tess. She had on black jeans and a purple T-shirt, which the jacket softly outshone. Tess held her palms together, the tips of her fingers at her smiling mouth. "You are simply beautiful," she said. She didn't see Charlotte rise from her chair and head for the bathroom off the front hall. Only Sarah saw her go.

When she returned, Tom tried to make up for her moodiness with praise for the table and its burden of beautiful food. Tess's contribution did deserve notice. Otherwise, it was the same table bearing the same china and the same well-laundered linens that were laid out for every festive occasion. Still, the strain lifted. All began chattering as they found their places and sat. Charlotte, though, remained silent as the meal progressed.

Whatever anguish David's adolescent storms had inflicted was finally over. It had taken a long time, but at least David and Charles had recognized and enjoyed each other once more before time had run out. David had been openly defiant well into his twenties. He took the car without permission; he used marijuana, hallucinogens, and too much alcohol; he slammed doors and raged at both parents, parading his existential angst through all the rooms of the house. He treated girls like candy, savoring every flavor he could find. Even holed up in his room, making not a sound and never showing his face, he could infect the household. Most poisonous of all was his contempt for his father—rigid, controlling, oblivious. But David had finally grown into himself with accelerating grace, while Charlotte, at forty-six, held onto old hurts, perhaps without even knowing what they were. Now her father, her chosen parent, was gone, and where did that leave Charlotte? With a mother she could barely tolerate and a daughter who didn't even try to tolerate her. The thought revived Sarah's guilt—both the old guilt, which spanned forty years or more, and the recent guilt over leaving Charlotte out of family business. For the first time, she wondered which of them had been the first to give up on the other. She had always thought it was Charlotte, but what if it had been Sarah herself?

Lottie waved a hand before Sarah's face, singing, "Oh, Naaa-naaaaa. You in there?"

Sarah blinked and saw all eyes upon her. She shook her head. "Daydreaming, sorry."

"We're planning Lottie's future," David informed her. "Since she doesn't seem to have any plans of her own." He winked at his niece, who made a face back at him.

"Too *many* plans, Uncle David, with which you are no help."

"Dream big," he replied. "Drama first, and *then* early childhood development, and *then* medicine. Then produce and star in your own movie about the children's ward in some big urban hospital." He grinned across the table at Charlotte. "What do you think, Char?"

"It's up to Lottie," Charlotte answered flatly. "I know *I* don't have a thing to say about it."

"You don't exactly *ask,* either," Lottie challenged. She lowered her eyes. "Sorry," she muttered.

Charlotte looked genuinely hurt. "You don't *let* me ask," she protested. "If I try, you just roll your eyes and sigh. What do you want from me?"

Lottie rolled her eyes and sighed. "Whatever."

Luke, who had followed the conversation avidly, mimicked Lottie's gestures and tone of voice as if taking lessons. "Whatever," he echoed.

"Luke, shut up!" his sister yelled. "Shut the *fuck* up!"

Luke looked slapped. Then, widening his eyes at Lottie, he breathed, "*Whoa!*"

"Lottie, leave the table," Tom ordered. "Now!" he added sharply, seeing her open her mouth to object. "But first, apologize. And mean it."

Lottie narrowed her eyes. "I am just so fucking sorry," she blurted, and ran from the room.

Charlotte wept without a sound. Tom put his arm around her shoulders, and no one said anything for several moments.

Finally Hannah crawled onto Tess's lap and said, "Why is Lottie so mad?" She burst into tears, not soundlessly but with open sobs that diverted everyone's attention from Charlotte and brought Lottie timidly back from the hallway where she'd been lurking.

She scooped Hannah up from Tess's lap. "I'm not mad," she told her. "I'm just sort of a mess." She choked back her own tears, trying to soothe the little girl.

Sarah leapt up, surprising herself.

"Oh, for crying out loud!" she exclaimed, then burst out laughing at her choice of words. Amusement bubbled in her throat like champagne, and she let it come, though she couldn't begin to locate its source. "Just look at this family!"

Around the table, angry, bewildered, or sorrowing eyes went blank and stared at Sarah.

"Lottie, you *are* mad. You're furious! You're surrounded by teachers and parents and rules, and they're driving you crazy.

Swear all you want to, I don't give a damn. Just be glad you live in a time when you can do anything you want."

Sarah circled the table. Heads and eyes turned to follow her. She could read these people. They were verses long ago learned by heart, which now came to her whole. Certainty coursed through her like clear, cold water.

"Charlotte," she said, "relax. Take the long view. I gave you too much room, I didn't know how to reach you, so I quit trying. I did that, not you." She stood still a moment, facing her daughter. "But now you're doing just the opposite with Lottie; you're hovering, you're trying to control her. Ease up, she might surprise you. Tom, quit protecting Charlotte from herself, it's condescending. Luke, don't be a smartass, it only makes things worse and you do it on purpose. And David . . . David . . ." Here Sarah broke into fresh merriment. "How did such a sweet little boy turn into *such* a pain in the ass? All that sulking and acting out and oh-my-*God* the superiority. And now look at you. Finally. See, Charlotte? All you can do is trust."

With this last, she winked at Hannah, who sat bug-eyed on Lottie's lap, her small chin thrust forward, her lips parted.

Sarah dropped back into her chair and surveyed them all. "I should talk. Sometimes I was a *horrible* mother"—here she looked directly at Charlotte—"but we can't any of us afford to get stuck in regret. There's no time for that." Sarah pushed herself up and started clearing away the last of the dessert dishes. "Let's move on."

Chapter 16

L OTTIE MOVED IN WITH Sarah on Saturday. She'd pleaded with Tom, who had approached Charlotte while she was still dazed by Sarah's rant at dinner. Charlotte readily agreed. "Give it a try. Nana's only two miles away. But I want you home for dinner at least once a week. You can't pretend we don't exist."

Lottie blissfully hugged both parents, catching Charlotte off guard. Luke was furious at the prospect of being an only child with no one to share the heat of his parents' scrutiny. Lottie thumbed her nose at him behind Charlotte's back.

Sarah wasn't so sure she wanted a full-time teenager, and she didn't want to become the new Charlotte in Lottie's eyes. It wouldn't be a permanent arrangement, though. Lottie would surely move back home when school let out. That was only six weeks off.

Sarah gave Lottie Stephie's old room at the far end of the hall from Sarah's and across from the bathroom that all her children had used. This way they would intrude on each other as little as possible. She knew Lottie would want privacy, as she did herself. She also didn't want to hear the music Lottie favored, with its thumping bass, its furious, incomprehensible lyrics, and its bizarre electronic noises—squeals, buzzes, howls. Sarah had heard enough of this noise at Charlotte and Tom's.

Lottie brought two suitcases, her computer and schoolbooks, a box full of CDs, and a pocket-size portable player with headphones. She unpacked in minutes and clattered happily down the stairs to help David and Tess, who were moving some boxes of Charles's goods. The others would stay in his office, safe from the damp and awaiting final disposition after everyone had searched for items they wanted. Right away Lottie claimed a baggy wool sweater, a heathery brown crewneck that Charles had loved. It matched her hair exactly.

Most boxes went into the back of Charles's pickup for delivery to the library, charities, or the landfill. They were labeled neatly and arranged by destination. Once they were delivered, Sarah would sell the truck, which was nearly new. She planned to keep Charles's car, a slightly older Subaru than her own. Lottie would soon have her driver's license.

Sarah stood in a patch of sun as she directed the loading of the truck. This was the warmest day so far, with the temperature heading into the low eighties though it was still only April. The snow was nearly gone; only thin patches remained in the woods and on the north sides of the house and barn. The mud would go, too, if this early dry spell held. It still lay wet in low spots, but in well-drained areas it was already hardening.

After the truck was loaded, and David had driven off to Cambridge with Tess and Hannah, Sarah invited Lottie to walk down to the cabin with her.

"What for?" Lottie asked. "I thought you never went down there anymore."

"Someone's moving in. But you can't tell anyone for a while."

"Who?" Lottie asked avidly. "Why can't I tell?"

"Peter Marks's cousin from Israel. He needs a place to write. And you can't tell, because then your parents won't think I need you for protection and might make you move back home."

Lottie shuddered at the thought. "Got it," she said.

They slogged through sopping brown grass in the low parts of the meadow, followed a path alongside the birches and hemlocks, and finally reached an overgrown stone walkway that led to the cabin's back door. Rough wooden stairs fronted a small porch about four feet square. Sarah was surprised when the aluminum storm door opened without sticking. The wooden inner door resisted, though, and Sarah bumped it open with her hip. She and Lottie stepped inside, leaving their mud-caked Merrells behind. Sarah quickly circumnavigated the room, sweeping twill curtains back along the thick dowels that held them. Sunlight poured in, brightening the dark interior through layers of dust on the windows.

"Musty!" Lottie said, and sneezed. "Mousy, too. Bet there are turds everywhere."

"No doubt," Sarah sighed. "How would you and some friends like to clean it all up?"

Lottie managed to turn her mouth down and wrinkle her nose at the same time. "Eeuuw," she said. "Is this my moving-in fee?"

"Of course not" Sarah said. "In fact, I was going to pay you, all of you."

"Sorry," Lottie said, abashed. "I didn't mean it the way it

sounded. You don't have to pay us." She thought a moment, eyeing her grandmother with a sudden calculating gleam, and said, "Unless . . ."

"Unless what," Sarah responded skeptically.

"Well. Do you think we could spend the night here, and get pizza, once it's all clean?"

"Who's 'we'? And how many sexes are we talking about?"

"Um. Two?"

"Tell me more."

Lottie counted on her fingers. "Me. Jenna Sterling, Lori Mellender. That's three girls. Then two guys, Tony Clausen and Guy Sproul. Five of us. No couples, Nana. We're all just friends. Please?"

"I'll have to talk with all the parents," Sarah said firmly.

"*Yes.* Thank you, Nana!"

"Including yours," she added.

Lottie started to roll her eyes, then caught herself. "Do you think my mom will let me?" she asked, screwing her face into doubt.

"I'll handle it," Sarah told her. "You just get the place clean — and I mean spanking clean, everything. Windows. Inside the woodstove. All the furniture and throw rugs. Take the mattress and rugs and cushions out onto the deck and beat them to death." She was smiling broadly at Lottie's pleasure. "I'll wash the curtains if you'll get them down."

The cabin was dirty and cobwebby and had the distinct odor of mouse that Lottie had complained about, but Sarah remembered how bright it could be and how safe it felt, tucked away out of sight, visible only to birds and other wildlife. Its main room was twenty by twenty-five feet, large enough for a dining area in one corner, a workspace in another, and a big, cozy seating area. Two down-filled sofas faced each other from either side of the big iron woodstove, which sat on stone tiles against the inside wall of the main room. The sofas were wrapped tightly in heavy plastic, drop cloths, and duct tape. Sarah hoped they were not nests for mice by now, in spite of these barriers.

Cut into that same inside wall was the entrance to a small kitchen, which opened into a bedroom and from there into a bathroom and miniature laundry and back out to the main room. Thus every room opened into the next, and they all circled the heart of the cabin, the woodstove. A good blaze, well banked, could keep the rooms warm all night long in the bitterest weather. The cabin's walls, with their siding of tight, squared logs, held the heat for as long as two days once thoroughly warmed. Theoretically. Sarah couldn't remember anyone using the cabin in winter, though someone might have before she and Charles had bought the property.

A big fan hung in the ceiling of the main room. She and Charles had used it on rare nights when the bedroom was stifling and they could catch no breeze on the deck. They had either dragged the mattress from the bed to the larger room, or they had collapsed onto the two couches. They had probably been in their forties the last time they had stayed out here for any length of time, but they were still young. Vigorous, happy, busy in their lives.

"What's wrong with this, Nana?" Lottie was standing inside the kitchen door, flipping a light switch to no avail.

"Burned out?"

"Nope," Lottie said. "I tried the light over the sink, too. And I plugged in the fridge. No juice. But the other rooms are okay."

"I'll check the breakers later." She'd better check the plumbing, too, and replace the propane tank for the stove. The old one had probably rusted through. "Are you sure your friends will be up for this?" she asked.

"Are you kidding? For a night away from home and no adults eavesdropping?"

Sarah leveled a stern look.

"Really, Nana, no funny stuff. It's just that parents are so *suffocating.* God!" She put her hands to her throat and thrust out her tongue, gasping harshly.

Sarah laughed. "What about grandparents? I could sneak down here and spy on you and you'd never know." No harm in planting that idea, though she was unlikely to carry it out. The fact was, she didn't believe there was much these kids could get up to. She was pretty sure that Lottie's crowd didn't drink much alcohol. She suspected they preferred pot, but Charles's change of heart about that had somehow eased her mind. Sex could be a problem, of course. Sarah was anxiously aware that early sexual activity was commonplace, but all she could do was talk to the various parents and make sure they understood the conditions under which their children would spend the night. Times had changed.

LOTTIE PAID A DUTIFUL call at home that Friday night, then returned to Sarah's on Saturday morning with her four friends. They arrived in Jenna Sterling's parents' truck, having picked up, at Sarah's expense, a rented floor polisher, a bag of apples, another of bagels, and a plastic tub of cream cheese.

Jenna had even brought her mother's handheld steam vac for rugs and upholstery.

Jenna was tall and Lori about an inch taller; both had thatchy hair whose natural color was dark blond, but according to Lottie, Lori's was a different color weekly. Today it was liberally streaked with blue. Guy Sproul was big-boned, rangy, freckled, and polite. His brown hair was shoulder length and straight; he wore a woven leather headband to keep it from his eyes. He was dressed in loose canvas pants and a threadbare T-shirt with *Phish* on the front. Tony Clausen—about five ten, slim, and handsome—had a band of Celtic knots tattooed around his left upper arm and wore five rings in his right ear that reminded Sarah of the spiral binding on a notebook. He was clean-shaven except for a small goatee, no mustache.

All five teenagers got down to work with industry. In only a few hours, the girls had moved the rugs, loose cushions, and mattress outside and had spot-cleaned and pounded the dust out of all of them. Tony and Guy had scoured the inside of the woodstove and washed down the outer surfaces. The stone tiles beneath it were free of dust and soot. Even the stove's glass doors shone clear, and the brass fittings gleamed.

The big windows were all clean, inside and out, when Sarah ventured down to the cabin with sandwiches and two big thermoses of soup. The girls had used a long-handled squeegee for the large panes, sponges and wadded newspapers for the smaller ones, and steaming vinegar water for all. They were about to start on the small, high windows when Sarah came through the back door with her arms full.

"Nana, where's a stepladder?" Lottie asked her, taking her burden of food. "We're almost done with all the windows, but somebody has to get the bugs out of the overhead lights. Kitchen stool's too rickety. If we had about *three* stepladders, we'd get done faster."

Sarah told them where to look under the deck and in the barn. She scanned the room and praised the fast progress. She ate lunch with her workers and took stock of what remained to be done. The kitchen and bathroom still needed to be cleaned, but that would occupy only some of the crew for only a couple of hours. It was clear, at the rate they were going, that there was time to put a coat of paint on the living room walls. She posed the question, adding, "I can run into town for paint and rollers and pans. And I would insist on paying you for the extra work. This wasn't part of our deal."

They settled on the terms, and Lottie offered to go with Sarah. "The paint will be heavy," she pointed out. She also wanted to drive. "I have my permit," she reminded Sarah. "But I hate driving with my mom. She's so critical. She even tells me how to hold the steering wheel. She makes me a worse driver than I'd ever be if she'd just leave me alone."

Sarah was glad for the company. The girl reminded Sarah of her own young self, anticipating New York and liberation.

Lottie got behind the wheel of Sarah's Subaru with a happy shimmy of her shoulders. She pulled the seat forward a couple of inches, saying, "Mom didn't get the tall genes from you and Papa, and Dad's too short to make up for it."

"I know, honey. It's just a shame you got saddled with those two, isn't it?" She cut her eyes sideways at her granddaughter. "Let's see, whose parents would you rather have?"

"Tony Clausen's," Lottie answered promptly, backing the car around so she could head out of the driveway facing front.

"Why Tony's parents?"

"Oh, they're so *cool,* Nana! His mom's a singer and his dad plays jazz piano and everybody in the family does music together. Tony plays drums, his brother plays saxophone. He has a little sister, and she plays piano, like the dad. His parents even made a CD a little while ago, and it's been getting reviews in *national* music magazines. And they live in this incredible house up near the Notch in Middlesex, with a waterfall right behind."

Sarah was suddenly less sure there were no couples in this team of workers she had hired. She said nothing, though. She would not perch on Lottie's shoulder.

When they returned from town, she noted with new interest that Tony Clausen ran out to help them carry the paint supplies, and she thought she felt a certain energy in the air that she had missed before. Or maybe she imagined it. Either way, she wouldn't interfere. If Lottie was in love with Tony, if the two of them were just beginning an attraction or had been acting on it for months, there was nothing any adult could do or say about it. Sarah didn't mind that thought. Lottie was a decent, smart girl, given to strong emotions but also to healthy self-scrutiny. She had her own life to live, and it stretched out before her in a grand, dim haze in which people and events would grow clear only as Lottie approached them.

Meanwhile, Sarah, looking back, had recently begun to perceive with fond amazement that many long-past people and events in her own life were regaining clarity. Where once they had seemed to recede into haze, something in the present had started burning the haze away. She wondered whether even older memories would emerge before long, perhaps the oldest of all, which she and Tess had been watching Hannah forget.

WHEN MORDECHAI ARRIVED at Peter and Vivi's in May, Sarah was invited over for dinner, two days before he would move into the cabin. She drove over in the mellow, early evening, her car windows down, a silky breeze winding around her neck like a scarf. She hoped Mordechai was not the kind of man who would get lonely and intrude on her shrinking privacy.

Vivi walked out to greet Sarah with Peter and Mordechai right behind. Sarah wished they'd given her a minute to steel herself, but her anxiety vanished in her friends' embrace. Emerging from the tangle of their arms, she came face-to-face with Mordechai, who smiled at her as though he had known her for decades. She took the hand he offered and smiled back.

Mordechai was an inch or two shorter than Sarah, stocky like his cousin Peter, with hair and beard that were salt-and-pepper instead of salt-and-rust. His eyes were brown but flecked with green and amber. He had a broad smile and a gap as wide as a matchstick between his front teeth, which were otherwise perfect. "I remember you now," he said to her. "And your husband, too. What a terrible shock to lose him after so many years together." Nearly everyone else had borrowed the same stock phrase from American television: "I am sorry for your loss." Mordechai was more direct, and his eyes were so kind that Sarah had to look away.

Flustered, she closed up the car and headed indoors, where she escaped to the bathroom to cool her face with a washcloth. She studied herself in the mirror and saw the pain in her own light eyes gazing back, renewed by a stranger's authentic condolence.

This was the first time Sarah had agreed to dinner at Vivi and Peter's since Charles's death. She had not wanted to revisit the scene of so many intimate evenings. Now, three months later, she sat here with a man she could not remember having met before. Throughout the main course—roast chicken and spring vegetables that Sarah barely tasted—Mordechai was like a wrong leg on the table, a mismatch that made everything wobble. Not that anyone thought he somehow stood in for Charles. It wasn't that. It was just that he was male and he was there, where Charles had always sat.

By dessert Sarah had begun to relax in Mordechai's presence. He came from a place where violence tore unpredictably through streets, lives, and bodies, and yet he was quiet and calm. He sat very still, listened attentively, and was in no hurry to speak. Sarah saw in his eyes only alertness and curiosity. She had worried that he might be jumpy, abrupt, or defensive, having lived with perpetual threat. She had dreaded being near someone like that.

Late in the evening Sarah learned that Mordechai was a social historian who studied immigrants to Israel from all over the world. He focused especially on whether their expectations had been met or undermined by the realities of Israeli life. He was now writing "an idealist's history" of the struggles between the Israelis and Palestinians. "What I mean," he said with his light Hebrew accent, "is that Israel was founded on strong ideals. Notions of freedom, identity, and healing. Above all, safety. And I am trying to understand what happens to ideals in the face of hatred and violence. And why it happens. And whether it must happen the way that it does."

"Whether the violence is necessary?" asked Sarah.

"Yes. Whether we are victims of our own worst nature or can transcend it."

Sarah asked him how long he thought it would take to finish his book.

"I have one year's sabbatical," he laughed. "So I suppose that is how long it will take."

Gradually Sarah warmed to the prospect of Mordechai's living quietly in her cabin, waking to the morning light and the pale, watercolor sky painted on the surface of the pond. She pictured ashes lying on the silty bottom of the pond, lifting in the currents made by small fish. Perhaps Mordechai would not disturb Charles even so much as that.

Chapter 17

O N THE LAST SATURDAY in May, Sarah and Lottie
went to the farmers' market in Montpelier, where
they roamed the booths and tents in search of new
perennials, already hardened off and ready to go straight back
into the chilly ground. With mud season gone, the earth in Sarah's
garden was damp but loose, ready to be worked.

They bought too many pots and flats for the two of them to
carry to the car, so Lottie went to drive it around — illegally,
since she was still driving with a permit, not a license. It didn't
even cross Sarah's mind to worry. She stood on the curb at the
edge of the busy market, surrounded by crowds giddy with
spring and burdened with plants, peasant breads, cheeses, or
crafts. Later in the season, the market would offer a seductive
array of plain and designer vegetables, but it was too early for
any harvest except greens and a few herbs.

Sarah was impatient to get back home to put in the new
plants. She'd cut back last autumn's dead stalks, making way for
the new growth that already stood well above the crowns. The

daffodils had finished blooming, and the tulips were fully open. Sarah was always in a hurry at the bare beginning of Vermont's short growing season, knowing it would rush away too soon. She wondered how she managed to forget, each winter, what lay beneath the snow, ready to revive. This year, when winter had finally receded for good, its cold tide had left behind the green tips of spring bulbs, already up.

Lottie drove up and loaded the Subaru's way-back. She slid behind the wheel again as a matter of course, now that Sarah let her drive whenever they went out together. She'd have her license in another few weeks, and Sarah would let her share Charles's old Subaru with Mordechai, provided her grades didn't suffer.

For Sarah the new living arrangement was still touch and go, complicated by her guilt about withholding certain things from Lottie's parents. Tom and Charlotte didn't know that Lottie had become Sarah's chauffeur. That was the least of it. They also didn't know that Lottie smoked marijuana, as Charles had suspected, that she was probably sleeping with Tony Clausen, or that she was pleading with Sarah to let two of her friends move in, just for a while, until they could calm things down in their stormy homes or make other arrangements.

The morning after the overnight in the cabin, Sarah had smelled smoke in Lottie's hair — not cigarette smoke. For an old woman, she still had a good nose, and she recognized the telltale scent from her own sweater after the dinner party last January. She could still see Charles's face, eerily lit from beneath by the kerosene lamp. His surprisingly easygoing attitude about Lottie, coupled with Sarah's disbelieving memory of having tried the drug herself, had made her unsure of what to say. The smell of the smoke had at first ignited a fury in her, the same fury she'd felt when David was a teenager and lied as often as he breathed. Hastily Sarah had doused her anger at Lottie in favor of reflection, which cleared her mind.

"Lottie," she'd said later that same afternoon, "we need to understand each other. There are certain conditions under which I will have you here with me. If you violate them, you'll go home."

Lottie, who had been lying on the couch in the great room, reading, sat up alarmed. "Nana? Did I do something wrong?"

"The law would say so. You were smoking marijuana last night, down in the cabin with your friends."

Lottie put on a show of indignation. "You really did spy on us? You snuck down there and *spied* on us?"

Sarah snorted. "Don't pull that on me, my dear. I'm not the one who's guilty here. And no, I didn't spy. I can still use my nose, and your hair reeks of smoke. Not tobacco smoke either."

Collapsing back against the loose couch cushions, Lottie sighed, "It wasn't me, Nana, honest. The others brought some weed with them, but they know I don't smoke it."

Sarah had not considered this and wondered if it were true. "I have no way of knowing, so I'll just tell you this. The first lie I catch you in, off you go. Back home. If you tell me the truth, no matter how dreadful, you will have at least a chance of staying."

Lottie was regarding Sarah seriously now, all defensiveness gone, anxiety and indecision shading her expression.

"Think carefully," Sarah went on. "If I ever, in the future, learn that you do smoke that stuff, I will have to assume that you were smoking it last night with your friends. I will have to assume that what you're telling me now is a lie, and out you will go, so fast the door will have no time to smack your butt. Though I myself might manage it." She sat straight in Charles's chair, next to the couch, angled slightly so she could look Lottie in the eye. Inwardly she was still angry and unsure of how to handle this moment. Outwardly she was stern and calm. It came as a relief to her when she saw Lottie's eyes fill and the tears spill over.

"I did *try* it, Nana," she whispered, not daring to look at Sarah.

Sarah had not planned Lottie's side of this conversation, and she had no idea how to respond to this bit of truth. Impulsively she told a truth of her own. "So did I."

Lottie gave her a look of utter astonishment, then rolled her eyes. "Oh, sure, Nana. When? Back in the fifties? When you were a—whaddyacallit, a *beatnik*?"

"Careful, Lottie," Sarah warned, struggling not to smile. "Don't get sarcastic. I hold all the cards."

"Well? When did you try weed, then?"

"Just a few months ago. With Papa and some friends." Surely this was a mistake! Hastily Sarah added, "But, Lottie, we're adults. *Old* adults. We know who we are; we have judgment you don't even know you're going to need in this life." *Lame,* she thought. *That sounded lame and ancient and prim.*

"Nana, I'm *so* careful. You wouldn't believe. I never, *ever* smoke where I could get caught, not in town, not at school, not while I'm in someone's car. And never, *ever* on a school night." She searched Sarah's face. "Nana, I *promise* I'm telling the truth now. I've smoked maybe a dozen times, starting almost a year ago. But I don't drink; I've never had more than a beer. I don't smoke cigarettes, I don't use any other drugs, not even *coffee.* Honest."

"Where do you get the marijuana?"

"Friends have it." She flicked a look at Sarah and dropped her voice. "Usually."

"And *un*usually, when your friends don't have it? Have you ever bought it yourself?"

Lottie sighed. "Once. But only from somebody I know at school who grows it himself. A kid my age. In the back of the loft of his barn, with special lights."

Sarah slowly shook her head at Lottie, not sure what to say next.

Lottie cleared her throat and ventured, "So. Did you like it, Nana? Weed? And *Papa* smoked it, too?" Lottie covered her mouth with both hands but could not hide her mirth. Her eyes widened mischievously, alight with hungry questions. "Did you *inhale*?" At this she burst helplessly into laughter, throwing her shoulders forward and stomping her feet in front of her. She fell over onto her side and buried her face in a cushion, muffling her glee. Peering out, she sputtered, "Who *else*? Not *Vivi*!"

Cracking a smile against her will, Sarah nodded, setting Lottie off again. Sarah's resistance caved. Her sudden burst of laughter startled Ruckus and Sylvie out of canine dreams near the woodstove. Ruckus sat up and yipped. Sylvie watched with her ears cocked as Sarah and Lottie struggled to get serious.

Sarah finally pulled a straight face and said, "Clean slate."

Lottie nodded, trying to keep the corners of her mouth still.

"But not one lie, ever again. I won't ask you anything more than I think I have to, but when I do ask, I'll expect the truth. All of it. I want more than anything to give you total freedom, but you have to prove you can handle it."

Sober now, Lottie agreed.

"And you have to make some promises," Sarah went on.

"Such as?" Lottie was not just going to cave. Sarah was glad to see that; it made it easier to trust this girl.

"Such as. And these are absolute. If you can't agree, you can't stay here, and I mean that." Seeing Lottie give a tentative nod, she elaborated. "*One.* You have to keep up with your classes. If I see even one grade slip, I bring your parents into the picture. We all go to school to find out what's wrong. *Two.* If you have sex you have to use condoms every single time, no exceptions."

Lottie opened her mouth to protest, but Sarah held up her hand. "I'm not saying you *are* having sex or even planning to. And I'm not asking, at least not now. But even I can feel the air hum between you and Tony." She smiled smugly at Lottie's surprise and seized her momentary advantage. "*Three.* You will not *ever* get into a car with friends who are in any kind of altered state, not from alcohol or drugs or even excess testosterone. If you're out with friends who are high and you need a ride, call me. Any time of the night or day. I will come pick you up."

"*Jeez,*" Lottie breathed. "I don't have much choice, do I?"

"Of course you do," Sarah snapped. "You have a perfectly good home and parents who love you."

Abashed, Lottie mumbled, "I know. It's just hard at home." She took a breath and said, "I promise, Nana. I agree to your terms."

"Not yet," Sarah replied. "You'll be tempted to lie if I ask you about things you don't want to talk about. You'll think you can get away with it. You can try that. But get caught, and you will be out of here before you can blink. Wait a few days before you decide."

Several weeks later Sarah was confident that Lottie had kept her promise once she made it. Her grades were good. She was openly paired off with Tony but in no way a fool for love. Usually Lottie saw her friends in groups of three or more, with and without Tony. She was busy nearly every moment, with no more than a waking hour or two to herself every day. She ate dinner with Sarah and talked with her freely, then went to her room to study, surf the Internet, and listen to music—often simultaneously. Sarah saw plenty of evidence that things were going well.

The one thing Lottie and Sarah had not yet resolved was the matter of Lottie's friends, the ones who wanted a place to stay until their home lives settled down or they had paved a way to more independence. Sarah had told Lottie she would think about this and make a decision by the end of the weekend, which was tomorrow evening.

Sarah still didn't know what her answer would be. Today in the garden she would let her mind work the problem while her hands worked the soil. She knew from a lifetime in gardens that physical labor could strangely untangle knots and dilemmas.

Now Sarah paused in her raking and pruning for a late lunch at the picnic table under the beech. She admired her progress. The fragrant, friable earth was nearly clear of leaves and dead prunings, which lay mounded on an old tarp. Lottie would later drag the tarp to the compost, down near the vegetable garden. Eventually Sarah would put in some tomatoes, bush beans, cucumbers, and squash. She would not try to match Charles's striking variety. No striped eggplants or fingerling potatoes, no melons, no artichokes, no exotic peppers, which in any case needed too much babying in the north country. It was never hot enough for them.

Charles had loved the gardens, both ornamental and edible. Sarah could feel him everywhere today. She could see his hands in the soil he'd worked, setting the seedlings he'd started, or painstakingly constructing the miniature stone walls that kept small, unstable banks from sliding or crumbling. She missed him frightfully, but today her longing felt oddly companionable. Lighter.

Sarah went back to work, fully in the grip of the energy that the flower garden spawned in her. The only blot on her day— many tiny blots—came in the form of the blackflies that arrived in Vermont each May to torment anyone who stepped outdoors. They weren't as bad in Sarah's garden as they could be near streams and rivers, but she cursed and swatted at them all the same, inadequately protected by an herbal repellent. Some year she would decide she was old enough for the hard stuff, with DEET, figuring something else would get her before its carcinogens could. But not yet.

By three, Sarah had dug several holes and sprinkled bonemeal inside before plopping a green inhabitant into each and backfilling carefully, leaving no air around the roots she had gently spread. Bonemeal. A meal of bones. The powdery stuff felt like Charles's ashes. She would like her own ashes planted someday around the roots of irises, lilies, campanulas, delphiniums. With this, she rose stiffly, pulling herself up by the handle of her rake. She brushed off her knees. She watered everything deeply, hoping for generous rain throughout the summer, and went inside for a bath.

As she eased herself into the tub, Sarah felt every muscle exact revenge for overuse. "Oh, quit!" she muttered and slid down until her chin rested on the rippling surface of the bathwater. Then she dropped her head back against the rolled rim of the clawfoot tub and exhaled, pleased with her day's work, picturing the garden filling in. Suddenly she thought of her house filling in, too, and realized she had decided to let Lottie's friends come. There were many kinds of gardens, after all, many growing things, and a meal of bones nourished them all.

Sarah's earlier life had died with Charles, and in this new one she would—the word came readily—husband life in the forms that it offered. Charles had always done this, in both his practice and his life. Sarah remembered his defense of those teenaged car thieves. Maybe they'd have been less desperate if someone had given them more room. This was what her own parents had done, sheltered people who had no place else to go. In doing so, they had given Sarah a richer life as well. Perhaps she was not too old to recapture that atmosphere she'd loved as a child.

Chapter 18

S ARAH STILL WALKED IN the mornings, after Lottie left
for school, and she took photographs almost every day
with Charles's Nikon. She liked to think of its lens as his
eye; she liked seeing through it the world he had shown her from
time to time, as he had that day in the woods above the deer run.
Recently Sarah had started venturing into the woods instead of
staying on the roads. Everything looked different now, with the
leaves unfurled, the undergrowth thick, the light filtered and
green. Everything was crowded together, enfolding Sarah wherever she walked. Her field of vision ended at the dense growth
around and above her. Now and then she felt something similar
in her mind—burgeoning new life filling her up.

On this June morning, the dogs darted in and out of the trees
as Sarah picked her way along the trails, avoiding the mud that
remained in the lowest, shadiest places. In her hurry to leave
the house, she'd forgotten, once again, to bring a walking stick.
She chided herself. Imagine if she fell, just like Charles. Imagine
if Sylvie had to rush home and lie in wait for Lottie. For some

reason Sarah was amused by the image of her own body lying just where Charles had come to rest. *Whither thou goest.*

Something caught her eye then, and she stopped and peered ahead where the trail bent around a stand of white pines. A tuft of color on the ground, something reddish and soft-looking. Sarah walked slowly closer, not quite sure what she was seeing until she stood right there, looking down at a scrap of blood-stained rusty fur and skin. Nothing else, no carcass, scarcely any flesh, just a three-inch ragged tear from the hide of a red fox, or maybe a red squirrel. Leaning over, Sarah saw scuffed tracks near the brush at the side of the trail. Only one print was relatively clear, and it was canine. The pad marks were barely visible, but symmetrical, and there were toenail impressions. The track was small, an imprint of a heavily furred paw, so a fox, surely.

Nearby she saw spatters of blood on some low leaves and a place where the brush had been flattened and small branches broken. Something had jumped the fox right here, muscled it to the ground, torn it, and made off with its body. The hair on Sarah's neck stood up, and she straightened, looking nervously about. The camera on its strap bumped her breastbone, and soon she was snapping away at the scene of battle. At the very edge of the trail, she found a single track of a much larger creature—bobcat, lynx? It was clearly a feline track this time. There were no claw marks, the heel pad looked large in relation to the toe pads, and the whole pattern was asymmetrical. Sarah remembered all that from outings with Charles.

Suddenly she remembered something else, rumors of cougar sightings, which sent fear slicing through her. Did catamounts eat foxes?

Sarah snapped the cap back onto the lens and called the dogs.

She walked rapidly toward home, wondering whether she should make as much or as little noise as possible. Would a catamount fear and avoid her? Or would it regard her as a feast, stringy as she was? She half ran now, feeling hungry yellow eyes upon her at every step.

When at last she arrived home, intact and ridiculously relieved, she went straight to Charles's office in search of his field guides. The fourth box she opened was the right one. A book on North American mammals informed her that the red fox had few enemies other than humans and that reports of cougars roaming northern New England had not been documented. It also said cougars were solitary beasts. They hunted both by day and by night but attacked humans only if threatened or exceedingly hungry. However, a tracker's guide said that two cougar sightings had indeed been confirmed in New England—it didn't say which state—and asserted that cougars did eat foxes. Sarah found no mention, in any other volume, of any other animal doing so. She knew from Charles that fishers could prey on foxes, but fishers were mustelids—weasels—and didn't leave feline tracks, let alone such large ones.

Sarah shuddered. If that piece of bloody fur indeed came from a red fox, then the only thing that could have eaten it, according to her limited research and the evidence at the scene, was a catamount. She would give anything to ask Charles about this. She knew nothing. She had let him go with his mind full of lore and his heart full of the woods and its secrets, and she had hardly ever asked him about any of it.

As Sarah's photographs accumulated, she kept them in a drawer, not bothering to show them to anyone. Most were of pleasing scenes and the progress of spring. One morning she caught a bobolink on a high branch, zooming in on him just as his mate hopped up to his side. Another day she photographed a fawn lying stone still in the deep grass of the meadow, waiting for its mother. More recently she'd started looking for interesting close-ups in the textures of bark, the zippered, herringbone fronds of feathers, or the random cubism of fractured rock ledges. When she succeeded in making a familiar thing abstract and unrecognizable, reducing it to pure color and pattern, she was pleased. She enjoyed making visual mysteries, images that reversed expectation, as in the photo she called *Terra Firmament,* which might be sky or earth, air or water. Such elemental reversals suited her mood when she was out walking. Somehow they offered her a view of herself as a universal being, one of billions here and gone, no more or less lost and sorrowing than others. It was how she had seen Charles on that long-ago day of her secret reconciliation with him, the day he had appeared both dear and anonymous against the looming hills. Outside, she, too, was small within the vast world, but alive and strong despite the grip of grief. Inside, she still felt reduced and faded.

Sitting on the steps of the backyard deck, Sarah examined five photographs taken hurriedly amid her catamount fears. She had never before focused on ugliness in the natural world. She had never examined things broken or decayed—birds' eggs, featherless nestlings, gnawed bodies, downed trees. These new pictures, though unusual for Sarah, were otherwise nothing much. The splash of blood, the tuft of fur, and the snapped branches were all swallowed by the overall complexity of light, shadow, stones, bark, undergrowth, and mud. But in one shot something stood out, a large feline pawprint, sharply visible in the glistening wet earth. Sarah didn't even remember taking that picture, and she certainly hadn't thought to place something next to the track to show its size—a wristwatch or film canister.

Catamount, mountain lion, cougar—whatever its name, it could reach eight feet long and three hundred pounds. Black bears did not compare. They were unaggressive and shy unless a cub was in danger, whereas a cougar, so the books said, would now and then devour a human. Sarah gave silent thanks that Charles had not died that way, torn by scimitar claws.

A clatter interrupted Sarah's grisly thoughts, and she was glad to see Mordechai come through the backyard gate, carefully closing it behind him. Everything Mordechai did was careful, but nothing about him was studied. Sarah had seen him little since he moved in more than a month ago, but when she had checked on how he was settling in, she'd liked the spare simplicity of his space. He'd added many books and a computer, arranging on his own for an Internet line. He'd taken down all the curtains that Sarah had laboriously laundered and rehung, letting the light in unimpeded. Two framed pieces of Hebrew calligraphy, some candles, and a small, padded stool were the only personal items Sarah could see. Everything was orderly.

He said, "Good morning, Sarah," in his lightly accented English. "Are you busy? May I interrupt for a moment?"

"Terribly busy, Mordechai, as you can see," she answered, stretching her arms lazily toward the sun. "What can I do for you? Is everything all right at the cabin?"

"The cabin is perfect, beautiful. I worry that you can hear me clicking away on the keyboard, even up here. It sounds so loud in the quiet."

"I don't hear a thing. Not even music. Don't you ever play music?"

"No," he answered. "I have a single focus to my mind. I read and write nearly all day, and I cannot listen to music at the same time. Because, well, then I listen to the music instead of reading and writing." He smiled broadly. "I am not what they call a multitasker."

"Good for you. I'm sure multitasking is just a way to get more work out of everyone. Eyes here, hands there, feet on the treadmill, everything in motion." Sarah fluttered her hands like startled birds.

"But not you," Mordechai ventured. "You seem to have a calm life." He gestured toward the garden and then the woods. "You make this garden. You walk. I see you with your camera every day, heading toward the woods or the road." Sarah's pile of photographs caught his eye. "May I look?" he asked.

"Oh, Mordechai, I'm no kind of photographer," she said, embarrassed. "I just take snapshots of things I happen to notice." She scooped the photos up, though, and handed them to him, not wanting to be rude or coy.

He sat next to her on the step and shuffled curiously through the pile, sometimes rotating an image in an effort to make sense of it. "This one is . . . ?" He stopped at a starkly simple photo of a flat rock face, cracked down the middle. Its colors ranged from rust to blue-gray to silver, and the jagged line that divided the whole gave it the look of a lithograph—something deliberate instead of accidental.

"It's just a pattern I liked in a rock ledge." Sarah pointed out what had pleased her in each shot. Then they came to the scene-of-attack photographs, and she told him about her fears of a catamount in their woods. "You should be careful if you go walking," she said to him. "You could always take the dogs. They love to ramble."

Mordechai put his hands up in front of his chest, palms out. His flecked eyes caught the light, and he squinted in the glare. "I'm not a woodsman," he said. "There are not so many trees in Israel as here, at least not where I've lived. I am shy of the woods; it's a dark world. I hear creatures at night. An owl, I think, and something that sings and yips — many voices, all together."

"Coyotes," Sarah told him. "They started appearing in Vermont about twenty-five years ago. You had left the country by then, of course. It was very exciting. They migrated slowly eastward. Some people say they bred with timberwolves along the way. Eastern coyotes are bigger than the ones out west."

"Ah," he said. "They make an eerie sound. The first time I heard it, the hairs stood up on my neck and arms."

"They sound closer than they are," Sarah said.

"Good," he replied. "I have lived in cities all my life. Except for a year or two on a kibbutz, a long time ago. And the animals there were tame. I rather like hearing the sounds of wild creatures at night now that I'm getting used to them, but I don't wish to meet them. I like those solid logs all around me." He clapped his hands suddenly, startling Sarah. "That reminds me! May I borrow some firewood? Some nights, even now in June, my desert blood refuses to keep me warm."

Sarah dropped her head into her hands. "I am an idiot," she said through her fingers. Looking up, she gestured toward the barn, where stacks of dry wood were ranged six feet high. "Take all you want, any time. There's a big garden cart in the barn, too.

You can use that to trundle the wood to the cabin." Impulsively she put her hand on his shoulder. "Mordechai, I'm so sorry. Have you been freezing to death all this time?"

Again he shrugged. "I thought it would get warm soon. It's a small thing. I could have asked at any time."

"It does get cold in Israel, though, doesn't it?" she asked. "Not like here, of course, but you do have winters?"

"Oh, yes. Damp winters, freezing rain. It gets into the bones." He looked at her with his brown-green-amber eyes, forest eyes in a desert face. "We have our wild creatures, too. Though for now, most are asleep. No car bombers, no attacks."

Sarah hoped Mordechai didn't think her a sheltered fool, yammering about catamounts and coyotes. "I'm glad for that, Mordechai. People must be so frightened in the bad times."

"Well. Frightened and determined. They will live in their promised land, whatever the cost," Mordechai said. "But here I am—completely safe in this beautiful country where I grew up. Which now feels foreign," he added. "It is very, very strange to be back." He rose and handed Sarah her photographs. She showed him where the garden cart was, ashamed that she hadn't given a thought to his comfort on chilly nights. There would be chilly nights all summer.

Chapter 19

SARAH RAN INSIDE TO grab the phone while Lottie's friends unloaded computers and boxes of clothing from a rattletrap van in the front driveway.

"Hello?" she said, panting.

Silence. Then a faint, ragged intake of breath, a shuddering exhalation. Sarah was about to hang up, thinking this was a crank call, when she heard a small, strangled voice say her name. "Mrs. Lucas?"

"Yes. Who is this, please?" More silence. "Hello. Are you there?"

She heard her caller take another shaky breath. She could almost picture someone closing her eyes, putting a hand to her breast to steady herself. Sarah's own heart lurched against her ribs.

"Mrs. Lucas. This is Sandy Hanks. I don't know if you remember—"

"Of course I remember you, Sandy. What's wrong?"

The story came out between jagged bursts of crying. There

was a fire, an electrical fire, the Hankses' trailer was gone. Bob was in the hospital in Barre. Sandy and Tyler had no place to go, could they stay with Sarah for a little while?

Lottie walked by carrying a box. One of her friends, similarly laden, was silhouetted against the screen door, shoving it open. Between Sandy's weeping and the chatter and heavy tread of teenagers, Sarah felt momentarily dazed. She had promised Lottie's friends, and they were half moved in, but she could not turn Sandy away. It was simple, but so complicated. Where would she put everyone? The house would be a zoo, all those teenagers, a four-year-old—probably five by now—and a distraught mother. She must be mad; if not now, then soon.

Sandy was still pouring out her story. Bob was severely burned. If he survived, he would be hospitalized for weeks or months. Sandy had few friends. Bob had only his mother, who lived in the far Northeast Kingdom and wasn't well. No one could put them up. "I can't pay you, Mrs. Lucas. But I can help out, I can cook, stack wood, clean. Anything."

Sarah started to speak, but Sandy kept on with frantic energy.

"We've lost everything, Mrs. Lucas—our home and clothes and furniture. Tyler's toys and books. His baby pictures!" Sandy wailed.

Sarah said briskly, "Sandy, you come on over, right now. Do you have a car? Are you steady enough to drive?"

Sandy did, and she was. She was calling from the hospital's burn center, where she and Tyler had spent half the night and all morning. The fire had broken out around midnight. Bob had hustled his wife out through a window and raced through flames to Tyler's room, sustaining burns over half his body. He had inhaled a lot of smoke as well. Everything was gone, but Tyler and Sandy were safe, and Bob was hanging on. Sandy thought he blamed himself. He was an electrician; he should have found the problem before it could flare. "He'll never believe it wasn't his fault," she cried.

Sarah spoke soothingly, urging Sandy to come over. She hung up and rapidly began to calculate and revise. She'd told Lottie that her friend Jordan could have Charlotte's old room and a boy named Angelo could have David's. All three of her children's rooms were to house other children now—nearly grown ones. With Sandy's arrival, though, Lottie and Jordan would have to double up. Sarah felt like an innkeeper. The Inn of the Desperate and Disaffected. Well, no matter their condition, they would all have to use the same bathroom.

She gathered Lottie and her friends and explained the situation. "Whatever," Angelo said, heading back to the van for another load of goods. The girls scarcely blinked, though Lottie said, "That sucks." Sarah assumed she meant this in sympathy, not complaint, since Lottie and Jordan promptly went upstairs to transfer Jordan's belongings.

Sarah watched them go. Jordan Tilley was a tiny girl. Her mop of dark curls tangled with a purple streak over her left temple, where it was all held in place with a filigreed silver comb. She wore a silver ring in her right eyebrow and a slender leather collar with small metal spikes. Her low-cut, tattered jeans, heavily decorated with inked curlicues, were held up with a studded belt. An expanse of smooth, flat, childlike belly showed between the belt at her hip bones and a cutoff green T-shirt that stopped inches below her sternum. Jordan had Betty Boop eyes and a soft, little-girl voice. Sarah had never met her before and did not know her family. She had spoken with Jordan's mother in advance of the new living arrangement, startled by the woman's harsh dismissal of her own daughter. "She's a pain," the woman had warned. "She does what she wants. I work two jobs. I don't have a husband. I have two other kids and no control over Jordan. She's on her own."

Lottie had sworn that Jordan would be no trouble, but Sarah knew firsthand that parents had their own stories to tell. Jordan would move in on trial, as would Angelo.

Sarah at first misheard Angelo Fiori's last name as "Fury," and he appeared steeped in it. He was a handsome boy, tall and skinny, with a smoky voice and a broody, scrutinizing look in his light gray eyes. His dark hair hung in a fringe over those eyes. Angelo bore none of the tattoos, piercings, or strange hair colors of most of Lottie's friends. In that, he was like Lottie herself. But he was unkempt and taciturn, and he didn't meet Sarah's eyes. His parents, Joan and Ed Fiori, had been nothing like Jordan's mother. Where she was cold, they were heartbroken; where she judged, they were merely stymied.

Joan had told Sarah, "We've tried everything, but he wants nothing to do with us. The only thing we can all agree on is that he should live somewhere else for now." Her eyes filled as she added, "I feel like a cuckoo, laying my egg in some other bird's nest. It's so unnatural."

The Fioris insisted on paying Sarah for Angelo's room and board. Jordan's mother had made no such offer, nor did Sarah want her to. Three kids, two jobs, no partner—an impossible situation.

Sarah wondered whether she would end up feeling like a single mother, too. It was hard enough to take care of herself. Some days she woke up and couldn't remember the last time she'd taken a bath or shower. Clumps of dog hair scudded before her feet like tumbleweeds before she finally vacuumed or mopped. The laundry piled up until she had nothing clean to wear. She did start cooking again, when Lottie moved in, but now they usually made sandwiches or foraged for quick-fix meals. They ate together most of the time, but not always. Lottie was often out. Sarah had not once stopped to consider that three teenagers in the house would mean more cooking and cleaning. Someone else would have to do that, she decided.

Sighing heavily, she went in search of Lottie and the others, who were making an unholy racket. Laughter and loud music blared; someone dropped something heavy, and Angelo yelled, "Fuck! That *hurt!*"

Sarah approached with her fingers in her ears, and Lottie quickly turned the music down. "Just for today, Nana. For the move. Peace and quiet again, once the boxes and stuff are in." She grinned and moved to the tamped-down beat of the music. She jerked her head sideways, slid an arm out in the same direction, and slithered her body along behind. Then she moved the other way.

Sarah eyed their progress, which had produced mainly chaos so far. "Sandy and Tyler will be here any minute," she told them. "The noise might be more than they can take. I didn't tell Sandy she'd be entering a rave." She left them, shaking her head. She said a wordless prayer for Bob and right away heard Sandy pull in behind Angelo's van.

CHARLOTTE CAME INTO THE kitchen through the mud-room and stopped in dismay. "Mom, this place is a *mess,*" she said. "Look at it!" She swept an arm out to encompass the sight in front of her. The counter was cluttered with jars and boxes that no one had put away. They sat amid crumbs and the sticky residue of unidentifiable substances. Dishes sat next to the sink and inside it, waiting for their turn in the dishwasher, which ran nearly all the time and was running now. The floor was gritty.

Sarah looked around. "It is pretty bad, isn't it? I don't notice it like I used to." She pointed her chin toward the hall. "You should see the great room. Tyler's toys everywhere, the dining table covered with artwork and homework and mail. Lottie and her friends leave a trail of shoes and books and clothes and CDs wherever they go. I don't know how they can tell whose stuff is whose."

Setting a brown bag down on the counter, Charlotte looked around disapprovingly. "It was never like this even when we were all living at home. Isn't Lottie helping out?" She hoisted her purse strap higher on her shoulder. "What about the others?"

"They're all better than I am," Sarah told her. "I just don't seem to care much about housekeeping anymore." She returned to what she was doing, tying long, supple branches together with fine wire.

"What's this?" Charlotte asked, looking over Sarah's shoulder.

"Oh, nothing really. I'm trying to build frames for some photos I took. I've had three of them enlarged, but I don't want to put anything formal around them."

Sarah spread them out, and Charlotte looked at them — *Terra Firmament,* the snowflake photograph, and a new image of lines in a rock face that approximated a human profile with a beaky nose. Sarah thought that one looked a little like Charles, which was why she wanted to frame it. Charlotte didn't pick any photos

up, but she walked around to the other side of the table, trying
to figure out what she was seeing. Sarah explained them to her,
then pointed to another photo, not an enlargement. "Think I'll
do this one next. Can you tell what it is?"

Charlotte could not.

"Moose marbles," Sarah laughed. The close-up of the round,
brown turds, clumped together and glistening after rain, could
be a stone wall, the convoluted surface of a mudflat, a cluster
of smooth beads or nuts. Without knowing, it was impossible
to tell what actually formed the bumpy, abstract pattern that
pleased Sarah's eye so much.

"Lovely, Mom." Charlotte grimaced. "Since when do you take
pictures of anything but your garden and all of us?" she asked.

"Since I started feeling like it," Sarah said lightly. "I'm discov-
ering a lot of new pleasures."

Charlotte sat. "Such as?"

"Oh . . . reading late into the night. Walking. I go for walks in
the mornings with the dogs. I take the camera. I find things in
the woods, or I see a bird or plant I don't recognize, and then I
come home and go through your father's books. I like identifying
what I'm seeing. I like thinking that Charles is pleased by this."
She gestured toward the rough frame she was constructing. "I
never tried this before. Usually I just put the photos in a drawer.
But Mordechai suggested blowing some of these up, and I like
them. Don't know what I'll ever do with all that stuff, though."
She nodded toward the bay window behind Charlotte. The sills
were crammed with things Sarah had picked up on her walks.
A brittle nest lined with feathers. A smooth, gray, heart-shaped
rock, almost perfectly symmetrical. The clean, tea brown skull
of a weasel, or at least what Sarah thought was a weasel. Feath-

ers, a cluster of leaves eaten down to their skeletons. Tumbled glass from a streambed, a rusted hinge, and a scratched, square-shouldered glass bottle from the site of a long gone farmhouse now crumbling and overgrown by young woods. The bottle bore raised letters that said TINCTURE OF CANNABIS, confirming something Charles had told Sarah, that this had once been a common household remedy, perfectly legal. An earthenware cup from the same place wasn't even cracked, though its base and handle were embedded with dirt where the glaze had worn away.

Frustrated by Charlotte's polite silence, Sarah said, "I'm thinking of getting a cat." Actually she hadn't thought of it at all until that minute, but she suddenly realized she was no longer living with anyone allergic. At least she didn't think so. She'd ask her boarders.

"Oh, great," Charlotte muttered. "Then Luke and I will never be able to set foot in here."

"Of course you will," Sarah said calmly. "I hear there are pills you can take now, in advance of being exposed to things that trigger allergies."

Sighing, Charlotte said, "Where's Lottie? She didn't come over at all last week. I thought we had an agreement."

"Lottie's out. I'll have her call you when she gets back."

"Well, would you just tell her we're expecting her tomorrow night? For dinner and the night?"

"No, dear. That's between you and Lottie. But I'll have her call."

Charlotte rose. "All right, then. I brought some groceries, a few extra things I picked up at the store. Those teenagers must be eating like termites."

"Thanks," said Sarah. "I'll put them away in a bit." She got up and walked Charlotte through the mudroom and barn. It had started raining heavily, and Charlotte had parked outside. "Need an umbrella?"

"No. I'll just run for it." She dashed out, ducking and waving.

Sarah went back into the kitchen but then moved out onto the big porch, where she sat in a wicker chair and watched the rain and the mist in the distance. The gap between two ridges to the southeast was a bowl full of fog. Vapor rose like steam from soup. The rain softly blurred the distant hills, and everywhere the moisture brought out the scent of wet bark, grass, earth, and leaves. Sarah loved the silence outside and the rarer silence in the house. Everybody gone. Charles's sudden death had gouged out the center of her life, and now the emptiness was filling up in the strangest ways, with people and pursuits she never would have welcomed before.

Perhaps this was why, as she thought about Charlotte — her air of disapproval, their inability ever to speak a fresh word to each other — she simply quit worrying. She made a pact with herself — no more of this. Then she headed back into the house and reached the kitchen just as Sandy and Tyler came in through the mudroom.

Tyler headed for the hall bathroom, and Sarah asked, "How's Bob doing today?"

"Oh, God, Sarah, I wish I knew." Anxiety made Sandy altogether less shy and polite than she'd been during the blackout last January. "It's been almost a month and he's still not out of the woods."

They heard the toilet flush, and Tyler came down the hall, wiping his hands on the front of his jersey. "Where's Angelo?"

"He's at work, honey," Sarah told him. "He works on Wednesdays, but he should be back pretty soon."

Sarah was glad the teenagers had jobs. Their schedules were impossible to track, but rarely were all three at home simultaneously, and that kept the noise level tolerable. At their expense, Sarah had had a new phone line put in for their computers. They didn't need it for calls because Angelo and Jordan both had cell phones, and Lottie used Sarah's house line.

It was a mystery to Sarah why Tyler was so enchanted with Angelo, whom he followed like a hungry puppy. Angelo was friendly with Lottie and Jordan in a sardonic and slightly superior way, but he barely acknowledged Sarah or talked with Sandy. Sarah witnessed few of his interactions with Tyler, so it was hard for her to imagine him as anything but abrupt.

Sandy said Angelo made up stories, which Tyler tried to repeat for her in Angelo's wry narrative style. It was clear from his efforts that Angelo laced his tales with bathroom humor, deadpan silliness, and a swear-to-God earnestness about impossible things. Angelo apparently didn't talk down to Tyler or dismiss his worries about Bob. He simply distracted the boy instead of offering false assurances.

Sarah had no reason to doubt Sandy's reports, but she also couldn't see that Angelo was really interested in a sad, pesky five-year-old. She mistrusted his aloofness. It was too hard to tell what went on with him.

Now Sarah watched as Sandy and Tyler climbed the stairs together at the end of the hall. Tyler held Sandy's hand, just as David had once held hers.

She wished David would call with the news of Tess's pregnancy. She must be well past the first trimester by now—unless she had miscarried. Or aborted. Perhaps she didn't want another child. There was nothing like an unplanned pregnancy, if it was one, to test a new love.

A DAY OR TWO later Sarah grabbed the Nikon and hiked into the woods with the dogs. This time she took a walking stick and slathered herself with DEET, having decided she'd rather risk that than the bugs. She was still haunted by thoughts of cougars, knowing no stick could help her if she encountered one but feeling safer for having it nonetheless. Halfway along her usual trail she spotted a young beech whose roots grew around a rock outcropping, gripping it like a gnarled hand. Looking closer, she saw that the hand held something else besides rock — it was a length of bone, pale and petrified against the bark and stone. How on earth? It looked like the thigh of a deer or young moose. Sarah couldn't fathom how it had lodged on top of the rock or why it hadn't been knocked from that spot by the grasping young roots of the tree.

She was taking the lens cap from the Nikon when something large moved with a lot of rough noise behind her. Sylvie and Ruckus set up a ferocious, warning challenge, and Sarah spun around, raising both camera and walking stick. She shrieked to find herself almost face-to-face with the creature she later figured must be Stallone, the bull moose Charles used to track. The animal stood barely ten feet from her, its big rounded muzzle higher than her head, its rack of velvety antlers nearly as wide as the moose was tall. The only parts that moved were its wild eyes and the fleshy, swaying bell at its throat. The moose reeked of piss and animal sweat and seemed no less a threat than the cougar she'd thought it was. Whuffing and snorting, it appeared every bit as surprised as Sarah.

The dogs moved between Sarah and the moose, charging and retreating, making a racket all the while. When the moose didn't respond, they stopped and stood their ground with their ears skinned back and their hackles up, growling low in their throats. They were gathering themselves to attack, and Sarah panicked to think what the moose would do to them. She froze for an instant; so did the dogs, and so did the moose. She could not hear a sound in the woods. Then — thank God! — the huge animal bolted, crashing across the trail, breaking branches with its rack, and nearly tangling its ungainly legs. Within seconds, it had vanished, and soon after even the noise of its leaving had ceased.

Sarah leaned heavily on her stick, breathing hard and staring into the woods where the moose had fled. When she was steady, she stooped to fondle the dogs and praise their courage. She started for home at a fast walk but soon broke into a run, giddy with relief that the moose had not charged her and trampled her. Sylvie and Ruckus cavorted like puppies, catching her excitement. She was sorry she hadn't photographed Stallone.

Chapter 20

TYLER STOOD ON THE DECK outside the kitchen door and hollered. "Lotteeee! My hands are *full*! I got *sooo* much stuff!"

Lottie, who was scrubbing pans that the dishwasher would not accommodate, dried her hands on her jeans and went to let him in. "What'd you find, kiddo?"

His T-shirt was stretched to its limit over the day's harvest. He struggled to hold the bottom edge tightly over its lumpy contents and in the process exposed his small belly, which pooched out as he arched his back to counterbalance his load. Edging past Lottie, he released his bundle onto the table. A colorful plenty tumbled out — peas, lettuce, beans, young carrots, radishes, and leeks.

"Wow!" Lottie cried. "Great! That'll do us for at least a couple of days." She ruffled Tyler's hair. "Thanks, boysie."

The boarders had taken over the vegetable garden. Sandy had volunteered almost the minute she moved in, now more than a month ago. It had been too late to grow anything from seed, so she and Sarah had bought starts for an assortment of vegetables as broad and exotic as Charles had ever planted. Sandy had mapped where everything would go, and Lottie had helped with the planting. Now, in the third week of July, new crops were ripening all the time. Lottie and Sandy did most of the watering and weeding, but they dragged Jordan and Angelo into the enterprise whenever possible. Even Tyler helped, picking the vegetables for dinner every night—now that there *was* dinner every night.

The chaos indoors had calmed after the first few weeks, and the boarders now kept a certain order and a variable routine. Sarah had almost nothing to do with any of it. She thought Charlotte must have threatened Lottie—keep the place clean, help your grandmother, or move back home. She knew Charlotte had complained to David and Stephie, because, of course, David and Stephie had said so. Sarah had been peevish with all of them. She liked the way she was living, especially now that the household ran more smoothly, on steam from others. On her own, she might have remained in permanent disorder after her lifetime of neatness and routine. Instead her house was cared for, and so was she. Some days she felt like a queen.

Angelo had withheld the royal treatment for several weeks, but gradually even he had begun to soften. A month ago Sarah had asked him a question about his job at a music store in town. She further asked what kinds of music he liked and whether he played any instruments. She was making conversation, trying to put them both at ease. In return he gave her monosyllables. *What business is it of yours,* he might as well have said.

She'd rolled her eyes. "Angelo, for heaven's sake. I'm not your mother, I'm not your enemy. You just happen to live in my house. Relax a little, I won't tell."

"Sorry," he said sullenly. Then he permitted himself a slow smile. "Force of habit."

LOTTIE SORTED THROUGH Tyler's garden haul, stowing some of it and washing the rest. She fixed dinner for the household—leeks, carrots, and peas from the garden, braised in broth and wine, with grilled chicken and biscuits. Sandy had taught her some culinary techniques, which she was proudly mastering.

Usually those who were home ate the evening meal together at the kitchen table. Whoever felt like cooking did so, often two or three at once. Even Mordechai joined them a few nights a week. He would bring wine or cider, bread or cheese, sometimes a plate of stuffed grape leaves or a cold soup. He would show up, unannounced but not unexpected, after the sounds of kitchen activity had drifted down to the cabin from the open doors and windows of the house.

One Sunday, Sarah went looking for Mordechai to extend a formal dinner invitation, before the day got away from her and she forgot. Vivi and Peter were coming over a few nights later, bringing Jonathan, who was back from Siberia. Jonathan was to be a surprise for Mordechai, so Sarah needed to make sure he would be available.

On the way to the cabin she stepped into the vegetable garden through the hurricane fence that kept out the ever-hungry deer. She walked down a neat pathway between mounds of prolific bean and squash plants to the far end of the large plot, where she picked three early tomatoes. She had to tug them from their moist hairy vines. They were medium size, warm from the sun, and heavily fragrant. It was a good growing year.

Holding the tomatoes in her cupped hands, smelling summer in their taut skins, Sarah rounded the cabin to the steps that led up to the deck. She liked skirting the pond and saying hello to Charles. It wasn't until she reached the top step, calling out Mordechai's name, that she saw him on the deck through the surrounding screen, sitting straight up and cross-legged on his wide, low stool. It was another second or two before she realized he was naked.

The sun angled through the screen just right, spotlighting him. Calmly he reached for a short robe. "Good morning, Sarah," he said, as if he routinely greeted company in the nude. "You wanted something?"

Sarah stepped through the doorway and held the tomatoes mutely before her.

Mordechai took them and inhaled their scent as Sarah had done. "Mmm," he sighed. "Thank you. I will have one with lunch today."

She blurted, "Mordechai, I'm sorry, I should never have come down unannounced."

His bushy eyebrows went up, and he smiled. "Don't apologize, Sarah. Goodness," he said, looking down at himself in his light, striped robe, "this is just a beat-up old package. Nothing much."

Sarah sat. Mordechai gently touched her shoulder. "People are so funny about bodies, don't you think?"

"Yes, I suppose. But what were you . . . ?"

"I was meditating. As I do every morning. Always in the nude, because it is conducive. Always outside — or as close to outside as the bugs will let me go. I should have warned you that if you came down in the early morning you would find a naked man with stick legs and a fat belly exhibiting himself." He laughed again.

Sarah asked, "Is meditation a Jewish practice? I know so little, I'm sorry."

"It's just part of my practice." He shrugged. "Maybe I am a Zen Jew. I look for the place inside me where there is no noise, only light and peace."

"Do you find such a place?" Sarah asked, interested. "I could use a map."

"Yes, I find it. Not every time, but often. Anyone can."

"When did you start?"

"A few years after my wife died giving birth to our son. Baruch. He died, too."

Sarah remembered then. "Vivi told me you had lost your wife and child, but she didn't say when. Or how. It must have been terrible."

Mordechai shut his eyes briefly, then went on. "I entered the IDF — excuse me, the army, the Israeli Defense Forces — soon after. I served three years, as everyone does. Rachel and I would both have served sooner, but she was pregnant, and I was recovering from a motorcycle accident, many broken bones." His gaze went distant. "Later, after the army, I went to teach at the University of Tel Aviv. I tried going out with a few women. Smart, lovely, strong. I liked them very much, but soon I knew I would never love anyone but Rachel." He focused on Sarah's face again, pulling himself back to the present. "It seems I married for life, for both our lives. I'm still married, still faithful to my wife after thirty years. Which is why bodies are just bodies to me. Nothing more."

"Was it hard to go into the army so soon after your loss?"

Mordechai sat back down on his stool and stared out through the screen. The surface of the pond registered small currents of air, which roughened some patches and left everything else a mirror full of high clouds.

"Sarah," he said, "you can't imagine. I was crazy with grief. I felt completely powerless—and then I was given weapons and trained to kill an enemy. For a while I fought the Arabs as if *they* had killed Rachel and Baruch. When I finally saw how illogical that was, I could no longer fight. I began working for peace. I became a pacifist. Or perhaps I learned I had always been one."

This surprised her. "What do you mean?"

He didn't answer directly. "My mother—the only time I ever heard her speak of the Holocaust, she said that war was never about ideals, it was always about hatred and greed. Years later, when Rachel and I left for Israel, the protests against the war in Vietnam were just beginning. If we had stayed, we would have been for peace. Instead, less than a year later, we were wildly celebrating the Six-Day War." He paused. "Isn't that a strange thing? If my mother was right, and war is always about selfishness and hate, then how could I oppose one war and support another?"

"What happened when you finally did go to war?"

He said slowly, "It was—it is—endless war. It has solved nothing. And there is nothing like actually killing people to make you a pacifist. If you are meant to be one."

"Are there many pacifists in Israel? We never hear about them."

Mordechai sighed. "Some Israelis have always called for peace, even in the worst of times. They aren't all pacifists, but the urge for peace is strong. It's why Barak won the election."

"You should have hope then."

He looked gravely at Sarah. "I do. But there is one terrible thing. Sometimes Israel is safer when there is no progress toward peace at all."

"Why, for God's sake?"

"Because fanatics on both sides hate the idea of reconciliation." Mordechai rose from his stool and leaned against the frame of the screen, his back to the water. "After a peace accord was signed in Oslo, a Jew went and slaughtered worshipers in a Muslim mosque. The Arabs retaliated. Another Jew, a student, murdered Yitzhak Rabin, who had signed the accord for Israel." He looked sadly at Sarah. "Some people just won't give up their hatred."

This was more than Sarah could grasp — hopelessness inside the very heart of hope. She watched the surface of the pond and scanned the air above it. A sparrow lit on the tip of a reed, its weight barely bending the stalk. Sarah, studying its lightness, had a sudden thought.

"Mordechai, did you hold your baby? Your son, Baruch — did you see him?"

He brought his hands together and touched them to his chin, as if praying, or thinking. "Yes," he answered. "He lived only a short time. They called me in. I knew Rachel was dead, and I knew Baruch would follow her, but I saw into his eyes before he died. I was a father for five minutes."

"No," she said softly, picturing the scene. "You were a father for nine months before that. You're still a father. Nothing changes that." She paused, remembering the look in Charles's eyes when he'd spoken so ardently about David with Hannah. She added, "Just like you're still a husband, all these years later."

She told him about Andrew then — how she had held his small body and wondered what he was supposed to teach her. "I still wonder, though sometimes I almost understand."

Mordechai said nothing for a long moment. Finally he murmured, "Thank you for telling me."

Stephie had once told Sarah that the worst and best of human nature lived in separate parts of the brain, the worst in the oldest part and the best in the most recently evolved. Mordechai, it seemed, had erased the boundary between them. Sarah, though, was still sometimes ruled by stark pain, lost to everything else. Grief slipped away, only to attack from behind. It changed shape endlessly. It lacerated her, numbed her, stalked her, startled her, caught her by the throat. It deceived her eye with glimpses of Charles, her ear with the sound of his voice. She would turn and turn, expecting him, and find him gone. Again. Each time Sarah escaped her sorrow, forgetful amid other things, she lost him anew the instant she remembered he was gone.

Chapter 21

SARAH SLEPT LATE ONE morning and woke at eight to hushed sounds that meant others were trying with some difficulty to be quiet. She smiled lazily and got up, and on her way to the kitchen she overheard Angelo's voice through the screen door that led to the front porch. Tyler's piping laugh chimed in as she turned in to the foyer and drew closer.

"So," Angelo was saying, "you know that feeling, right? When you have this insane itch that you can't reach?"

"Or you can't scratch it cause . . . cause . . ." Tyler was trying to talk past the giggles. He took an audible breath. "Once I was in Sunday school and my butt itched."

"Uh-oh," replied Angelo. Sarah stayed out of sight, but she could picture a glint in Angelo's eye. "Whadja do? You couldn't scratch your butt in Sunday school."

"I wiggled!" Tyler said, howling with glee. "And the teacher kept telling me to sit still!"

Angelo snorted. "Teachers. *Jeez.* But hey, I know a story about a dragon that had this *really* terrible itch. Wanna hear it?"

Tyler did, and Angelo proceeded. He launched into a tale about a friendly dragon who lived in the woods and guarded a cave full of treasure. "Not boring stuff like jewels, you know. People's dreams. Babies' first words. Memories. Things like that."

The dragon lived among forest animals who loved him but couldn't help when he got a searing itch right between his wings. Their claws and teeth couldn't penetrate the dragon's scales to reach it. He tried scratching the itch himself, against trees and rocks, but the trees just snapped under his weight and the rocks crumbled.

"What did he *do*?" Tyler asked.

"Well," said Angelo, warming to his tale. "He had to go see this horrible witchy person on the other side of the forest. Nobody even knew if it was a he or a she, but we'll call it a she just because that's kind of traditional for witches."

Sarah crept closer to the doorjamb and leaned against it.

"So the dragon found this witch and begged her for a magic potion. She smelled bad and looked worse. But she finally said she would cure the dragon's itch for a price."

Tyler took a sharp breath. "His treasure, right?"

"Right," said Angelo. "Stupid witch had *no* imagination. She'd never want the dragon's stuff, but he couldn't convince her of that."

"So did she get his treasure?"

"Nah. The dragon was too smart for her. He pretended to go along, but while she was in her cottage mixing up the potion, he thought of a plan. He kept working on it as they flew back to his cave. The witch rode between his wings, smack on top of his itch, which was suddenly ten times worse. He began to think she had caused his itch in the first place."

Sarah couldn't see Tyler, but she could imagine just how he looked, his small, squarish knees drawn up, his eyes on Angelo's face.

"When the dragon landed beside his cave, the witch scrambled down from his back and started to run toward it. But the dragon yelled, '*Wait, Witch!* How do I know your potion will work?'

"The witch was furious, but she scuttled back and motioned for the dragon to kneel down. Then she put the tiniest possible drop of potion on his itch. It worked just long enough to convince him before the itch came back worse than ever.

"The witch spun around and headed for the cave again.

"'*Wait!*' the dragon yelled. 'One more thing!'

"The witch glared, but the dragon let a tiny tongue of flame come out of his mouth. The witch noticed this. The dragon pointed out that she had never signed an agreement with him. He said he needed her signature on a piece of paper. Not even that—just her initial. *W,* for *Witch.* He'd fill in the details later.

"The witch was crazy with greed, so she conjured up a scrap of paper and a quill pen and scribbled a messy *W* and threw it at the dragon.

"The dragon acted fast! He snatched the paper, grabbed the potion, yanked the stopper from the bottle, and dashed a dollop into the witch's ugly face.

"And guess what?" Angelo said in a throaty, conspiratorial voice.

"What?" Tyler whispered.

"The witch disappeared, right in front of the dragon's eyes. She just went *poof*!"

Tyler let out the breath he had been holding. "Why? How?"

"Well," said Angelo. "What do you get when you take *W* away from *Witch*?"

Tyler barely paused to think. "*Itch!*" he hollered, triumphant. "He turned her into an itch!"

"And then he gave her the old heave-ho," Angelo confirmed.

"The old heave-ho!"

Sarah stifled a delighted gasp.

Awestruck, Tyler said, "Did you make that story up?"

"Nah." Angelo cleared his throat. "My mom did. She used to make up stories a lot. But that one the other day? About the war between the donkeys and the monkeys over how to say their names? That one I did make up."

"Oh, yeah! Dawnkeys and mawnkeys or dunkeys and munkeys. That was *funny*."

Once again Sarah had the sensation of standing still while time flowed around her.

A FEW NIGHTS LATER, still thinking of stories, still remembering down in her bones and belly how Charles had found out her own most private tales, Sarah glimpsed herself naked in the big bathroom mirror. Look what she had come to. Her impulse was to turn away and duck hastily into her nightdress. What was there to see in an old woman? Then she paused. What indeed? Slowly she put the nightdress on top of the hamper and began to look at herself from every angle. "God," she groaned. She was melting, coolly and in slow motion, everything heading toward the floor. Even the skin of her knees sagged. Her breasts were scored with wrinkles. Her belly was slack, her throat webbed, her long arms mainly bone and loose skin, their once firm flesh eaten by time.

When exactly had she become old? Sixty? Seventy? Even in her fifties, maybe later, she had seen her younger self underneath the years. She had remembered her face and body when they could make Charles moan and he in turn could make her cry out, his passion electric on her skin. This was so powerfully true in their early years together that she would jump if he kissed her while her hands were in dishwater, as if the current of his love could deliver a sizzling jolt.

Sarah took in the evidence of age not knowing whether to laugh or cry. How many girls and women she had been — she carried a multitude inside who shared only memory and character traits.

I am *a memory,* she suddenly thought. *And half the time I can't tell what's real from what I've made up.* She slid her nightdress on and felt as if some other Sarah's head emerged through the satin edging the neckline. As she buttoned the yoke, pushed up the loose sleeves, and brushed her teeth and hair, she had the odd feeling that some brand-new piece of her singular, shifting, multitudinous self had bumped lightly into place, moving the others, making more sense of the whole — the irreducible, authentic Sarah, who weathered perpetual change and yet persisted. More would happen to her. She wasn't finished yet.

Chapter 22

DAVID, TESS, AND HANNAH arrived unannounced just as Jonathan's homecoming dinner was winding down and the arguments were heating up. Peter was goading Mordechai — "Isn't a pacifist in Israel a bit like a hen in a foxhouse?" — when David walked in with Hannah sleeping on his shoulder and Tess beside him.

"We heard Jonathan was in town," David said, amid a clamor of greetings. He and Tess met Mordechai for the first time, Tess met Jonathan, Hannah woke into full, excited alertness and asked for Sylvie, who at that moment came racing into the great room with Ruckus skittering behind her. Lottie took Hannah from David, and Sarah offered food, drinks, or coffee.

"For heaven's sake," she said abruptly, "where will you sleep? The house is full!" Surely she had told him about all the boarders. Except for Lottie, they had discreetly or coincidentally gone out to jobs or movies or friends' houses.

"Thought of that, Mom. Thought we'd camp in Dad's office, if that's okay."

Sarah drew up short for a second. "Oh. That never . . . Yes, of course that will work."

They drifted to the other end of the great room, leaving the dining table still cluttered with dessert plates and wadded napkins. Charlotte and Tom, the quietest pair in the gathering, sat on the loveseat together. Lottie took Hannah onto her lap in the rocker, while Sylvie and Ruckus fell into sighing heaps at their feet. The others settled themselves with coffee or drinks.

"I heard Peter yelling as we came in," David grinned. "Which hobbyhorse was he whipping this time?"

"Oh, let's not start that again!" cried Vivi, mock horrified. No one but Sarah paid any attention in the renewed uproar. She knew Vivi was glad for Mordechai, whose presence eased Peter's loneliness for Charles.

Peter cracked up, pointing at Mordechai. "My esteemed cousin over there, the one whose last name means 'nut case' — oh, excuse me, 'nut *tree*' — believes Israel's new prime minister will do everything he promises. Unite the Jews among themselves, then make them brothers with the Israeli Arabs. And fit everybody into a place smaller than Vermont, which has only a half million people to Israel's six million and counting."

Mordechai applauded, sardonic. "Very clever, Peter, you manage to exaggerate and oversimplify at the very same time."

Jonathan, usually so easygoing, said scornfully, "Peace, ha! Never happen. No way."

Mordechai blew out an exasperated sigh. "Jonathan. You are young. If the young cannot believe in peace then the world is lost."

"It's probably lost anyway," Tess said abruptly. "People will always find reasons to kill each other. It's human nature; it's in our blood."

Charlotte shuddered, and Tom put a hand on her knee. They all looked at Tess as if they had forgotten who she was.

David half smiled at her. "Excuse me, aren't you that Quaker pacifist I live with?"

She bristled. "It's not funny, David. And it's not simple. A lot of Quakers have fought in a lot of wars. They have to weigh the ideal against the risks, and sometimes the risks are just too heavy."

Mordechai nodded, interested. "But that is the key, you see. Weighing the risks. The ones that are right in front of you will always feel heavier than the ones your own defenses might lead to—which is precisely how sticks and stones have become nuclear armaments."

Gathering herself, Tess said, "Mordechai, I am a pacifist, like you. But I can't forget that ninety-five percent of Jews who should be alive today have been killed or have never been born at all. There should be two hundred million Jews in the world." Her voice dropped; she looked down at her hands. "But there are only twelve million," she murmured. "*Twelve.*"

Tucking her arms into the sleeves of her loose sweater, as if she were freezing on this warm night, she looked straight at Mordechai. "Hatred in the Middle East started thousands of years ago. It's not about principles, it's not about ideals, it doesn't mean anything. It blows *families* apart. And when it's your family . . ."

The story of Ian's murder came out then. David told it, to let Tess collect herself.

Mordechai told his own story in return, succinctly but

without discounting the hatred he had once harbored. "I know how you feel," he said. "It is very hard."

"It's very hard for me to imagine *you* filled with hate. At least from the little I have seen of you tonight."

Mordechai laughed. "Ah! Thirty years ago, I fought ferociously. I hated and killed Arabs because they hated and wanted to kill me. They wanted to destroy the little I had left, the small things I still loved." He paused, then threw his hands up in disgust. "Pah! To hate in the name of love, to kill in the name of safety. There will be no peace anywhere until we unlearn such stupidity. No safety. Not for Jews, not for Palestinians, not for anyone."

"Oh," sighed Tess. "That much I do know. There is no safety. So how can you believe in peace?"

"By choosing to," he said. "By needing to. We all have to choose, minute by minute." He paused and looked them in the eyes, each in turn. "Hatred is a reflex. Peace is a choice. It's intentional. It takes constant thought and work."

"What choice did Ian have?" Tess insisted. "Attacked out of nowhere, unarmed."

Mordechai nodded. "If he'd had a gun, he would have been justified in using it. Innocence and guilt were perfectly clear. But then Ian would have carried the burden of another's death. Believe me, that is an immensely heavy burden. It changes a person forever. It harms him, turns him to ice or burns him alive, slowly, from inside."

Sarah wondered, *Which is Mordechai today, fire or ice? Ice,* she thought. *Warm ice, a conundrum.*

The air went out of Tess. She closed her eyes for a second or two, then regarded Mordechai thoughtfully. "Quakers believe the light of God burns in every person, no matter how hateful."

Mordechai said, "Yes. Go on."

"I have asked myself, if Ian had killed his murderer's light, would that have killed his own, too?"

"No," Mordechai answered. "As you say, he would not have chosen to kill but would have had it thrust upon him. To save his own life, to keep his family from suffering."

"That's what I want to believe. Ian was a good man." Tess looked down, pressing her lips together to stop their trembling.

David took her hand. She cleared her throat and went on. "I don't hate anymore. I managed to stop for Hannah's sake. But I am angry, and I can't forgive," she said. "I've tried, Mordechai, but it's not in me. Even now, with David . . ." She broke off and looked at him. Then she looked around the room and rested her gaze on Sarah. "God help us," she breathed. "We're going to bring another child into this world."

As SARAH LAY IN bed that night, Charles felt as near as her skin. It was maddening that she could not touch him. He would have known what to say to her; he would have cooled and calmed her. What pain she had seen in all those faces! They would grieve their losses forever, just as Sarah would. And poor Tess, announcing her pregnancy. No one had known whether to rejoice or to console her—no one but Mordechai, who had stood up and raised a glass and beamed at Tess and David.

"This," he had said, "is why I believe in peace."

Sarah could not believe. Her faith in human nature was thinner than the skin of her own eyelids. She thought suddenly of Angelo—Angelo with his stories for Tyler—the war that his gentler self must have to wage behind his mask of cool scorn. The mask had slipped, thank God, but his stories, though designed to instruct and delight, were all *about* wars. Donkey and monkey wars; dragon and witch wars. Evil is vanquished, good prevails, but it takes a battle to make that happen. Angelo's stories drew on habits of mind as old as the first humans.

Everything lives on the death of something else.

Sarah lay awake as images came and went before her—Tess's hand in David's; Mordechai, so gentle with Tess; Lottie, silent and intent; Tom and Charlotte, taking it all in. And then there was Charles in his hospital bed, laughing or choking, grinning or grimacing, she would never know. Her own infinitesimal life turned off center, within wheels of unimaginable size.

Eccentric, she thought idly. Ever since Charles died. All I want is to tramp the woods and take pictures, tend my garden, let my mind roam. I don't care anymore whether the sheets are smoothly folded or stuffed crumpled into the linen closet, whether dog hair piles up in the corners of the hall, whether the kids leave their books and socks strewn about, whether the stove is wiped down every time someone uses it. Those things mattered to Charles. I thought they mattered to me. She breathed in and caught the scent of the woods through the open window near her bed. I would like to be a leaf, turning toward sunlight without the least intention, so easily.

Sarah slipped into sleep, her thoughts becoming dreams. Charles appeared beside her bed and put his hand on Sarah's forehead. "Hot," he said. He touched her again and chuckled. "Cold!" She startled awake. She sat up, her hands to her mouth. "Come back," she whispered, then wondered whether he would still know her.

SARAH WENT DOWNSTAIRS early the next morning, but David was already there, awake before even Hannah or Tyler had stirred. He had fresh coffee waiting. He sat at the kitchen table, his back to her, staring out the window. Sarah watched him yawn, roll his shoulders, and tilt his head from side to side, stretching his neck. His coarse hair was snarled and tufted, uncombed. Sarah remembered him, just so, as a small boy. Bedraggled. That was their joke. She spoke to him, and he started, as she had started at Charles's touch in the night.

"Morning, Mom," he said, and yawned again.

"Morning." She poured herself some coffee and sat next to him. A bunch of her photographs lay spread out before him.

"Where did these come from?" he asked, sweeping over them with his outstretched hand.

"I took them. I carry your father's camera with me when I'm out walking."

"And those?" He pointed to several that were framed with twisted branches or weathered, peeling wood from old windows. Lottie and her friends had hung them in the breakfast area. Others hung in Sarah's office, where David must have found the unframed ones on her desk.

"Mine."

"I thought all you took were pretty garden scenes. But these. Not exactly pretty. More beautiful, and strange. Really, Mom. Some of them I can't figure out what I'm seeing." He sorted through the pile. "What's this one?"

He held up a photograph that had unnerved Sarah in the taking. She had felt the back of her neck prickle, as if the air still vibrated with the suddenness of killing. That was impossible, because the bones she had found were old, stripped almost clean and weathered to a light, mottled brown. But something in the way they were scattered telegraphed a ripping of limbs. She had thought lynx, preying on snowshoe hare—the small, catlike skull and long hind legs of the broken skeleton. She had imagined the pounce, the squeal, the white fur soaked in red.

She helped David make out the image—edges of bone, unidentifiable, overlaying a melange of leaves and earth, making clean, sharp lines against the chaotic ground. Strangely, Sarah found the lines disturbing, the disarrangement behind them peaceful. She tried to explain this to David.

"Mmm," he said, still sorting through Sarah's prints. "The ones you can't quite make out are the most unsettling. You know they're actual images, but images of *what*? It's kind of a tease, but serious. Menacing, even."

Sarah shooed his comments away with a fluttering hand, though she noted with pleasure how different his reponse was from Charlotte's. "David, they're not *art,* you know. They're just, I don't know. Necessary. To me, for some reason."

"Since Dad died."

"Yes."

"What's this one, then?" He held up a swirled, pink and brown image flecked with tiny light spots, like grains of sand. Or stars. Diffuse light glanced off whorled edges, suggesting a nebula.

Sarah burst out laughing. "You'll never guess!"

"So tell me," David prompted.

"It's bear shit! Raspberry bear shit!" She pointed. "See the seeds?" She showed him the photo of the moose marbles, too, and another of fisher scat stuck through with bloody porcupine quills. Only a fisher would eat a porcupine.

David snorted. "Bones and shit and dead things. You sure you're all right?"

"Absolutely. I don't know why I'm so drawn to this stuff. I just know I'm not afraid to go into the woods anymore. With the dogs, of course. I never would have dared while your father was alive." She told him about meeting Stallone. She told him there might be a catamount in their woods, but he seemed not to hear.

He sobered. "That wasn't the most joyful announcement last night, about the baby. Tess felt bad about blurting the news that way." He regarded Sarah anxiously.

She put her hand on his. "David, is Tess all right? Are you?"

"She's all right now," he said. "But it was tough. This pregnancy was a surprise, whereas Hannah was planned. Tess and Ian were both so happy." He drank some coffee, lowering his eyes, but Sarah had seen the shadow in them.

"And now you and Tess . . . are you happy?"

"Yes," David said. "Now we are. But Tess wanted an abortion at first. She was terrified, of what I'm not sure. More love, maybe. She panicked."

"She's afraid of loss."

David nodded. "That was part of it. She also didn't know whether I could live with Ian's death. His ghost, rather."

"Can you?"

He nodded again. "Yes. Surprises the hell out of me, I'd never have thought it. But something shifted, just like that, soon as I knew Tess was pregnant, soon as I saw how high the stakes were.

I just suddenly started thinking of Ian as if he'd been my friend. A close friend. It was easy because we *would* have been friends, if we'd ever met."

"What changed Tess's mind about the baby?"

David looked directly at Sarah. "They caught Ian's murderers." Quickly he added, "We were going to tell you last night, but things took that whole other tack."

Sarah closed her eyes. "No wonder Tess had Ian on her mind."

"There were two guys. They almost killed another driver — a woman — in another carjacking. But she survived, she identified them."

"And Tess feels safer now?"

"Something like that, I guess. It's still a bit of a tangle, but Tess is tugging away at it."

"She's a good person, David. You both are."

David's eyes lit up. "Hey, Mom, I'm gonna be a daddy."

She beamed at him. "David, you're already a daddy. You're Hannah's daddy now."

"Well, then," he said. "December. Maybe we'll have a Christmas baby."

His look of amazement reminded her of the sudden surprise she herself had felt back in April, beside the pond. "David, . . ." Sarah began.

He glanced over at her. "What?"

"David, I've known for months that Tess was pregnant. I was wondering why you hadn't said anything."

"Mom, we never told a soul."

Sarah lifted her hand lightly off the table and let it fall again, a small wry gesture. She described the moment near the pond, when Hannah buried her face against Tess's belly. "I just knew. I mean, I really *knew,* David. I could almost see that baby inside her. That tadpole, I should say."

David grinned. "Aha! Ponds! Tadpoles! The connection is made!" That set Sarah off, chasing the last of her midnight fears.

Chapter 23

LOTTIE AND HER FRIENDS were up to something. They fell suddenly silent around the kitchen table when Sarah entered. Lottie ran to her room with Sarah's cordless phone when calls came in for her. Lottie and Tony brought bulky packages in through the front door and hustled them upstairs. Sarah pretended not to notice, but she was curious.

Two days before Sarah's birthday, she overheard urgent whispers and muffled laughter coming from Lottie and Jordan's room near the front of the house. The sounds drifted downstairs only faintly. Sarah couldn't hear, even standing stock-still in the hallway, straining her ears. Whatever was going on involved all of them—Tony, Angelo, and both girls. She heard a loud baritone guffaw at one point and a rumbling chuckle, then more stifled talk and giggling.

Then she heard the girls' bedroom door slam and four sets of feet come tramping toward the stairs. She darted back to the kitchen and sat down with her coffee and a book, facing the garden. She spun around when they all entered, trying to sing "Happy Birthday" while cracking up. Tony, Angelo, and Jordan each carried a cupcake with a lighted candle. Angelo's candle went out and trailed a long scribble of waxy smelling smoke. Lottie carried a big box, open at the top. She plunked it unceremoniously down on the table, in front of Sarah, and said, "Meet your new boarders, Nana!"

Sarah peered down and saw two pale orange kittens, fat fluff-balls with amber eyes registering alarm. They huddled together in one corner of the box and stared up at Sarah. One of them opened its pink mouth and mewed at her, demanding and in-dignant. Sarah laughed out loud and scooped them both into her hands and held them close to her chest. "Oh!" she cried, bending her cheek to their soft bodies, "I've been wanting cats! You knew!"

The teenagers looked pleased with themselves. Angelo said, "We named them. If you approve. Neo and Retro."

Sarah blinked. "Neo and Retro," she repeated, looking from one kitten to the other in some bewilderment. "Perfect. Who's who?"

"Neo's the one with the white paws," Lottie answered. "He's very adventuresome. Retro is quieter. Neo beats up on him." Neo demonstrated his boldness on cue, climbing Sarah's T-shirt to sit on her shoulder. He mewed again, loudly, right at her ear.

"We have all the supplies upstairs in Angelo's room. Litter and box and food and dishes and toys. We had these guys up there for three days, Nana! We couldn't wait any longer—we were *so* sure you'd hear them."

"I never did," Sarah said, setting the kittens down on the

table. She hugged the teenagers all in turn. They hugged her back, even Angelo.

Tyler and Sandy came in from the vegetable garden then. Tyler spotted the kittens immediately. "Neo! Retro!" he cried, running toward them. They arched their backs and stood stiff-legged as he approached. Neo hissed at him. "Oh, silly!" Tyler chided, picking him up and cuddling him.

"I see," Sarah said, mock stern. "Everybody was in on this." She picked Retro up with her hands around his rib cage and held him before her at eye level. He batted softly at her nose.

Sarah turned to Lottie. "I am officially in love," she announced. Then she added, "They'll have to be indoor cats, given all the fishers in this neighborhood. But that's okay. We'll just be careful, all of us." Turning to Lottie, she said, "Your mother and brother are going to have a fit."

Lottie smiled wickedly. "I know. Isn't it awful?"

"Well, they can take allergy pills before they come over. If they ever come again."

Sylvie scratched at the mudroom door, and Ruckus whimpered behind her. "What about the dogs?" Sarah exclaimed. "They haven't been around kittens for years!"

"All taken care of. Or mostly," Jordan answered. "We snuck the dogs upstairs four or five times and just sort of threw them together with the kitties. When you were out."

Sarah sank into her chair with Retro on her lap. Tyler dropped Neo down next to him. Both kittens purred loudly. Neo wrapped his front legs around Retro's neck and vigorously washed his face.

"I like to feed them," Tyler said, putting his finger in the way of the sandpaper tongue. "Can I be the person who feeds them?"

Tyler had flourished here, with the gardens, the dogs, and the people—especially Angelo, his surrogate big brother, and Mordechai, who told him stories of a different sort than Angelo's, stories about Israel and kibbutzim and history. Tyler was no longer shy. He was outspoken and eager to help. He was more independent. He was happy to stay with the others when Sandy visited Bob.

Bob's condition was still unstable, and the daily treatments for his burns caused him terrible agony. His medications didn't touch the worst of his pain. Twice he had begged Sandy to help him die, but that was weeks ago. Now he just endured, speaking to her little. She thought he was willing himself to die, pulling away from everything he loved. He wasn't angry, just weary.

Sandy managed to protect Tyler from the worst of her fears. Often she was weary herself, but she revived in the vegetable garden, which was immaculate. Not a weed escaped her sharp eye and plucking fingers. The tomato vines never trailed on the ground, nor were their dropped fruits allowed to lie rotting. Sandy carefully husbanded every growing thing inside the tall fence, harvesting squashes, beans, and tomatoes, shining eggplants, artichokes, and even peppers of many colors and shapes, for which she had fashioned portable greenhouses from wooden dowels and clear plastic.

Sarah felt she could live on vegetables. She and the others feasted on them nightly, adding little or no meat, just rice or couscous, bread or pasta. They grilled them, steamed them, roasted them, ate them raw. They made cold soups and endless salads. They dipped raw vegetables in hummus or baba ghanoush or guacamole. And still they could not eat them all. Sandy was canning, pickling, and freezing the garden's excesses. She made dilly beans, tomato sauce, corn chowder, vegetarian chili.

The summer was flying. August was well under way, the gardens were browning at the edges, and roadside vegetation wore an ever-heavier coat of dust. In only days or weeks, the nights would start bringing a deeper chill. Sarah wanted to lasso time and tie it down. She wanted to hold onto this summer, to hoard the long days, the voices of her boarders, her growing friendship with Mordechai. They were all her teachers. They all gave energy; they brought her out of herself.

Sarah had told Mordechai about recent reveries in the window seat, hours she'd spent gazing into the night, surprised by calm. He had informed her that she was meditating. "It is not mysterious, Sarah. Someone had to start this practice, eons ago. Some ordinary person had to notice that certain states of mind bring peace and a finer awareness of the world. The trick is to do it on purpose, and then to guide the mind without pushing or tugging on it."

Sarah wanted to be able to induce the state that sometimes overtook her without notice. She needed its healing effects. So Mordechai had been helping her with that a few mornings a week when she joined him for meditation on the cabin's deck. He was teaching her to focus her attention without directing her thoughts or trying to stop them.

Sarah too often came up against a tumult inside her, a rush of noise and images that led not to clarity but to chaos and fret. She would rise out of herself, short of breath and frustrated.

"I'm getting nowhere," she complained one morning. "Why

is it I can bypass all this . . . this *traffic* in my head . . . when I'm not even trying to, but the minute I sit down on this deck, it turns into gridlock?"

Mordechai raised his eyebrows. They'd had this conversation before.

"I know, I know," Sarah groaned. "I need to quit trying. But, Mordechai, I'm trying not to try! I'm trying to trick my mind into thinking I'm just letting it go its own way. But all the while I know perfectly well what I want, and that's to elbow my way through all this noise to that quiet place."

Mordechai was amused. "You still believe you can solve the mystery of your mind with your mind, Sarah. You wish to comprehend instead of apprehend."

Sarah glared at him. "You told me you actually find peace and light through this process. You sit down here every morning and you mean for that to happen, do you not?"

"I do not. I invite the peace, that's all. Which sometimes comes and sometimes does not."

"Oh." She tilted her head and gazed at him, letting his words sink in. "Oh." Then she closed her eyes and let her shoulders drop.

Now she could empty her mind for whole moments at a time. She never caught herself doing this; she noticed it only after the fact, after she had returned from her excursions into places both in and beyond her being. She was beginning to see paradox all around her.

MORDECHAI HAD BOUGHT A car almost as soon as Lottie passed her driving test back in June. This freed the Subaru for her alone, though state law allowed her no passengers until

December. It frustrated her that Tony drove whenever they went out together. "Guys *always* drive. My dad drives when my parents go out. Papa always drove, too. Angelo drives with his girlfriend. I keep telling Tony, when my six months are up, I'm driving *all* the time! Unless he gets his own car. Then he can drive."

The Subaru was Lottie's reward for her energetic help. She and Sandy ran the house now. Lottie, with help from Angelo and Jordan, managed the general housecleaning, and Sandy took care of the kitchen and the grocery shopping. Jordan liked the lawn tractor. She mowed everything outside the backyard fence except the long meadow, which a nearby farmer hayed twice each year. Angelo hauled trash to the recycling station, stacked wood, and weeded Sarah's perennial garden, assuring her that he used to help with his mother's. Tony helped randomly but often, with whatever chores needed doing.

Sarah now headed for the toolroom in the barn to look for her triangular hoe, ready to attack a patch of weeds that Angelo had not yet discovered. Tony and Lottie pulled into the front part of the barn from the village road just as she was about to leave, and, hidden from view, she saw Tony lean from behind the wheel to kiss Lottie, cupping the back of her head and pulling her close.

Sarah remembered Charles's kiss in the woods, the way he had stirred her banked passions with surprise. As she carried her hoe outside, among the tall phlox, she remembered other kisses and everything they had led to, her body tangled with Charles's time and again. She conjured the soft friction of the hair on his young legs, then saw that dense cover disappear slowly over the years, worn away by the rub of trousers and socks and by vigorous toweling after showers. Charles's body had sagged, like her own, though he was so lean. No gut had ever lapped over his belt nor had love handles ballooned above it; but his backside all but vanished, his scrotum drooped, and the skin went loose over his muscles and bones. Charles, young, had been wiry and strong, with the long lovely body of a swimmer. He had been tireless in his desire to please Sarah with that body. She had loved the way her belly contracted under his touch and the swollen feeling of her mouth and cunt. The word startled her, forming uninvited in her mind. She had never said it out loud in her life. "*Cunt!*" she whispered, grinning. She could recall the rush of blood that swelled her flesh and the way Charles pulsed with each burst of his ejaculation. "Oh!" she cried softly, straightening over her work.

"Nana? You okay?" Lottie and Tony came out of the barn, their hair disheveled, their own lips swollen from kissing.

Sarah smiled at them. "Yes, dear." *You've no idea.* She watched them mount the stairs onto the deck and go inside. How it all goes on, she thought. She had known six generations of relatives and friends, and here she was in the middle of them, her time drawing short. She could remember one great-grandmother, dimly, from her earliest years. She had known all four of her grandparents. It was possible she would know one more generation before she died, if William or Paul became a father by then, or Lottie a mother. Seven generations, three on each side of her own. Her own was now called the Greatest Generation, which exasperated her.

Yes, by their teens, Sarah and her peers had seen worldwide economic depression. By their twenties, world war, rationing, carnage, and loss. But Sarah questioned this popular notion of unique greatness. Her doubts took her back repeatedly to the destruction of Hiroshima and Nagasaki and to the dreadful, postwar revelations of the Holocaust. Everyone had reeled before the images of calculated mass slaughter. Everyone had wept over the sticklike bodies piled up, the hollow-eyed heads lolling upside down against the starved bellies or sunken chests of strangers.

Lottie and her friends had never known real trials. They'd been born well after the struggle in Vietnam, the race riots at home, the worst of gender inequity. In their childhood the Berlin Wall tumbled, the Soviet Union broke apart, and the economy prospered. Starvation, war, genocide, and massacres had taken place elsewhere, in the Middle East, the Balkans, Somalia, Rwanda, China. Americans had rarely fought on their own soil, but this generation seemed more removed than ever. Was it just that so much time had passed since real dangers had arisen at home? None of the young people Sarah knew seemed to expect to fight, ever. Sarah hoped they would indeed, miraculously, avoid war, but she had little reason to expect it.

Hearing Tony and Lottie laugh inside the kitchen, scuffling near the open windows, Sarah wondered, *Will it all go on?*

That, she suddenly knew, was why hers was not the greatest generation. They had courageously stopped unprecedented slaughter, at dreadful cost to themselves. They had cleaned up after the horror. But they had not prevented it. If any generation could make the leap away from the primitive human past, if it could neutralize hatred, if it could make peace a way of life and not just a passing dream between wars — *that* generation would be the greatest.

Vivi and Molly picked Sarah up at six on her birthday. They were heading to Adelaide and Leila's for dinner, eager to celebrate. Sarah had not had a birthday without Charles since her twenty-fourth.

Leila welcomed them into the big kitchen of the house where Addie had grown up and offered them drinks. Adelaide was at the counter, wielding a chopping knife so fast it was a silver blur above falling slices of cremini mushrooms. She was an adventuresome cook who kept learning new cuisines and then crossing or mingling them freely—committing culinary miscegenation, she called it.

Now she was making a reduction of red wine, pomegranate jelly, shallots, and butter to adorn filets mignons. The mushroom slices, nearly paper thin, were the final ingredient, to be added at the last minute. "Everything's all but ready," she said, turning away from her work to hug Sarah and the others. "Let's go sit." She led the way to the screened porch that looked out over an expansive lawn and a pond bordered with gardens. The blackflies were long since gone, many of them eaten by dragonflies. Deerflies and mosquitoes were still a nuisance, and it was a pleasure to be screened away from them, watching the bees nuzzle the monarda while the phlox swayed in a light breeze.

The five women reminisced. Addie and Leila once again told the story of their move from New York City to Vermont after Adelaide's mother had died and deeded the house to them, in both their names. That was eighteen years ago, but their amazement had never faded. "We've never been able to figure out if she knew we were lesbians or just thought we were friends for life," Leila said. "And she first made that will in the midsixties, when nobody was thinking about gay rights except gay people, and even gay people didn't think they'd ever get any."

"She knew perfectly well what she was doing," Sarah chimed

in. "Your sharp-eyed mother. And she'd love it that you've spent all these years guessing about her."

"Well," Addie countered, "why did *you* think I lived all those years in New York, when I missed Vermont and my mother so much?"

Sarah gave them a wry smile. "What was I going to do in those days — confront you, once I figured things out? I assumed you stayed because you were happy in the publishing world, you and Leila both. You could have lived here. You couldn't expect people to approve, but you could expect them to keep their noses out of your business."

"She's right," Vivi said. "But I don't blame you for wanting to live a little more openly than that."

"All I can say is, you're lucky, you two." Molly scowled at them. "Once upon a time, I'd have given most anything to find the right person. Male or female, didn't matter. But I'm probably better off on my own. Never could stand anybody fussing at me."

"You mean you're *bi*?" Leila squealed. "You've had, you know, both men and women?"

"Back when," Molly confirmed. "That stuff hasn't interested me in about fifty years now. Too damn complicated."

The other four exchanged wide-eyed glances and shrieked with laughter. Sarah suddenly wanted more than anything to share this juicy news with Charles. "Molly," she said, leaning over to stroke the back of her spotted hand, "you are a treasure. Too bad nobody had the good luck to share your life with you."

"Too bad for them," Molly agreed.

They went in to dinner then, and the others presented Sarah with gifts and cards after dessert. Sarah felt buoyant, mellow in the evening shadows and slanting rays of the day's last light. Suddenly she sat up straight in her chair. "I just remembered something!" she cried.

"What?" the others chorused.

"It's been bugging me for months." She told them about the night she was sick, way back before Thanksgiving, when she had tried to reclaim her sleep from nausea. She told them about trying to remember a bend in a road, a small cottage next to it, a causeway ahead, her sense that it all had meaning for her. "Maybe it was a premonition," she said slowly. "I drove that road with my mother just after my father died. She wanted to see a friend who lived on an island off the coast of Maine. So we went together while Charles and Charlotte stayed home. I was pregnant with Stephie, but only just."

Sarah looked around the table. "The woman we visited was my mother's best friend since childhood. Nell. She was a widow, too. And Nell's daughter was a very young widow, younger than I was. She lived in that little cottage tucked into the trees. The daughter, I can't remember her name, she had no children. She had lost her husband only a year before. And I was so worried that all that would push my mother over the edge. Seeing her friend and the daughter . . . They had all lost their husbands. I was the only one who hadn't." She looked around the table at her friends. "Now, I'm the only one who has."

Sarah's memory at last released vivid details about that long-ago road trip, the cottage, the causeway. She recalled the hum of tires on the metal grid that spanned the water. She saw, as if on film, the weathered house stacked up among others on the steep little island, the view of water, and the scattering of other rocky islands. She heard again Nell's soothing words to Louisa, Sarah's mother. "I promise, you will survive this," she had said. "Not only that, you will be glad to survive. You will love him forever, but you will learn things you could never have learned when you shared your life with him. You will become yourself."

Sarah turned to Molly. "Do you think you might have been a different person if you'd lived with someone all this time?" She hesitated. "Do you think I'm different since Charles died?"

"No," said Leila and Addie.

"Yes," said Vivi.

Molly said, "You're probably just more of a good thing."

"No, really," Sarah insisted. "My house is a mess unless the kids or Sandy clean it up, and just the fact that I'm *living* with the kids and Sandy . . . well, that's totally unlike me. Or so I would have thought. I read until one or two in the morning, and I sleep later than I ever have in my life. I don't want to take care of people, but I love tending the garden and the dogs and my cats. Did you know I have cats? I'm snippy when people cross me, and I have no patience with ditherers. Yet I dither all the time in my own mind. I don't know whether I'm becoming the real me or slipping into senility. I must walk miles every day, and I'm obsessed with photographing the ugliest stuff I can find in nature, except that I don't think it's ugly, I think it's all beautiful and important. The thing is," she said, pausing for breath, "I'm happy. I miss Charles all the time and I'd give all this up for one more hour with him, but it doesn't hurt so much anymore. Not in the same way."

Molly applauded almost silently, and the others joined in, smiling fuzzily from the pot and the wine, the food and their fondness for Sarah. They sang "Happy Birthday" to her, softly, in harmony, almost like a chant, ending with, "Hope you live to be a hundred, a hundred years or more."

LATE THAT NIGHT A violent thunderstorm woke Sarah. Rain pooled on the floor beside her bed, and the covers on Charles's side were damp. She closed the sash, picked up Neo and Retro, and went across the room to the window seat and wrapped herself up in the quilt. She opened the casement, safe from the rain on this side of the house, and lay back to watch the brilliant streaks in the sky, to hear the roar of wind and water. The wild weather both thrilled and unsettled her. When she was small and afraid of storms, her father would tell her jokes and stories, distracting her, making her feel safe inside the circumference of heat from his body. She would wonder how his voice, quiet and deep, could outtalk the thunder and wind. Sometimes he made up stories on the spot, just for her. The stories had sunk far down in her memory, beyond retrieval, but Sarah's body remembered everything else. How one ear against her father's chest could hear his voice rising from some cavernous space inside, while in her other ear the sound registered normally. How his beard could scratch, and how he smelled of soap and pencils. In her throat, still, she could feel the laughter that rose as he told her tales about herself, Sarah at age three swinging like a monkey, tree to tree, until she reached California—that one she suddenly remembered whole.

Then Charles was there, as real in Sarah's memory as her father, as tender and masculine and warm. His clean, earthy smell, the snaky veins on the backs of his hands, the shiny pale shrapnel scars on his back and shoulder, markers on his path into medicine. Charles with Charlotte and Stephie, and lately with Hannah, was just as Sarah's father had been with her. The two edges of life, age and infancy, came together again and again, making a smooth seam, weaving sense out of everything. The seam had almost broken the day Hannah had fallen into the pond, but Charles had stitched it back together. Now it was torn beyond mending, but this time the appropriate edge, his edge, had pulled away, the one that was already faded and fraying, ready to go. Or almost.

Chapter 24

THE THIRD SATURDAY IN August was sultry, the air alive with the rise and fall of a cicada chorus. At nine in the morning it was nearly one hundred degrees on the screened deck of the cabin. Mordechai and Sarah sat in silence, he on his padded stool, Sarah on a low bench. Rivulets ran freely down their faces and necks. For a while, Sarah sank beneath her discomfort into a stillness that separated her from her thoughts and self. She was in, but not of, her skin and surroundings. She noticed everything—the raised grain in the wood of the deck, the mirrored surface of the pond and the haze above it, the shrill of the insects, and the scent of grass mingling with her own scents, female, human, old. Yet she partook of nothing. She was just a thing, like a sound or a scent.

Then a raven called hoarsely from the woods. A sudden ache thrummed between her shoulder blades, and Sarah's concentration shattered. She rose too fast to the surface of her mind, like a diver with the bends, and the heat was suddenly unbearable. Moving stealthily to avoid disturbing Mordechai, she took off her T-shirt and used it to dry the sweat under her breasts and on her neck. Her nakedness felt natural and sensible. She barely thought about it. She dropped her shirt into her lap, rested her hands palm up on top of it, and lowered her eyelids. Slowly she made her way back down to the quiet, imagining herself sinking into the pond without a ripple, settling along the bottom like the porous ash that had been Charles's bones. Cool water moved in her mind and lowered the temperature of her skin.

In her trance a story entered her mind, one that Mordechai had told her about cornering a Palestinian boy no older than fifteen. Mordechai was an Israeli soldier. The boy was cut off from his taunting, rock-throwing friends, and he cowered before Mordechai's Uzi, pleading and stuttering in Arabic. Mordechai did not understand the language, only the message, which was terror.

"If I did not shoot him—this *child*, Sarah—he would one day shoot me, or another Israeli. I *meant* to shoot him. I aimed my gun at his chest. And then I heard in my mind the wailing of women, and I knew this boy was someone's son. I remembered Baruch, whom I would never know, and I lowered my gun and shooed the boy away."

Mordechai and Sarah had sat on her back deck while he told her this. "That day I realized I could no longer kill. I began to weep instead, for my wife and child, for myself, even for my enemies, I had no idea why. I only knew, when I could *stop* weeping for whole moments at a time, that I was exactly like those I hated, who hated me." Here Mordechai paused, and Sarah saw the memory of his grief well up in his eyes. "We were all afraid," he went on. "We were ruled by terror, and yet we inflicted terror on others in the name of love—love for our people, our causes, our country. This was a revelation. I saw in one flash that the most courageous thing a person can do is to love without being afraid."

Other stories entered Sarah's meditations. Floating on the rough wake of Mordechai's were her father's tales, Angelo's itchy dragon, the Nana Who Ruled the Sun, and Papa the Moose Papoose. Sarah's life was all story, all memory, edited and incomplete, yet whole between the lines. *Perhaps,* she thought, *our minds know what they're doing when they deliver up a piece of memory here, an exaggerated anecdote there. Perhaps they edit with a purpose—to challenge, illuminate, soothe.*

Something in Sarah gave way, finally, and she saw herself from a place outside her skin. There she was, only one person, one old woman unwilling to buckle. She could tend only to her family, her friends, her cats, dogs, and garden. In the time she had left, that would have to suffice. The very thought drew her further into peace and light.

HALF AN HOUR LATER, Sarah was again jerked back into the rush of time and waves of heat, this time by someone opening the screen door to the deck. Before she could cover her nudity, there was Charlotte, gaping at her.

"Good morning, dear," said Sarah, pushing her head and arms into her shirt. She tugged at the hem, pulling it down over the folds in her belly.

Charlotte managed to splutter, "*Mother!* What on earth are you doing?"

"Meditating. Until I was so rudely interrupted."

"In the *nude?*"

"Yes, dear, it's hot. Nude is more comfortable."

"And where's Mordechai? Is *he* nude, *too?*" Charlotte sounded very much like Lottie.

"I'm right here," Mordechai answered from the cabin door, "and fully covered, as you can see. Would you like some iced tea?"

"No!" Charlotte cried. "No thank you. I'd like to know what's going on."

"I told you, Charlotte," Sarah answered, holding fast to the edge of her patience. "You can think what you like, but if you would kindly remember everything you've ever known about me, you will see that you're being ridiculous in the extreme." Now there was a prissy sentence, she thought, nearly giggling.

"What I *see,*" Charlotte burst out, "what I *saw,* was that you were sitting out here with nothing on."

"Nothing on top," Sarah corrected her. She softened toward Charlotte, then, and pitied her bewilderment. Remembering her vow to herself, that she would change toward her daughter, she said gently, "I once startled Mordechai while he was meditating nude. Totally nude. I was embarrassed, too." She turned to him. "May I tell Charlotte what you told me then?" she asked.

He nodded. "I'll get the tea. Perhaps Charlotte will change her mind."

So Sarah told her about Mordechai's lifelong faithfulness to Rachel. Charlotte had known about the death of his wife and baby since the night Jonathan and Tess had challenged his pacifism, but she had not known the rest of it. Sarah also described her morning and evening meditations and their benefits. "I've found endurance I never thought I had," she said. "I'm not nearly as afraid of dying as I used to be. And it doesn't torture me to keep loving your father, not anymore."

Charlotte stared mutely at Sarah and nodded slowly. Tentatively, she touched Sarah's shoulder, probably appeased more by Mordechai's celibacy than by Sarah's own account of herself. Still, her indignation was gone.

"What did you want, Charlotte?"

"Oh." Charlotte seemed to give herself a quick mental shake. "I forgot. I . . . I was looking for Lottie. We were supposed to go to Burlington . . . to shop for shoes, and Tom's birthday present. She forgot, I guess. Jordan said she might be down here."

"No, she's hiking with Tony." Sarah studied her daughter. "You must feel so angry when she does that kind of thing."

But Charlotte didn't look angry; she looked sorrowful. "I guess," she said. "But I'm so used to it, I barely notice. She wants nothing to do with me." She slumped down onto a bench inside the deck railing and sighed. "I just hope she'll come back."

Sarah started to say that Lottie would be back in a couple of hours, but of course Charlotte meant something more than that; she was hoping she had not lost Lottie for good. Sarah saw in Charlotte's eyes exactly what she had finally seen in Charles's, that day in the woods when he had let himself mourn the lost time with David. She remembered her own sadness over this daughter who sat before her. But Sarah was sad no more, not just now. She leaned over to Charlotte and brushed the hair back from her eyes. Then she chanted softly, "Leave her alone, and she'll come home, wagging her tail behind her."

The two of them walked back to the house together after iced tea with Mordecai. Charlotte remained subdued, and Sarah saw that it was probably harder for her to have Lottie out of her house than in it. From Charlotte's perspective, Lottie had simply and totally defected—to Sarah, to her friends and

Tony, even to Sandy and Tyler. Lottie loved them all without reservation.

Charlotte said, "Mom, really, how can I just let Lottie go and do exactly as she pleases? Are you saying she doesn't need parents anymore? She should just make all her own choices at sixteen, including sex and drinking and drugs and . . . just everything?"

"I'm saying she'll do that in any case. And she'll make mistakes. But Charlotte, you and Tom have already said everything you have to say to her. You've set good examples. You've loved her, you will always love her, and she knows that." She paused. This was more than they'd said to each other, about anything real, for a long time. Sarah didn't want to jeopardize their small progress, but she added, "Lottie has already let go. The best way to invite her back is to let go yourself. You already began that process when you agreed she could stay with me. It takes time. But Lottie's a good person, and you've had a lot to do with that."

Throughout the summer, Sarah had sometimes wondered whether her relationship with Charlotte might have been different if Charlotte had spent a couple of her adolescent years away from home. It was easy for Sarah to have three teenagers living with her, now that she wasn't mother to any of them. They were on their best behavior, as children often are in other people's homes. Angelo had lost nearly all his prickliness, and Lottie loved being at Sarah's amid friends. Only Jordan wasn't entirely at home. She was too diffident, as compliant as a windup doll. But she'd have time to settle in. She and the others would stay on with Sarah for the next year, until graduation. This summer they had given her more than she'd given in return.

Hot as it was, school had started two days earlier, on the thirtieth of August. Labor Day weekend had begun. Sarah was cutting back the perennials that were finished for the year, leaving sedums, monardas, asters, and a few others that still bloomed above their browning stalks and leaves. The air smelled different now, full of dust and pollen that hung suspended in the motionless heat. The vegetable garden would yield right up until the first killing frost, which could come any night now, or hold off until October. Sandy had been putting up the harvest at a faster pace, trying to keep up with the abundance. When frost threatened, she would finally pick all the tomatoes that were left on the vines. The household would feast a time or two on fried green tomatoes, and the rest of the late-season yield would ripen in brown paper bags for stews and sauces.

Already Sarah missed the random patterns of her boarders' comings and goings. The teenagers' new schedules were tighter and more synchronized. They would be gone from seven thirty until four or five or six, depending on their after-school jobs or activities. Tyler would enter morning kindergarten next week, a prospect he faced with mingled excitement and dread. Sandy would continue to spend her days at home or at the hospital.

Bob was dying. His doctors were still treating his burns, but they told Sandy he just wasn't fighting to survive. There was little hope. Sandy sat beside him every day in an effort to revive his will. "Sarah," she would plead, "why isn't it enough that I love him, that Tyler needs him? Why doesn't he want to stay with us?"

Sarah thought it likely that Bob no longer recognized himself. He was helpless and disfigured; he was in perpetual pain; he was exhausted. The Bob Hanks she had met for those few days last winter had been constantly in motion and always in control. He was passionate about hunting, fishing, driving his snowmobile in the woods and meadows. He took care of his family. He was proud of them and of himself. Now he was piling up bills, a mountain of debt that he could never conquer, especially impaired. If he recovered, it would be months before he could work again, if he ever could work at all. He was blind in one eye and three fingers on his right hand were webby stumps. He would need long, painful rehabilitation.

Vermont was full of people who lived on the edge, but Sarah had never been so aware of this, nor so close to it. Everyone in her own household lived near the edge of poverty, the edge of old age, or the edge of adulthood—dangerous in itself. More and more often, she recalled her childhood and that other household filled with people balanced precariously between survival and disaster, sanity and despair. This time around, things were less desperate. Sandy's need was greatest, and everyone supported her. If Bob died, as he seemed determined to do, his life insurance would leave Sandy and Tyler better off financially, but the price of this was high nonetheless.

Sarah straightened up from her garden work, soaked with sweat. She thought of the cold to come. So many kinds of cold, always lying just under the heat of sun or skin or human tenderness. She raked the last prunings onto a tarp, pulled its corners together, and laid her rake on top in case a breath of air should stir the pile.

Inside, she went upstairs, stripped off her sticky clothes and dropped them into a heap on the floor. She stepped into the shower. It felt cool on her overheated scalp but ran warm down her back, carrying the heat away with it. She scrubbed soil from her nails and hands, her arms and legs. She had worked as unclothed as possible in the garden, just a tank top and shorts and sandals, so she was black and gritty in her many creases. Good dirt.

She was rinsing the last of the shampoo from her hair and soap from her body when Sandy knocked loudly. "Sarah! Can you take a phone call? It sounds important!"

"Damn!" Sarah muttered, shutting off the water. But she called out, "Yes! All right, I'm coming."

She opened the door, wrapped in a towel, and took the cordless phone from Sandy, mouthing, "Thanks."

It was Josie Koval's mother, Rose, breathless and upset. "Sarah? Oh, Sarah, I've got to ask you the most enormous favor, very fast. Right away. I really need your help."

"Rose," Sarah said calmly. "Slow down. I'll help if I can. What's wrong?"

Rose was calling from a hospital in the town of Berlin, closer than the one where Charles had died and where Bob was now. Sarah remembered Sandy's frantic call in June, and she braced herself. Indeed, this was another disaster, though not as bad as it could have been. Josie's partner, the father of the baby she had been carrying when she'd lost two toes to frostbite last January, had attacked her and threatened their child. Josie needed a place to stay where Roger would not think to look for her. It wouldn't be for long. He'd been arrested right after the incident, just an hour or two ago. He was in custody, and Josie was determined to press charges, but he still could get out soon if he was granted bail. Rose was furious at the thought. "Goddamned idiots!" Sarah had known Rose casually for at least thirty years and had never before heard her swear.

"Oh, Rose, dear, let me think." Sarah said. "You know I have a house full of refugees?"

"Yes. Word travels. It's why I thought of you, that and the fact that Roger doesn't know you. But perhaps you just can't fit Josie in. I'll understand, though I don't know . . ."

"No, no, just *give* me a minute," Sarah snapped. Instantly contrite, she said, "Rose, I didn't mean that the way it came out. I'm sorry. Let's see." Mentally she ran through a half-dozen excuses. The last thing she wanted was another boarder. Then she heard herself saying, "Maybe I could put a couple of the kids out in Charles's office. Or Josie and the baby could squeeze into my office off the kitchen. Oh, I don't know—we'll work it out. Just send her over, Rose. Or bring her. When will they release her?"

Rose exhaled audibly, a gust of relief. "Sarah, thank you! They're just finishing the cast—Roger broke her arm, that son of a bitch. The baby's fine but screaming his head off. Oh, God, I shouldn't tell you that, you'll never let him in your house!" Her voice cracked on a hysterical giggle.

"Rose," Sarah said sternly. "Calm down. I'll get a room ready for Josie. Just get her over here in one piece."

Sarah hung up, and for a furious second or two she chastised herself for agreeing to one too many people in her house. One and a half too many. Then she addressed the problems at hand. She figured she and Sandy would have an hour to decide where to put Josie and start preparing the space. *Lord!* she thought. *A baby! Probably more noise than all three teenagers.* She hoped fervently that Roger Whatshisname would stay in jail long enough for Josie to make other living arrangements. Then she realized that even with Josie and the baby she would have fewer people, under easier conditions, than her parents had had in the Depression. So be it.

"All right," she told Sandy. "We'll put them in my office for now. The baby can sleep in a file drawer or a big box if need be, and the daybed will do for Josie. I'd really like to keep Charles's office free for David and Tess."

Sandy shook her head. "I'll move down here with Tyler," she offered. "We'll get a little cot or mattress for him."

"Why on earth?"

"Nobody's after us. Josie will be safer on the second floor."

Sarah kissed Sandy on the cheek. "You are a sweetheart. It won't be for long, I'm sure. You'll move back upstairs before you know it."

Chapter 25

ROSE CAME AND WENT in a flurry of anxious energy. "I don't want to leave my car outside your house for long," she panted, struggling with a large duffel that she had hastily packed for Josie. "Who knows who might see us and then tell Roger?" She looked around apprehensively, but there wasn't a single other car within sight or earshot.

Josie carried her son and a shoulder bag full of his supplies. The baby was squalling and looked as if he'd been doing so for a long time and intended to keep on. Sarah stopped herself from sighing.

Then Rose was gone. The teenagers would soon be home from school. Tyler was at a friend's house for the afternoon and a sleepover—his first, and good timing, too. Mordechai was at work in the cabin. Surely he would hear the baby's crying.

Sandy sat Josie down at the kitchen table and poured her some iced tea while Sarah stood outside, saying good-bye to Rose and promising to call her. "Don't you call me," she said, searching for a credible reason. "In case . . . well, you know, in case Roger is released and somehow gets his hands on your phone records and tracks Josie here." Rose was hysterical enough to swallow this. The truth was, Sarah didn't want Rose phoning every five minutes.

Back inside, Sarah found Sandy holding the baby and Josie looking darkly into space. She shifted her gaze to Sarah, but it did not lighten. "Thank you," she said stiffly. "I'll try not to be any trouble." Glancing at Sandy, who was doing the mother shuffle with Josie's howling son, she added, "I'm sorry about the baby. He's upset. He'll quiet down."

Sarah sat down across from Josie. "Is your arm hurting a lot?"

The young woman shook her head. "Not now. Not until this big wallop of Vicodin wears off."

"You can take that stuff and still nurse? If you're nursing, I mean?"

"Yeah, I asked. They said it was okay but to get off it as soon as I can. Which will be now. I'm not going to take any more."

Sarah examined her. She had a long scratch down her right cheek and scrapes and bruises on her forearms and neck and around her mouth. Her lower lip was puffy. Her left eye would probably be swollen shut by morning. Still, she was sharply pretty, with a strong square jaw, straight eyebrows, and a wide, thin-lipped mouth. She had short, spiky, very dark hair, and flawless olive skin, just now muddy from shock. She looked harder than Sarah remembered. After her near fatal walk in the cold, she'd been abashed, mocking her own carelessness as she admired the yarn Sarah had brought her. Sarah could see no humor in her now, but that was not surprising under the circumstances. Josie was too thin, except for her breasts. The baby was probably due for a feeding. Andrew. The child had the name Sarah had given her own son, the stillborn little boy whose birth and death had woven a single, seamless patch of cloth.

"Well," said Sarah, getting back to her feet. "Let's show you where you two will sleep." She hefted the baby bag while Sandy gave Andrew back to his mother and struggled with the duffel. "Sandy, wait till Angelo gets home, why don't you?"

"It's okay, Sarah," she answered. "Maybe Josie could use a few things out of here."

"Thanks," Josie said dully, jouncing her baby in her uninjured arm.

Sarah thrust the baby bag at her and motioned for her to take the strap onto her shoulder. "Can you manage this? I'll help Sandy with the duffel."

Thus burdened, the three of them climbed the stairs, Sandy and Sarah huffing, Josie following silently behind them, and Andrew still wailing, but less hysterically. His cries were subsiding into monotonous drones punctuated by hiccups.

Sandy and Tyler's things were piled neatly on the bed, but there hadn't yet been time to move them down to Sarah's office. It was clear to anyone with eyes that Josie was displacing Sandy, but she said nothing, just dropped the baby bag on the floor beside the bed. She looked around the big room, then down at the bed. "Can I push this against the wall?" she asked. "So Andrew won't roll off?"

Sarah pointed to the small daybed across the room, where Tyler had been sleeping. "Don't you want to put him there?"

Josie shook her head. "He's used to sleeping with us . . . me. He'll cry all night over there."

It was a reasonable request, which Sarah nevertheless resented.

Sandy said, "Sure, let's move the bed. That's all right, isn't it, Sarah?" Without waiting for an answer, she took the baby from Josie, plunked him into Sarah's reluctant arms, and started shoving the heavy bedstead. "Give me a hand, Josie."

Josie put her hip to the task instead, and together she and Sandy managed to move the bed. There wasn't a speck of dust on the carpet where it had stood, just four dents left in the nap by the casters. Sandy was meticulous about this room, and Sarah hoped Josie would follow her example.

Raucous laughter drifted up from the driveway, followed by the slam of the front door. Angelo, Lottie, and Jordan came trooping up to their rooms to drop their backpacks before heading for the refrigerator. Sandy stepped into the hall to intercept them and explain the situation.

"Thought I heard something yowling," Angelo said. "Knew it couldn't be one of the kittens."

"Big lungs for such a little guy." Sandy lowered her voice, but Sarah still heard. "Thank God he's quiet now. I thought Sarah might throttle him."

"You mean my Nana didn't googoo-eye the wittle snuggums?" Lottie asked. Sarah snorted, glad Andrew was still making enough noise that Josie wouldn't overhear.

Jordan nudged Lottie and giggled. "Let's go see. Might as well say hello to the new castaways."

During the introductions, though, Jordan sobered and looked away from Josie's injuries. Sarah hustled the teenagers out of the room, her hand on Jordan's arm. "Let's let Josie and Andrew get settled," she said, following them. Andrew had finally fallen asleep against his mother's shoulder. Sandy stayed behind to help Josie ease him onto the big bed, with the wall on one side of him and the duffel on the other. He looked as if he'd sleep for hours. Sarah hoped Josie would sleep too, so the baby wouldn't wake in a strange place alone.

TEN PEOPLE SAT AROUND the dining table that night, including Mordechai and Tony. The group had outgrown the kitchen table, which sat six if they rubbed elbows. Andrew nuzzled sleepily at Josie's breast. He was propped on pillows while she attempted to eat one-handed and balance the baby with her other arm, in its cast. Angelo intently averted his eyes from this maternal tableau, even though only a modest inch or so of Josie's breast was exposed. Tony, on the other hand, seemed entirely at ease, talking eagerly to Josie about people they knew in common. Her mother lived only half a mile from Tony's parents, and they were well acquainted. When he asked about her injuries, and she told him about Roger, he said, "Jeez, I'm sorry. That totally sucks."

Tony's questions gave Josie a chance to open up. She blamed herself for losing control of her situation. She knew about the rate of domestic violence in Vermont, and she had been wary of Roger in the wake of a layoff and his growing dependency on booze. Drinking gave rise to quiet, menacing self-pity in which Roger steeped until he could stand it no longer. Then he would yell, break things, turn on Josie, blame the world for his disappointments. But today was the first time he'd ever hit her, and she'd told him it would be the last. No second chances. She had left him on the spot, grabbing the baby and running to a neighbor's house for help.

JOSIE RELAXED A LITTLE more each day, largely because of Sandy's persistent, gentle overtures and Tyler's fascination with Andrew. Tyler was a born nurturer. He was faithful about feeding Neo and Retro, just as he had promised, and he seemed to have limitless patience with Andrew. The first time he made Andrew laugh, he was hooked. From then on, he did everything in his power to repeat the effect. Andrew cooperated, with a baby's dawning delight in an older child. He threw his toys on the floor again and again, as if he could not believe his good fortune when Tyler obediently picked them up and gave them back. Sandy saw the glint of infant power dawn in Andrew's eyes. "Oh, Josie, you're in for it with this one!" she said.

Josie regained her color and managed her pain as best she could with over-the-counter medications. Her black eye gradually faded to purple, then yellow. The swelling around her mouth disappeared. Her arm was mending, though the cast would stay on for several more weeks, and then she would need physical therapy.

Josie's anger was the slowest of her injuries to heal. In only the two months since Roger's layoff, her life had been torn apart and all her assumptions had disintegrated. She was worried about Andrew and their future and thrown by her misjudgment of Roger. She had thought him incapable of violence; she had thought he loved her. But when Roger broke her arm, he forever shattered her illusions and her affection for him. She did not want family counseling; she did not want to be with him at all. She had loved a fantasy.

Sandy indoctrinated Josie to the ways of the household, soliciting her help instead of waiting for Josie to offer it. She gave her tasks that would not strain her arm or aggravate the slight limp left by her lost, frostbitten toes. In return, she helped with Andrew—especially with bathing and changing him—but she also expected Josie to help with Tyler. Josie would never have joined the household fully without Sandy to pull her along. Sarah wondered at first why Sandy bothered but soon saw that the two women needed each other. Sandy had few friends, none of them close. Josie had a handful of friends, but she couldn't tell anyone where she was staying, and she couldn't safely go out.

THREE WEEKS AFTER Josie and Andrew moved in and a week before Roger was due in court, Rose Koval called in a panic to say that he'd jumped bail and disappeared. She called from a pay phone in town, and Sarah felt a little guilty that Rose had taken her so seriously about the phone records. "I *knew*," she wailed into the phone. "I *knew* they should have kept him locked up."

Sarah reassured Rose that Josie and Andrew could stay. There was no safer place for them. No one knew they were here except the members of the household and Sarah's own family. The teenagers had no reason to tell anyone and were, besides, too involved in their own lives to think of mentioning it. Mordechai, of course, was as trustworthy as a vault, and Sandy would be the last person to reveal Josie's whereabouts. Sarah reassured Rose with all of this. Nothing had changed really. Roger might look for Josie, but he would not find her.

To her own surprise, Sarah didn't worry much. There would always be reason for dread, but that only hardened the imperative for inward steadiness. She had thought, once, that her fears would automatically dissipate as she established a new life, but Mordechai had taught her that it took work and focus.

The solitary life Sarah had anticipated as a widow had filled up with pleasures and frustrations. She had allowed people to move in, and they had brought their baggage, some of which was heavy. Now Josie had brought new trouble. It wasn't her fault that Roger was loose, that he might come looking for her. Josie formally asked Sarah to let her stay at least until her arm healed. She even thought out loud about getting a gun, but Sarah wouldn't hear of it. Then Josie had shrugged off her own worries. "I'm overreacting," she confessed. "I know Roger, and he's long gone by now."

Chapter 26

J OSIE'S CONFIDENCE WAVERED and Jordan nearly panicked when a rash of thefts broke out in the Rockhill
area. The general store and several remote, well-hidden
homes were broken into. The small crime wave soon spread to
Montpelier and other towns. Lottie's friend Jenna Sterling was
mugged getting into her car one night, right in front of the library. This was unheard of. The newspaper said police suspected
drug-seeking teenagers, but Jordan was sure it was Roger. At
least some of it was Roger; how else would he get money and
food? Jordan worried almost as much as Rose did, while Josie
kept uttering her frayed assurances.

These gave way entirely when Sandy told Josie that someone
had stolen at least a bushel of produce from the garden. "But it
couldn't be Roger," Sandy said. "He wouldn't be so stupid, not
with so many other gardens around. Why ours?"

"To scare us," said Josie, gone white. "He's trying to scare us."

Everyone in the house adopted edgy new habits. They locked
their cars. They locked the doors when the last of them went

to bed. The girls, especially, came and went with a buddy after dark. They reminded each other of these safety measures, unused to thinking of such things and resenting the need. They didn't blame Josie, but they were all nervous.

September gave way to October and the first hard frost. Sandy, Josie, Sarah, and Mordechai hurriedly gathered the last yield from the garden while the others were in school. Josie's cast was finally off. Her arm was weak, but she could use it, and she helped Sandy can a mountain of vegetables.

There was no sign of Roger. The thefts and muggings dropped away. Everyone breathed more easily in the autumn air and forgot to be quite so careful. Lottie and her friends came and went more freely. They studied, ate voraciously, squabbled like siblings, and invited troops of their schoolmates to the house. No one seemed curious about Josie. Introductions never went beyond first names.

Sandy began going out more often than she had since moving in. She still visited Bob nearly every day, but she also saw one or two new friends—a nurse from the hospital, another mother she'd met at the library. Sometimes she and Josie went all the way to Burlington together, out of the likely range in which Roger might lurk. They ate at inexpensive ethnic restaurants or went to movies when someone at home was willing to babysit. More often, though, they rented videos, creating a new household pastime. Once Tyler and Andrew were asleep, whoever else was at home would gather in the great room with popcorn, ice cream, or sandwiches. They often missed dialogue amid arguments over the plot or performances, the directing or the script. They judged films against the books they were based on.

One night, when Andrew wailed over Josie's portable intercom, interrupting *The Sheltering Sky,* Sarah went up to comfort him. She'd been distracted during the movie, and besides, she liked sitting with the baby in the rocker she had moved into Josie's room. He was still inclined to be fussy when overtired, but he was gregarious and clearly liked having a lot of people around. He willingly went to any of them.

Andrew was seven and a half months old. He had changed rapidly in the weeks since his arrival at Sarah's. It was easy to forget the blink-of-an-eye progress from infancy to babyhood. Just in the past week, he'd been getting ready to crawl. From a prone position he could stick his butt into the air, then push up onto his hands. He would rock and wobble, then fall into a heap and rest before trying again. He had begun to utter syllabic sounds, which he inflected with passion and meaning, waving his hands in the air. At dinner, in the high chair Sarah had dragged in from the barn, he held forth with glee, egged on when Jordan mimicked his gestures and tones and everyone laughed.

When Sarah went in to Andrew now, though, he was sitting up in the big bed, bolstered by pillows, snotty and aggrieved. When he saw Sarah, he reached up for her, and her heart turned over. He felt feverish when she picked him up. His crying sounded like sick-baby sorrow, not anger or fear, not hunger or wetness. He did need changing, though, and Sarah tended to that before giving him a dose of PediaCare. Then she rocked him and thought about her own Andrew, as she often did these days, but since she'd let herself fall in love with Josie's child, she had finally stopped aching for her own.

Andrew quit crying and drifted into a light doze, but he whimpered and squirmed. Sarah examined him in the dim light streaming in from the hallway. He lay across her lap, his head on her arm, his hair damp, his thick, upcurving lashes resting on his cheek. Sarah's much tinier Andrew had lain just so, contained within his permanent sleep, newly arrived and departed. No time to stay. No time to show Sarah what he had brought with him—knowledge of the place from which he had come. The odd thing, as she entered further into old age, was that Sarah caught glimpses of that place, or some place. These were not images so much as sensations, flickers at the edge of her eye. Perhaps they really were memories of her own origins, returning at last.

Andrew stirred in his sleep and flung his arm out sideways, into the dark. His eyelids fluttered but did not open. Sarah murmured to him and brushed the hair from his forehead. She traced the whorls of his ear and thought about her own Andrew, and Hannah.

Hannah was fearless, despite her cold submersion in the pond, despite her full and final initiation to a world of hazard. Hannah kept her innocence. Sarah had lost hers, along with much of her native courage, when her infant son had both lived and died at the moment he passed from her body to the world outside. What Hannah's courage induced in Sarah was both a longing for her own fearless self and a prayer for Hannah, who would face more challenges to her tough, eager spirit.

This awareness sank into Sarah without a ripple. She accepted it fully and felt at peace. Nothing in the world was sweeter than sitting in a darkened room with a sleeping baby in your lap. Soon it would be Tess and David's baby.

Let there be babies in my life until I die, Sarah pleaded to the sky outside.

• • •

"WHERE'S NEO AND RETRO?" Hannah demanded, scampering inside before David and Tess had even closed the car doors. They had driven up for the weekend, while Tess's due date was still more than two months off. They might try for Thanksgiving, too, but that would depend on her doctor's say-so.

Sarah swooped in on Hannah and gave her a quick squeeze. "You know, we have a baby for you to meet, too. And his mom."

"Kitties, first, please," said Hannah, who knew about Andrew and Josie but understood more about cats. According to David, she was having second thoughts about a baby brother — the same doubts Stephie had had about him when she was about Hannah's age. David was aware of the story, and he tried to reassure Hannah with it. "Stephie likes me a *lot*," he would say, never mentioning that Stephie had taken two years to decide.

Tyler had run down the stairs at the sound of Hannah's voice and skidded into the kitchen holding each kitten with an arm around its ribcage. Their hind legs swung like pendulums; their eyes were wide but unalarmed. They seemed content to dangle.

"Look, Hannah!" Tyler said excitedly, pointing his chin to each kitten in turn. "This one's Neo, and this one's Retro. I feed them two times every day."

He set the cats down. They were about four months old now, getting leggy and thinning out. Hannah squatted down next to them, her corduroy knees almost to her chin. She wrapped her right arm around her legs and extended her left hand tentatively toward Retro, who crept forward, stretching his head out to sniff. Hannah wiggled her fingers, and Neo leapt forward to swat them. Retro took confidence from that and went for Hannah's shoelace. She squealed delightedly. "Can I pick them up?"

"Yes," Tyler said. "Let me show you how." He reached under Neo, supporting his ribcage and haunches. "See? They don't like it if you pull them up by their arms." Hannah tried it with Retro. "There you go," Tyler said proudly. "You've got it." They started upstairs together, each carrying a kitten, while Lottie, Jordan, and Angelo rattled past them on their way down to the kitchen.

Greetings filled the room as Tess and David took off their jackets. Had Renoir painted pregnant women, Tess could have modeled. Her fair hair shone, and her belly rose high and shapely underneath a collarless cotton dress with small buttons down the front.

That night, everyone would be home for dinner, including Mordechai. Charlotte and Tom were coming with Luke. Lottie had invited Tony. Sarah put an extra leaf in the dining table and counted—sixteen people on a no-occasion evening in October. Most nights, at least six or seven were at dinner, more than when Sarah's children had lived at home. Her life was more heavily populated now than it had ever been since she'd grown up. She never would have thought.

Tess helped her set the table. The late-day sun slanted in, lighting up the linens and place settings. Points of light caught on glasses, flatware, and ceramic glazes; the whole table glittered. Outside, fall color had burst wide open. Each year it was sudden, surprising, and new.

Sarah still walked in the mornings, her eye for detail now fine and focused. She noted the departure of the migrating birds and the signs of animals wintering down, the bears gorging for their long sleep, especially evident around ancient apple trees, where even the rotting fruit on the ground did not escape their hungry scavenging. Bears sometimes got drunk on fermenting apples. Sarah pictured them reeling happily into their dens, to collapse and outsleep any hangover. The females would bear their cubs without even waking. The cubs, tiny and hairless, would crawl blindly toward their mothers' nipples and suck the winter away, growing fat and furry. Their mothers would wake in the spring to greet their chubby babies with all the hard work done. Bears had it easy when it came to childbirth.

Sarah turned to Tess, who was folding cloth napkins. "How've you been feeling?"

"Good," Tess answered, smiling. "With Hannah, I had terrible morning sickness. With this one . . ." she put a hand fondly on her belly, "not a twinge."

Tess and David had announced weeks ago that their baby was a boy. They wanted to know the sex so they could begin knowing him better. It also helped Hannah. It made the baby seem more real to call him "he" instead of "it." They were working on names now.

"Actually," Tess confided, "I think we've known all along. But I want to know what you think."

"I'll think it's fine," Sarah assured her. "I know you'd never call him—oh—Ambrose, or Bonaventure."

"We want to call him Charles," Tess told her. "Charles McDermott Lucas."

Sarah's eyes stung and she blinked hard. "Tess," was all she could manage.

"Charlie," Tess said. "There really was no other choice, not given who Charles was, not after he saved Hannah. It was David's idea to make McDermott his middle name. It was Ian's name, and David thought we should keep Ian in the family."

"You take my breath away," Sarah sighed, touching Tess's cheek.

"We think we'll get married, you know."

"I didn't want to ask. And I didn't think it mattered much these days. But I'm glad."

"We'll all be Lucases. Hannah has agreed to that as long as she can have McDermott as a middle name, too, like Charlie. What do you think?"

"I think it's grand." Sarah put her hand shyly on Tess's belly. "Hello there, Charlie."

LATER, AS LOTTIE and Sandy were getting ready to carry serving dishes to the dining room, and Mordechai was slicing bread, David stood near the kitchen table with Sarah and watched the activity. "Mom, you're running a commune," he said, shaking his head in wonderment. "Every time we're here, there are more people in this house." He looked down at her. "It's great. You're really helping these kids. And Sandy, too, and Josie. They're helping you, too, I see. You haven't lifted a finger except to set the table, you sly thing." He nudged her.

"I'm no fool." She nudged him back.

"Something else has changed around here, too," he added. "Charlotte. She's different."

"How can you tell? She and Tom only got here half an hour ago. You've hardly had a minute with her."

David tapped his temple. "I am astute."

"Then tell me, Stoot, what is it you see?"

"I see that she has dropped her shoulders, lifted the corners of her mouth, and lowered her voice by several decibels when talking to Lottie."

"My," said Sarah. "You don't miss a thing."

"So, what's the deal? Who slipped the tranks into Charlotte's hors d'oeuvres?"

"I believe she did that herself," Sarah told him.

They fell silent as Charlotte came into the kitchen. David watched her as she left again, carrying a tray of condiments. Keeping his voice low, he said, "Maybe Dad's dying scared her."

"Could be," Sarah agreed. "I think she's blown some dust off her heart. She and Lottie are doing better — being apart has brought them closer." She almost added that she and Charlotte were slowly spanning their own chasm, but she didn't want to jinx this tentative process. The chasm was forty years wide and deep, and Sarah didn't have another forty years for bridge building. If all she could manage was a swaying, precarious thing made of rope, then that would suffice.

Everyone drifted toward the dining table from the kitchen and the rooms upstairs. They inhaled the seasoned steam from a half-dozen dishes lined up along the center of the long table. Lottie lit candles and dimmed the overhead light. Mordechai poured wine and offered a brief, spontaneous blessing, delivered without any bowing of heads, without amens. He merely wished them peace and offered thanks amid a sharing of glances and a chorus of assent.

They had just finished eating and were starting to clear the plates and serve dessert when footsteps and a heavy thump reached them from the front porch.

Jordan's eyes went wide. Josie took Andrew out of his high chair and held him close. Angelo, Tom, and Mordechai exchanged glances.

"What's going on?" David asked.

"Nothing," Sarah answered, rising from her chair. It was not Roger. It wasn't.

"I'll come with," said Lottie.

"Me, too," added Angelo.

They went down the hall, listening hard and exchanging nervous glances. More footsteps, another thump. Sarah, suddenly impatient, switched on the outside light. A woman was just heading down the stairs, having left two large boxes at the top.

Sarah yanked the door open and called, "Hello? Did you want something?" Angelo loomed behind her, with Lottie at his side.

The woman stopped on the steps and held onto the railing, as if deciding whether to keep on going. She turned, though, and came back up. She was somewhere in her thirties. She wore heavy makeup, tight jeans, and a loose sweatshirt printed with a cartoon of a small boy scowling and pissing. Her hair was curly and short, like her daughter's.

"I'm Lorraine," she said. "Jordan's mom. I just came to drop off some stuff of hers that's been lying around."

"Well, come in, Lorraine," said Sarah, holding the door open. She took a big breath of autumn air, her anxieties fleeing like the leaves in the wind outside. "Please do. We're all finishing dinner. Why don't you have dessert with us?"

Lorraine drew herself up. Her eyes moved rapidly among the three who faced her until she reached her decision. She looked straight at Sarah and said, "All right. I will. Thanks."

Angelo headed back to the dining room to alert Jordan. Lottie stepped in front of Sarah and stuck her hand out. "I'm Jordan's friend Lottie," she said, speaking like an etiquette instructor and drawing Lorraine inside. "And this, as you've probably figured out, is my grandmother, Sarah Lucas." She gestured toward Sarah, who likewise held out her hand.

Lorraine offered a listless grip in return. Sarah and Lottie traded looks and led the way to the dining table in the great room. Lottie called ahead with a further warning. "Jordan, your mom's here."

Jordan was on her feet by the time they entered the room. She looked ready to run.

Lorraine scanned the faces around the table as if they were billboards.

Sarah made the introductions, and David brought another chair from the kitchen. Lorraine sat down stiffly, her eyes taking in the room and the furnishings. She glanced again at the fifteen unfamiliar faces, including Andrew's, but she avoided Jordan's eyes.

"Hi, Mom," said Jordan finally, her voice barely audible. She cleared her throat and spoke up. "Angelo said you brought some of my stuff."

"Yeah. Yes. It's on the porch. The kids and I are moving. I cleaned out your room."

"Moving?" Jordan's big eyes were bewildered. "Where? When?"

"First of the month, just over near Barre Street. I'll let you know. It's smaller. Less rent."

Sarah took her meaning—there was no room for Jordan. Hastily, hoping Jordan wouldn't tumble to this, she said, "I'm glad to meet you at last, Lorraine. We all are." She gestured around the table, where an awkward silence reigned and Jordan looked trapped. "You should be proud. Jordan is doing so well. We're all glad to have her here."

A hearty chorus seconded this, and Jordan blushed. Lorraine shifted uneasily in her seat.

Charlotte and Lottie, serving dessert, moved quietly and eyed Lorraine. Lottie looked ready to pounce if need be. Instead she set a bowl of Cherry Garcia before her and offered a plate of Milano cookies.

"Thanks, no," Lorraine said gruffly, not meeting their eyes. She saw that others were digging into their ice cream, so she picked up her spoon.

Sarah was suddenly touched to the bone by Lorraine's tense, defensive manners. She must wonder, how did her difficult, wayward daughter end up here, at ease in this family of strangers, while Lorraine worked her butt off and barely got by? Why should Jordan have all this support and affection, while Lorraine had none?

There would be a scene. Lorraine would scorn and belittle Jordan, she would disgrace herself, she would never contain her bitterness. It was why she had come inside. Sarah knew this absolutely, just as she had known that Tess was pregnant.

She stood, catching Lorraine's eye, and said, "I would like to propose a toast, if there's any wine left and if somebody could find Lorraine a glass."

Tentative conversations died around her, and only Mordechai caught on. He provided a glass, and shared out a half bottle of merlot that still sat on the table.

With Lorraine eyeing her skeptically, Sarah hastily said, "I would like to thank Lorraine for Jordan. It's as simple as that. It can't be easy raising three children on your own, and Jordan is proof of Lorraine's courage and success."

"Hear, hear!"

"To Lorraine and Jordan!"

They all drank.

Lorraine was the last to take a sip, and she put her glass down after barely a taste. "Well. Right. Jordan's dad left just about the time Jordan started to . . . just when Jordan turned twelve. Not that he ever did a lick. I pretty much supported us all. He's one less to feed. And he was mean." She downed the rest of her wine and jerked her head toward Jordan. "I guess she turned out okay. I'd best be going, see to the kids."

Jordan and Lottie saw her out and came back looking dazed.

Sarah met Mordechai's smiling eyes, then glanced around at everyone else, pleased with herself. It was the job of the old to help the young.

Chapter 27

F INALLY!" JOSIE SIGHED, coming into the great room
with an exaggerated stagger. "The little bugger's out
cold." Tyler had been asleep for over an hour, since
eight o'clock. Andrew, however, had decided to revive his talent
for squalling, which they all thought he had forgotten. Something had set him off at dinner, and he'd screamed for a solid
hour, then fussed for two more, through his warm bath, between
swallows of Josie's milk, in Sarah's lap and Sandy's and even
Tyler's. Nothing soothed him. Sarah remembered her annoy-
ance on the day of his arrival. Tonight his crying had brought
tears to her eyes.

"Thank God," she breathed into the blessed silence. "I wonder what got into him. He's been on such an even keel."

"Wish I knew," said Josie, plumping herself down onto the big
couch between Jordan and Sandy. Sarah sat in a wing chair close
by. The dogs lay at her feet, dead asleep, not even twitching in
their dreams. Popcorn, fruit, and a pot of tea sat on the coffee
table, next to a video.

"Are we ready?" Jordan asked. Sarah glanced at Josie for confirmation, then gave a thumbs-up signal. She grinned at Jordan, pleased to see how comfortable she was in this small group. Angelo was running the projector at the art theater in town, a new job since school started. Lottie and Tony were out with friends. Mordechai was in the cabin. Not long ago, Jordan would have hidden in her room with Lottie gone. But since the night Lorraine had backed down before winding up, Jordan had come further into her own.

She slipped the tape into the player while Sandy poured tea. Then they sat back to watch the movie, which Sarah had chosen. She had already seen *Strangers in Good Company* at least four times, but she never tired of it. She wanted these younger women to watch with her, to see how funny and brave a clutch of old women could be, stranded in the remote Canadian countryside with only their wits, each other, and the stories of their lives.

One of the women in the movie, a large, laconic Mohawk named Alice, was sitting by a stream fashioning a fish trap from her enormous, wide-stretched pantyhose, when Andrew began to wail through the intercom. Sarah paused the player as the other three women groaned in unison. "No!" cried Josie, yanking at her hair.

"Never mind," said Sarah, over the static and the baby's hollering. "I've seen this movie plenty of times. I'll go see to Andrew. *Bad* Andrew," she laughed, handing the remote to Jordan.

When she reached the stairs, her laughter died. The baby was shrieking fit to rattle the windows. *Night terrors?* she wondered. He was beside himself. Sarah hurried.

She had only the light from the hallway as she entered the

room in which Andrew howled. It took a moment for her eyes to adjust, and as they did, she saw a shadow moving toward her.

Roger was barely visible, but Sarah understood absolutely that it was he who inhabited the darkness, holding the hysterical child over his shoulder, patting him awkwardly and dancing in place. His dance was jerky, his movements abrupt. Andrew twisted in his father's arms, screaming more urgently than ever.

Rapidly Sarah gathered impressions. Roger was much taller than she, and muscular. He smelled unwashed. He smelled of fear.

His eyes were wild; he was tense with roiling energy. He looked angry, dangerous in his confusion over some plan gone awry. Had it never occurred to him that babies cry and people come to comfort them? Sarah wondered desperately why he was there, whether he meant to take Andrew and leave, or whether he was after Josie through Andrew. Perhaps all along he had meant for Andrew to cry and for Josie to come — not Sarah. If so, Sarah was an obstacle.

Roger loomed over her while Andrew sobbed and struggled, and only then did she sense that Roger was struggling, too — trying to assess his situation, trying to gain control, but also trying to comfort his baby. That was futile. Andrew absorbed his father's emotional chaos from his scent, his stiffness, his tight grip. The baby was terrified.

Roger motioned for Sarah to come close, and that was when she saw the gun in his hand. He used it not as a threat but as if it were his fingers or wrist. He made come-here circles in the air with its barrel, and Sarah wanted to comply, but her eyes were frozen on the weapon. She felt faint and feared she would fall, until Roger whispered plaintively, "What does he want?" Roger was panicked, too.

Quickly Sarah reached for the intercom and snapped it off. The last thing she needed was for Josie to rush upstairs. She hoped the others had not heard Roger's voice over the sounds of the movie.

She gestured shakily and said to Roger, "Give him to me, I can calm him down." Keeping her eyes on this frightened and furious man, she saw every emotion in the welter that had claimed him, but she was helpless to tell which outweighed the others. Her thoughts jumped and she remembered the teenage car thieves, then the Palestinian boy who escaped death when Mordechai's hatred suddenly ebbed.

Sarah could barely stop herself from grabbing Andrew and screaming for help, but her mind played this scene in fast-forward and showed her how panic could push Roger to violence. She couldn't afford fear. Andrew must be her whole world just now, the very center of it; all else must turn somehow toward the fixed goal of keeping him safe, here in this house.

Slowly she extended her arms, and Roger hesitantly settled his son into them. The baby's cries diminished as he clutched onto Sarah. They did not subside altogether, but they began to take on a rhythm, a decelerating tempo.

Sarah moved to the rocking chair with the baby and crooned to him through his sobs. Something cold took hold of her then and spread like frost on a window pane.

Roger had drawn close enough to touch, now that Andrew was growing steadily quieter. He caressed his son's head with a tough, broad hand. Sarah reached out slowly, past Andrew's hot, damp little body, to finger Roger's sweater. "Josie made this for you."

Roger glanced down as if to check what he was wearing, and Sarah thought it was too bad this lovely piece of work was infused with the odors that he exuded.

She continued speaking in a clear and rhythmic voice, "I gave her that yarn myself, after the night she got stranded in the cold. Andrew could have frozen to death, inside her." She kept her eyes on Roger's face. "You must have been mad with worry, and so relieved when Josie and the baby survived. You came close to losing them both that night."

Roger drew back from her, raising his gun hand. Was this reflex, or intention? He was so unsteady, she didn't know what he would do next.

He strode away from her, then spun back. "I've lost them anyway!" His voice cracked with rage or grief, Sarah couldn't tell which.

"Not Andrew, Roger. You haven't lost Andrew. You're in danger of losing him, but you still have a chance."

Roger shook himself like a dog. He squeezed his eyes closed and then opened them wide and stared into Sarah's face. "What do you know? Who the hell do you think you are?"

Sarah shrugged lightly and let one corner of her mouth turn up. She was benign, she was no threat. "Just an old woman with a houseful of other people's children. I know how to take care of people, Roger. I can help you take care of yourself, and Andrew."

Sarah kept her eyes from the gun with difficulty. She was never unaware of it. In only a few glimpses, in this dim room,

she had memorized its every detail. It was dull gray, not a re-
volver but one of those pistols that held a clip. The grip was
crosshatched and rough. The hole at the end of the barrel was
alarmingly large. Sarah couldn't put the gun from her mind, but
she could keep her mind in a place where the gun became just
an object. She had found the motionless center of her self. Her
mind was clear.

She said, "Let me tell you two stories, Roger. Both are about
you and how you can leave this house. You have two ways out.
You choose. You can take Andrew—but of course you will have
to do that over my dead body. A gun makes a lot of noise, as you
know, so that will reduce your odds of an easy exit."

Roger stood before her. She had his attention.

"If you do escape with Andrew," she continued, "you will
naturally have to run and keep running and still take care of
him—feed him, change him, keep him on a reasonable schedule. You will have to live with him underground—hoard him,
hide him, and raise him without his mother or any of the other
people who love him. Maybe that will seem like an adventure
to a growing boy. Maybe it will toughen him. But you can be
sure the police will not stop looking for you. Running and hiding will make it very difficult for you to give Andrew a normal
life."

Roger leaned down and glared into Sarah's face. "I'll figure it
out," he whispered harshly. "Nobody is going to keep me from
my son. Not you, not his *mother*." He spat out this last word.

Sarah held up a hand and silenced him. "You broke Josie's
arm, but maybe that wasn't enough for you. Maybe you want
total revenge—for what, I don't know. It's not like Josie laid you
off or forced you to hurt her."

He started to speak, but Sarah waved his words away before he could form them. "Whatever," she said, just like Lottie. "You could still kill her, if that would make you feel better. Or you could make her watch as you take her only child away screaming. She would see that forever. She would never have peace again."

"Good!" he muttered savagely. The barrel of the gun scribbled the air, and Sarah watched it with distant curiosity.

"Not so good, Roger. You *will* get caught, sooner or later. And then you will lose the last of everything you love. You will lose your son."

"I've already lost him! She took him away from me."

"That's because you showed yourself to be a threat. But you can change that. Leave here. Leave Andrew with me, and leave the gun, too." Sarah gestured with the hand that was not supporting the baby's bottom. Andrew had stopped crying altogether, and Sarah spoke softly, still rocking so as not to startle him. "Roger, the gun will only bring you trouble."

He said scornfully, "You're just gonna let me walk out of here and take off."

"Yes," Sarah said. "I am. I'll help you get out of the house and on your way. I will not call the police."

"*Shit*," he cried, raking his hand roughly through his dirty thick hair.

Sarah felt like the witch whose intentions were challenged by Angelo's dragon. She felt like the dragon, too, as she followed the plan that formed just ahead of each move she made.

"You'll have to trust me, Roger. I will not call the police. You will do that yourself. Actually, you'll go and turn yourself in. Not for this, tonight, but for Josie's arm, and jumping bail."

"Why the hell would I do that?"

"Because of Andrew. Because you want to be part of his life. You can't do that, you can't do what's good for either of you, if you're on the run."

He paced the room, back and forth, his big shoulders swaying at every turn. Keeping his head low, he held tightly to the gun, but Sarah could see that his fingers wrapped only the grip, not the trigger.

She went on. "I'll vouch for you, Roger. I'll tell the police you came here to see your son, you couldn't stand being away from him. I'll say you asked me what to do and took my advice. You had no intention of hurting anyone or doing anything wrong, and you are sorry for hurting Josie and want to make amends. I won't say a word about the gun, provided you give it to me right now."

She gestured for the weapon and Roger hesitated, casting his eyes about as if for assurances strewn on the floor or the furniture.

"Roger. You can have allies or enemies. Choose."

He stopped pacing and stood in the middle of the room. In the light from the hall, Sarah could see him decide, saw relief enter his eyes. He placed the gun in her lap, beneath the feet of his child, who now slept against her breast. He dropped his hands to his sides and said, "Are you sure I can get out?"

Sarah rose from the rocking chair, careful not to disturb Andrew. She slid the gun into the pocket of her loose pants.

"Go downstairs as quietly as you can. You'll still be this side of the great room once you're at the bottom. Slide out the screen door onto the porch. The hinges don't squeak, you can get out without a sound. I'll be right behind you to make sure you leave safely."

So they exited the bedroom together. On the way out, behind Roger's back, she took the gun from her pocket and placed it under the mattress of the big bed. In the hall they squinted at the brighter light, and Andrew cried softly in his sleep. Roger turned at the sound, his eyes full of longing.

"Go on, Roger," she whispered. "I'll take care of him."

He moved to the top of the stairs and started down silently, taking a last look at Andrew and Sarah before gathering himself and descending swiftly, soundless as a cat for all his size. Sarah waited a beat or two and followed. By the time she reached the bottom, Roger had turned into the foyer and its shadows. By the time she got there herself, he had slipped through the door and down the porch stairs, into the moonless night. She sent a prayer after him. *Let him do what's right.*

Adrenaline ebbed in a dizzying rush. Weak in the knees, her heart pounding and skipping, Sarah found Andrew heavy as stone for the few steps to the great room. No one even heard her coming. Josie, Sandy, and Jordan were cheering the arrival of the plane that would carry the stranded old women to safety. Their heroism was out in the open, their fears of death now small beside it.

The young women were astounded, therefore, when Sarah staggered up to Josie, plunked the still sleeping Andrew into her lap, and fell to the floor. She knew she was about to fall, but she lost all sensation before she hit. Her arm knocked the coffee table as she went down. Tea soared in a sparkling river through the air.

Chapter 28

SARAH'S THREE CHILDREN SAT at her bedside. She could hear them talking in low voices but couldn't see them. She couldn't open her eyes. "Where," she croaked, and went under again.

MORDECHAI CAME, AND SARAH could finally see. "Andrew." She whispered.

"Andrew is fine, Sarah. So is everyone else." He held her hand. "You are a hero."

"No," she said.

"Yes," he insisted.

"No, just one . . . old . . . one."

"Exactly the right one."

AT LAST SARAH LEARNED how things had unwound. The others knew only the version that Sarah and Roger had agreed on, because he had told it to the police exactly as Sarah had laid it out in Andrew's room.

Mordechai, however, sensed that there was more to the story. Sitting beside Sarah's bed with David and Charlotte, he grinned at her and said, "I think you held a peace conference, Sarah."

She rolled her eyes. "Tell me everything." So they did.

Roger couldn't remember how he had finally discovered Josie's whereabouts. Someone he knew had told someone he knew. All of Vermont was a village.

The night he'd meant to kidnap Andrew — rather, as he told it, the night he had needed so badly to see his son — Roger had entered the house well acquainted with its layout. He'd circled the perimeter night after night to get the floor plan down, always waiting until the dogs had taken their final constitutional in the dark. This time he left the dogs a late feast of raw meat laced with sleeping pills. Then he waited, knowing just who was home and who was out, knowing that Josie and the others were in the great room with the television on. He came in through the mudroom and the kitchen and moved silently down the hallway, hugging the shadowed wall opposite the great room. It was easy, then, to glide up the stairs to Andrew's room.

After Sarah's collapse, Jordan screamed for Mordechai, and Sandy called 911. Andrew woke and cried, and Josie strode up and down the room, jouncing him and fearing for Sarah. No one had any idea what had just happened upstairs. They knew only that Sarah had blacked out.

The EMTs spent an hour stabilizing her before taking her to the hospital in Barre, and in that time the police arrived, to the astonishment of the others. Roger was in custody and had told his story. The police wanted to question Sarah but had to settle for calming everyone down and piecing things together with them.

As Sarah would learn days later, the police had not believed Roger's version of the night's events, not with his history of violence and flight. They confided their doubts to Mordechai, who shared them and eventually laid them before Sarah. Knowing she could trust him, she finally told him everything and found relief in the true tale. But she would not tell the police.

Now Mordechai said, "When I found out what Roger had done, that he had put you in danger—I wanted to kill him, Sarah. I was suddenly an Israeli soldier again."

Sarah smiled. "Well, Mordechai, you're only human. You really need to get used to that."

Pushing herself higher in bed, she marveled that Roger really had turned himself in. She had said nothing to the police about the gun, which she would retrieve from the mattress, and somehow dispose of, the minute she got home. She meant for no one except Mordechai to know how dire the situation had been. Even Sarah didn't know for sure. Maybe Roger would never have used that gun at all; maybe he only meant to hold Josie and the others at bay while he took Andrew away.

Charlotte gestured at banks of flowers in Sarah's hospital room. "Rose and Josie sent at least half of these. Rose is nearly hysterical with relief." She rolled her eyes, adding, "Rose is nearly hysterical all the time, isn't she."

"Those are from Jordan," Mordechai said, pointing to a pot of lilies. "She took up a collection at school, so, really, they're from all of her friends, too. Angelo and his parents sent those roses, over there. Two dozen roses!"

"Yellow," smiled Sarah, gazing at the huge bouquet. "Beautiful." She fell back against her pillows, weak with relief and exhaustion. "Everyone's okay," she breathed.

Mordechai asked, "Don't you want to know about you?"

"What about me? I fainted, right?"

David explained, "It was a little more than that, Mom. Your heart started fibrillating. You were fighting for breath. Mordechai did CPR until the EMTs got there, but you scared the bejeezus out of everybody. You need to stay here for a day or two of tests."

Sarah shot a grateful look at Mordechai but dismissed David's concern. "It wasn't an actual heart attack, then, was it."

"No," he grinned. "It wasn't. You're a tough cookie, Mom."

"So, what else?"

Tyler had slept through everything in the room off the kitchen, which Roger had stealthily passed. Tyler asked about Sarah all the time.

Sarah closed her eyes. "Sandy?"

David shook his head. "Bob doesn't have long. She's having a hard time but trying not to show it. She's torn between grief over Bob and delight that you're safe. She's comforting Tyler, taking care of the house, putting the garden to bed. She planted about a thousand daffodils down by the cabin and the pond. Good thing the ground's not frozen yet."

A field of yellow dazzled through Sarah's mind. Suddenly, though relieved and happy, she could take no more news or company. She pushed the button to lower the head of her bed. "Sorry," she said. "Need sleep." Charlotte stood at the end of the bed. David kissed Sarah, and Mordechai touched her cheek. Then they left, promising to return in the morning.

TWO DAYS LATER, Sarah packed her belongings and waited for Mordechai to pick her up and take her home. She was warned to avoid stress, and even to stay away from her trails and garden for a while.

She puzzled over Mordechai's remark about a peace conference. That's not how either Roger or Sarah was telling the story, and yet it was true. Sarah was old and weak but not dead. She had kept the seam of life intact. It might have turned out differently, but it had not.

Mordechai arrived just as Sarah was zipping her small suitcase and wondering who had packed it on the night she'd been brought in. She turned to him happily, then saw his face.

He took Sarah's hand. "Bob died last night. Sandy got the call around eleven."

Sarah clutched Mordechai's hand, tears in her eyes. They had known this was coming. Bob had grown weaker every day. He had stopped speaking to Sandy when she visited, turning his face away. Sandy was no longer hurt by this. She didn't support his unspoken decision to die, but she understood it, finally. He was who he was, and he clung to that.

A WEEK LATER, Thanksgiving came and went. Angelo joined his parents for the day, and Josie and Andrew celebrated with Rose, but everyone else gathered at Charlotte's. Sarah, Charlotte, Tom, Lottie, Luke, Jordan, Mordechai, Sandy, and Tyler sat around the table. Peter, Vivi, and Jonathan joined them. They were all a little subdued, still shaken by Bob's death and Sarah's collapse, but thankful for blessings beyond measure.

Then it was nearly Christmas. Another holiday loomed without Charles. Sarah missed him, as she always did, but not more, because more was not possible. Twice he had come smiling and proud to her hospital bed, in dream or some other realm, but he had said nothing. Since then, Sarah talked to him often, his presence surrounding her like air.

Life would not hold still, even in Sarah's old age. It was never just one thing, whole and comprehensible. It was a tapestry, yet so fluid its strands might as well be water. The picture was never the same twice, any more than Sarah's view of the mountains or meadow was the same two days in a row. No joys were pure; they all partook of sorrow. No sorrows lacked joy.

Some of this Sarah learned from Sandy in the days after Bob's death. Sandy had taken the news in full, mourning it while accepting it and being glad that he was out of pain. None of it seemed more than she could handle, though she wept often, allowing Tyler to see her weep. "We need to cry," she told him, "so your Daddy will know how much we love him. But we can't cry forever, or he will be terribly sad."

Tyler cried a great deal at first, nearly bursting with grief. He was too young to understand the monumental events in his life. He and Sandy had moved back into their room upstairs, at Josie's insistence, and Sandy let him sleep with her every night, instead of on the narrow daybed. She let him cry and pound the bed in anguish, she let him ask her the same questions ceaselessly. Their conversations became storylike, almost liturgical.

"Why did we have to have a fire?"

"I don't know, honey. Bad things happen."

"Why are bad things so big?"

"Maybe all our bad things just came one after another."

"Is Daddy in heaven?"

"Maybe. I don't know what the place is called, but he's safe there."

The questions came steadily for a week, and then Tyler

stopped asking. He went back to Angelo, and Angelo's brand of story. He started feeding the cats again. He spent time with Mordechai and watched videos with Lottie and Jordan, who had an appetite for animated films as great as Tyler's own. It seemed he still pondered his father's death at moments when his eyes would fix on midair, and he would sit motionless until something else captured his attention. But he had already lived without Bob for five months and had settled into Sarah's large, busy household like a cuckoo in a nest of warblers.

Most of those who lived at Sarah's were cuckoos. Sarah and Lottie were the only birds native to the nest, and they were outnumbered seven to two, though soon the numbers would change. Sandy and Josie were going to look for jobs and a house to share. With Bob's life insurance and Rose's help, they would probably move soon. Sarah's house would echo with their absence, even with all three teenagers still there. But it would fill up again.

Molly was convalescing from knee surgery. She would stay with a nephew over Christmas and then move into Sarah's old office. She didn't need nursing. She just needed people around until she healed well enough to cook for herself and drive again. Her only condition for moving in was that she pay Sarah generously. When Sarah protested, Molly confided that she was "rich as a coot," though she was mum about the source of her wealth. For all Sarah knew, the old renegade grew marijuana for profit. Molly was certainly sold on its medicinal virtues, and Sarah could perfectly well see her branching out from her sales of legal tinctures and oils. She would never sell to kids, but there could be quite a market among seniors.

Other people needed temporary shelter, too. Adelaide had

asked whether a young gay couple from New York could stay with Sarah while they went house hunting in Montpelier. Another friend, who worked for the state, had called to find out whether Sarah might briefly accommodate a retired couple who had to evacuate while the housing authority removed the lead-based paint in their house. If Sarah agreed, the state would surely call on her again.

Not every boarder would become family. Sarah had been lucky with her first batch. Others might be demanding or rude, but that kind would come and go quickly. Sarah needn't live with people she didn't like, but she did need to offer a stopover. It was the least she could do. It was what her parents had done, and what Charles had done in a different way, each time he took barter for medical services. Now it was Sarah's turn, and someday, she hoped, it would be her children's turn, and then her grandchildren's.

CHRISTMAS SAW THE house overflowing. Stephie and Jake came three days before the holiday. Paul and William showed up next, with sleeping bags that Mordechai invited them to spread on the couches in the cabin. David, Tess, and Hannah drove up with Charlie, born two weeks early but thriving. He was a peaceful baby, a good sleeper, born to breastfeed. David's family, made whole and coherent by wee Charlie, took over Charles's old office, where they set up a cot for Hannah and a portable crib for the baby. Tess and David had married at Thanksgiving at Tess's parents' house with no officiating clergy. The two recited their vows directly to each other, using traditional Quaker language. Then they sat down to dinner with twenty-seven of Tess's relatives. David had both invited and

excused his own family. Sarah had been advised against travel-
ing in any case. Christmas would be their celebration.

Jordan was staying through all of Christmas, too. She had
established contact with her brother and sister, whom she met
faithfully at least once a week. She had bought gifts for them
and also for Lorraine, who was distant but seemed no longer
hostile.

Mordechai placed a menorah on the mantel in the great room
during Christmas week. "Hanukkah is only a minor holiday,"
he said. "But it comes near the solstice, when the light begins to
return. It feels good to mark that with a new candle each day."

Sarah was the only one who knew that Mordechai was staying for good once his book was finished. He had given her the
news just after she told him the whole story of her encounter
with Roger. He said it was time for him to live among family
and friends, time to settle where peace might not be perfect, or
dangers lacking, but where life went largely unimpeded.

"I am not leaving the struggle," he had said, "only moving it.
To write and teach here, in this country that has such power,
such potential. And it has you, Sarah." Silencing her protest, he
added, "You who do what every person must, if we are ever to
have peace."

On Christmas Eve, everyone gathered at Sarah's. On this
night, no one wanted to be anywhere else. Peter and Vivi
came, accompanied by Jonathan and Molly, who walked with
a cane, scowling at the inconvenience of it. Together they to-
taled twenty-four—eleven cuckoos, thirteen warblers. Birds of
a feather, nonetheless.

When the evening was over and warm bodies lay strewn
about on beds and cots and couches, in the house and the cabin

and over the barn, Sarah took up her spot at the window seat. She wrapped herself up in her quilt, opened the casement to the earth and sky, and breathed deeply, steadily, inhaling the cold and the smell of cold, envisioning the light from the stars entering her lungs. In and out she breathed, dropping further toward her center with every exhalation. Images came and went. Charles, tall and fond; her son Andrew, still as a stone behind his eyelids. All her offspring, and theirs; all her forebears, and theirs. Moose, coyotes, fishers, and blue jays; her photographs, the pretty and the ugly, the leavings of animals and evidence of slaughter. Charles would have been astonished by her photographs.

Sarah was unafraid, and strange in her own eyes. She was a tramp in the woods, a sharp eye through a lens. She could see the elements inside out, dust in mud, drought in rain. She could see the sky and earth gone topsy-turvy, could see gravity in the image of a snowflake, falling or rising, obeying or defying the laws of nature. Again and again, she heard Charles's final words to her, and she still did not know what they meant. What she believed, however, what she took on faith, was that he had seen a light and had decided to follow it.

Sarah's grief, which now felt like Charles himself hovering just out of sight, had taught her that love always brings loss. Nevertheless, love was where she would put her energies, because that was where her powers lay. There wasn't a thing she could do about loss.

EVERY LAST CUCKOO

Questions and Topics for Discussion

Questions and Topics for Discussion

1. We first see Sarah Lucas as she is racing into the Vermont winter woods on the heels of her dog Sylvie. What was your first impression of this seventy-five-year-old woman?

2. What do you think the woods represent to Sarah? How has her relationship to nature changed since her childhood? What caused it to change?

3. Rural Vermont is rugged, poor, and sparsely populated. How do you think this environment has affected Sarah throughout her life?

4. Sarah's long marriage to Charles was mainly happy and successful, but it did have rough periods. How did the two of them weather these times without lingering resentments?

5. After Charles dies, Sarah goes numb, avoids people, and doesn't even cry. What breaks into her suspended state? Once her numbness wears off, does her grief take on new aspects and forms of expression, or does she just set grief aside and get on with things?

6. What do you see as milestones on Sarah's pathway to a new life and perhaps even a new identity? Have you ever reinvented yourself? What were your milestones?

7. On impulse, Sarah takes Charles's old camera with her on a late-winter walk. How does photography help to change the way she sees? What does she examine with her new eyes?

8. Why, over time, does Sarah enjoy taking increasingly puzzling and ambiguous photographs?

9. Charlotte and David respond very differently to Sarah's photographs. How do their responses reflect their relationships with her?

10. Sarah's view of her world is somewhat altered after hearing about the murder of Tess's husband and Mordechai's experiences in Israel. How do these things affect Sarah's actions and assumptions?

11. Why do you think Sarah agrees to take new people into her life? For instance, why Mordechai, and then her granddaughter and the two other teenagers?

12. What enables Sarah's teenage boarders — who had been so unhappy and even angry in their own homes — to calm down in Sarah's?

13. Why do you think it upsets Charlotte when her predictable mother starts behaving unpredictably?

14. What is the basis for the deepening friendship between Sarah and Mordechai?

15. As the seasons change throughout the novel, so do all the characters' lives, both inner and outer. Sarah's changes are the most obvious and dramatic, but which of the other characters' lives changed the most, and which changes were most vivid to you?

16. What might Sarah have done differently in her encounter with Roger? How different might the outcome have been?

17. Throughout this novel we see natural hazards in the form of violent storms, life-threatening cold, and animal predation. We see human hazards such as domestic violence, murder, and warfare. What is the connection? Are humans given to violence or destruction because we are part of nature? Or can we choose otherwise?

18. What would Charles have thought of the Sarah we see at the end of this book?

GREG SCOTT

KATE MALOY is the author of the memoir *A Stone Bridge North: Reflections in a New Life*. Her work has been published online in *Literary Mama* and *VerbSap*, and in *The Readerville Journal*, *The Kenyon Review*, and the anthologies *For Keeps* and *Choice*. She lives with her husband on the central coast of Oregon. For more information, visit www.katemaloy.com.

Other Algonquin Readers Round Table Novels

Mudbound, a novel by Hillary Jordan

Mudbound is the saga of the McAllan family, who struggle to survive on a remote ramshackle farm, and the Jacksons, their black sharecroppers. When two men return from World War II to work the land, the unlikely friendship between these brothers-in-arms—one white, one black—arouses the passions of their neighbors. In this award-winning portrait of two families caught up in the blind hatred of a small Southern town, prejudice takes many forms, both subtle and ruthless.

Winner of the Bellwether Prize for Fiction

"This is storytelling at the height of its powers . . . Hillary Jordan writes with the force of a Delta storm." —Barbara Kingsolver

AN ALGONQUIN READERS ROUND TABLE EDITION WITH READING GROUP GUIDE AND OTHER SPECIAL FEATURES • FICTION • ISBN 13: 978-1-56512-677-0

Water for Elephants, a novel by Sara Gruen

As a young man, Jacob Jankowski is tossed by fate onto a rickety train, home to the Benzini Brothers Most Spectacular Show on Earth. Amid a world of freaks, grifters, and misfits, Jacob becomes involved with Marlena, the beautiful young equestrian star; her husband, a charismatic but twisted animal trainer; and Rosie, an untrainable elephant who is the great gray hope for this third-rate show. Now in his nineties, Jacob at long last reveals the story of their unlikely yet powerful bonds, ones that nearly shatter them all.

"[An] arresting new novel . . . With a showman's expert timing, [Gruen] saves a terrific revelation for the final pages, transforming a glimpse of Americana into an enchanting escapist fairy tale."
—*The New York Times Book Review*

"Gritty, sensual and charged with dark secrets involving love, murder and a majestic, mute heroine." —*Parade*

AN ALGONQUIN READERS ROUND TABLE EDITION WITH READING GROUP GUIDE AND OTHER SPECIAL FEATURES • FICTION • ISBN-13: 978-1-56512-560-5

Breakfast with Buddha, a novel by Roland Merullo

When his sister tricks him into taking her guru, a crimson-robed monk, on a trip to their childhood home, Otto Ringling, a confirmed skeptic, is not amused. Six days on the road with an enigmatic holy man who answers every question with a riddle is not what he'd planned. But along the way, Otto is given the remarkable opportunity to see his world—and more important, his life—through someone else's eyes.

"Enlightenment meets *On the Road* in this witty, insightful novel."
—*The Boston Sunday Globe*

"A laugh-out-loud novel that's both comical and wise . . . balancing irreverence with insight." —*The Louisville Courier-Journal*

AN ALGONQUIN READERS ROUND TABLE EDITION WITH READING GROUP GUIDE AND OTHER SPECIAL FEATURES • FICTION • ISBN 13: 978-1-56512-616-9

Saving the World, a novel by Julia Alvarez

While Alma Huebner is researching a new novel, she discovers the true story of Isabel Sendales y Gómez, who embarked on a courageous sea voyage to rescue the New World from smallpox. The author of *How the García Girls Lost Their Accents* and *In the Time of the Butterflies*, Alvarez captures the worlds of two women living two centuries apart but with surprisingly parallel fates.

"Fresh and unusual, and thought-provokingly sensitive."
—*The Boston Globe*

"Engrossing, expertly paced." —*People*

AN ALGONQUIN READERS ROUND TABLE EDITION WITH READING GROUP GUIDE AND OTHER SPECIAL FEATURES • FICTION • ISBN-13: 978-1-56512-558-2

The Ghost at the Table, a novel by Suzanne Berne

When Frances arranges to host Thanksgiving at her idyllic New England farmhouse, she envisions a happy family reunion, one that will include her sister, Cynthia. But tension mounts between them as each struggles with a different version of the mysterious circumstances surrounding their mother's death twenty-five years earlier.

"Wholly engaging, the perfect spark for launching a rich conversation around your own table." —*The Washington Post Book World*

"A crash course in sibling rivalry." —*O: The Oprah Magazine*

AN ALGONQUIN READERS ROUND TABLE EDITION WITH READING GROUP GUIDE AND OTHER SPECIAL FEATURES • FICTION • ISBN-13: 978-1-56512-579-7

Coal Black Horse, a novel by Robert Olmstead

When Robey Childs's mother has a premonition about her husband, who is away fighting in the Civil War, she sends her only son to find him and bring him home. At fourteen, Robey thinks he's off on a great adventure. But it takes the gift of a powerful and noble coal black horse to show him how to undertake the most important journey in his life.

"A remarkable creation." —*Chicago Tribune*

"Exciting . . . A grueling adventure." —*The New York Times Book Review*

"Gripping . . . Echoes the work of Cormac McCarthy."
—*The Cleveland Plain Dealer*

AN ALGONQUIN READERS ROUND TABLE EDITION WITH READING GROUP GUIDE AND OTHER SPECIAL FEATURES • FICTION • ISBN-13: 978-1-56512-601-5